Circlet of Thorns
Book Three

SACRIFICE

R. S. Kaio

Printed in the United States of America

First Printing, 2015

ISBN-13 978-0692498446
ISBN-10 0692498443

Library of Congress Control Number: 2015947917

Table of Contents

Introduction

We are travelers – just passing through. That's all we ever do: just pass through.

We were created for a single purpose: to lead humans to our Master. We are sent by his son, the Commander, to Earth, where we become his messengers and guardians of the living ones. There, we are only allowed to stay until the lesson is learned, until the Earthling is protected, until the Commander's work is completed.

The Commander: He sends us, wrapped in the guise of the universe as mere common living ones, to Earth. There we remain until he calls us home, to our planet Wynaeria.

It is for our benefit as much as the Earthlings' that we are sent. On Earth the Commander fills us with his love and enables us to lead the humans to him and his Father. We are sent to protect them from the Adversary – the Commander's and ours.

Our Enemy, Malevolence, only wants to destroy the Earthlings, to drag them down to Vyke where he belongs. His character is putrid with evil and he disguises it. He comes to the Earthlings as an angel – a wise, kind counselor. How little they know his ways! It is his desire to entangle them in his evil to keep them from the Commander, who longs to be restored with the Earthlings. The Adversary is ultimately deceptive.

It is from this Adversary, the Burning Ember, that

Wynaerians are to protect the humans, and it is only through the Commander that this goal is achieved.

Sometimes we are defeated by our Adversary. Sometimes we are destroyed and we leave our charges, the Earthlings, defenseless and alone. Yet the Commander's work is always completed – by whichever means he allows, through triumph or failure.

All is not so clear to behold, however. There is a snag that entangles us messengers, the Wynaerians. This snag is concealment. The Commander has forbidden any of his followers to Reveal to the Earthlings.

Revealed is the way we live on Wynaeria where the Commander beholds us personally. It is our form of being in our own world: nearly like giants to the humans, with bronze skin and sharper features. We are most comfortable in our natural forms, even on Earth, but on that beloved planet we are forbidden. If one of us were to Reveal against our Commander's command, we would be destroyed, for the danger our disobedience would pose to our guardianships. He is just.

While on Earth we remain only a mist to the humans – a breeze, a whisper, a thought, a feeling. True contact with their knowledge is forbidden. So our work is quiet, secret. It is with this secrecy that we evade, and sometimes battle, the Embers, our Adversary's cohorts, and lead the Earthlings to their maker.

Only when our keeping of a charge has been completed does the Commander call us home. Though even then, we only stay until our next assignment.

We don't mind. It is the way we were created.

We are travelers – just passing through. That's all we ever do: just pass through.

Prologue

A thrill of excitement ran through him. He stood alone at the top of the valley, looking down upon the grassy plain. Trees shaded him, keeping the sun's heat from beating on the back of his head. The valley he overlooked was full of white sticks, all dry as dust. Many crackled in the heat of the sunlight. A gentle wind blew among them, creating a low moan.

The Ember smiled. He was tall and lithe, with his arms hanging by his sides. At the ends of these appendages, rather than hands, protruded two jagged swords, wreathed in flame. Lights sparkled out from where his eyes should have been, one red, the other violet. Black smoke enshrouded him in wispy shadows. His sneer was joyous, revealing sharp, silver teeth. His whole appearance was that of utter darkness and evil.

Lightly, Malevolence skipped down into the valley and walked among the white sticks. There, he saw them for what they were: bones, blanched by the exposure to sunlight and brittle to touch.

The Ember scanned the massacre-ground with evident pleasure, turning slowly amid the carnage to take in all. His enemies: how far they had fallen! Gleefully, he began to dance: a slow, unnerving movement, casting shadows and sparks out to land on the dried bones.

Then, raising his jagged swords, he looked up into the sun and grinned. Head tilted back, he began a shriek, high and lilting, that penetrated the atmosphere around him.

From far away an answering shriek sounded, and then others. Soon they were surrounding him on the hillocks of the valley. As one, shadowy figures materialized beneath the shade of the trees. They waited for their master to command them and watched, eagerly switching from foot to foot in restlessness. There were hundreds of them, all with blades for arms and violet eyes. Some had sharp, pointed teeth and long, narrow faces; others, sinewy wings wrapped around their bodies and clawed feet. At least one claimed spikes along his body and a clubbed tail.

The Ember in the valley paused in his dance and looked down at the bones he was crushing into dust. With little thought, his sword-arms disappeared, extinguishing the flames, and transformed into hands with long fingernails. He reached down to pick up a long, slender bone. Delicately, he ran his thin fingers along the surface. It was smooth, as though it had been sanded, and had a soft texture of dust over it.

Malevolence lowered himself to the ground and bent over the bone. With legs crossed, he dropped his eyes and began scraping it with his fingernails.

Shrak. Shrak. Shrak.

The high-pitched tone would send a chill down any human's spine, had any been around. However, it didn't bother the Embers: they didn't have spines and were less substantial than a breeze.

Malevolence whistled tunelessly as he worked, only just a breath in the air. The bone he worked on was light and hollow, like that of a bird's, but it was not to a bird that it once belonged. With deft fingers, the Ember carved into it. White shavings fell to the ground before him like snow and gradually the bone began to shrink in size. Using his pointed fingernails, he cut off the end of the bone and began scraping out the trusses that made it airy. That done, he punctured holes along the ridge at intervals. Finally, he shaped a mouthpiece on the opened end.

The bone now in the shape of a flute, Malevolence raised it to his mouth and began to play. Along with notes, words flowed from the instrument, strong and deep. They came from Malevolence and were his voice in the form of Reverberation, a way to bounce the song through the air.

Among the decimated
laughter will reside:
bounding along the wind
until they're cold inside.

Come to me, my family;
shriek with lifted voice.
Raise your ears to hear me:
you have no other choice.

Dance over our defeated!
They go down to Death:
their fearsome, angry foe
who steals their final breath.

Sing with me, bonded friends:
cry with joyous shout.
Play upon their bones:
scrape and hollow them out.

Revenge on those who hate us!
Spite our Enemy!
Kill his chosen ones
and come celebrate with me.

Among the decimated
laughter will reside:
bounding along the wind
until they're cold inside.

The music that drifted through the valley was that of an eerie celebration. With one hand, the Ember continued playing; with the other, he motioned his followers to join him. As one, they flooded into the valley of bones until it was full of darkness and shadows.

As their master had done, and commanded them to do, the Embers concealed their bladed limbs and began selecting bones to form into instruments. There amassed an assortment of flutes, recorders, maracas, rain sticks, and shakers.

One by one, they began joining their master's song, until the dell was rife with it. Within moments all that could be heard was the unearthly tune, rising up into the heavens.

~ ~ ~

A hundred miles away, standing at the top of a mountain peak, the Commander overlooked the disturbing scene. A fire like hatred burned in his eyes.

Chapter 1
Lost Opportunity

The land of Wynaeria glowed clear and bright that morning. The world lit up by starlight, there could only be joy for those who belonged to the Commander.

I sat alone at the uppermost point of a double valley, overlooking my homeland as a guardian for the Commander. There was no true need for vigilance over Wynaeria and her inhabitants, as there had never been a threat to our country. The practice was allowed merely as an exercise for those of us who journeyed to Earth. There, we were commissioned to lead our charges to the Commander. Such an opportunity had not been afforded to me for several years, and I yearned for one.

As often happened during my watch, boredom reigned in me. For several hours on this beautiful day I'd stood alone at my station, with only the creatures of the valleys to keep me company. I had recently reverted to sitting on the hillock, twiddling with the grass between my fingers.

As the light beat down over the land, I reached into my silver tunic and unsheathed my knife. Up, I released it from my fingers to glint golden in the starlight; down, it fell into my open palm and balanced. Smirking at my deftness, I looked past the toying weapon to observe the landscape.

Before me, to the north, spread the double valley at whose peak I stood. Down rolled the lush, grassy knolls, leveling out in a short plain and then plunging once more.

To east and south, jagged cliffs dropped down into a raging sea. The country Wynaeria was surrounded on all sides by the ocean, which no one ever crossed. There was never a need, as the island was the only land on the planet. A multitude of creatures dwelt in the sea, large and striking, though nothing a Wynaerian could not easily defeat.

In the west, running down the edge of the double valley, stretched an immense forest. A stream flowed out from the trees and curved through the valley, down into a waterfall to rejoin the sea. Beyond, slicing into the horizon rose mountains, strong and proud watchers over the world. Dragons resided in the foothills, only rarely coming further inland.

In daylight, the valleys were full of life. Bright fairies danced among the toadstools, gnomes played in the shade of the trees, and a white tiger crouched in the wood, ready to pounce.

The only village on Wynaeria nestled beneath the double valley, cut into the hills. It rose and fell with the landscape. The streets were made of cobblestones or dirt, threading through mud huts with thatched roofs. Everything was plain and simple, to allow for concentrating on the Commander's love without distractions.

There was no sun that shone on Wynaeria, as there was no need for one – the light that emanated from surrounding planets and stars shone through Open Space to illuminate the world. It was a stationary planet, with only one season – summertime. When night came, it was by the Commander's will, when he allowed the brightness of Open Space to diminish around us and provide darkness.

Rainbows stretched across the clear blue sky above, the fairies' masterpiece. As ever, nothing suggested a threat.

I sighed, tossing my blade up to catch again.

"Suri."

The blade slipped through my fingers. I bent to retrieve it, shifting into a kneel, and bowed my head. "Commander."

Light shone on the ground before me, radiating from his being. He had come in person, not just as a voice or the Beam of Light, but as a Wynaerian.

An unspeakable desire to please him rose in me. I waited for him to speak.

"Devastation is coming against Wynaeria," he stated in an imposing voice, infused with thundering waterfalls. "You will be found unprepared. They will look to you for guidance and protection. Only when one stands against the darkness and sacrifices his life will the darkness depart."

"I will, Commander," I said before he could ask me, excitement curling through me. "I will stand against the coming evil and sacrifice my life for you and my country."

"Will you?" A wistful tone laced his words.

His countering question stalled me for a moment. "Commander," I spoke before he left, remembering my request.

"My son."

"Will I have another assignment?"

The Commander's soft chuckle washed over me, still tinged with sadness. "Yes, Suri." His voice wrapped into itself and dissolved with his light. Then he was gone.

I rose from the ground, smiling, and twirled my blade around my fingers. It occurred to me that Wynaeria had never been assailed before. The idea of standing guard no longer seemed inconsequential to me. I returned to my task with a new vigor, envisioning whatever danger would approach.

~ ~ ~

The afternoon was waning when my watch ended. I had exhausted all thought of the Commander's adventure, and now pushed it from my mind. A fellow Wynaerian, Lyler, took my position and I skipped lightly down into the valleys. Threading through the tall grasses, jumping the stream, I hummed my way along to the village.

At the edge of the second valley, the land sloped downward into rolling hills. These stretched out to the forest, mountains, and horizon beyond. I stopped at the peak of the second valley to overlook the village, contentment settling in me.

Starlight filtered through the streets, casting golden beams through the air. Aromas of baking bread, sizzling meats, and cooking vegetables wafted through the air. Gardens were plentiful this time of year and at the evening meal, produce abounded in kitchens.

In the streets of the village, men and women milled to their respective homes, daily duties finished. Children ran along with dogs, laughing and shrieking in the dying day. Behind some houses, I could distinguish maidens harvesting their gardens and young men chopping firewood for the coming winter.

I headed down the hill into the village. Down several hills, and around bends in the dirt streets I walked, occasionally trading hellos with men, or running with a group of children after their runaway dog. Soon I reached my own solitary hut, built into the side of a hill.

"Nuncle Suri!" a voice cried.

Two small children came running to meet me from the doorway of my hut. I bent to receive them, an unbidden smile stretching across my face.

"Mena! Poil!"

The two barreled into my chest, knocking me over backwards in their enthusiasm.

"Nuncle Shuri!" Poil panted, a small, tousle-haired boy of three years. His cheeks were dimpled and red, freckles dotting his nose. His eyes shone out blue and sparkling beneath his mop of brown curls. He pulled on my arm to help me stand.

Mena sat on my chest, preventing her brother's efforts. Dark-haired, her eyes shone deep brown, looking down into my face. She was the older of the two, a little mischief.

"Le' 'im up, Men!" Poil demanded, still pulling furiously on my arm.

"No," she retorted, lying down on my chest and curling up with her head under my chin. "He hasn't kissed me yet."

I chuckled, raising a hand to smooth her hair, and kissed the top of her head. "There," I pronounced. "I've kissed the princess. Am I free to go now?"

Mena sat back to give me a studious glare. "I suppose," she said hesitantly. "If you say yes to Papa." She grinned, eyes dancing, and jumped off of me. She, too, grabbed my arm and tugged.

I allowed them to help me up, and, swinging a child on each arm, walked toward my hut. I didn't get far before being hailed again.

"Suri!" a booming voice called.

I lifted my gaze to the doorway of my house.

"Caught by the princess, eh?" Juris chuckled, banging on the arched door frame of my hut. Tall and broad, he took up the entire entry of my home. His face was round and red with dark sparkles peeping from tiny eyes. Out of those eyes shone a brilliant light, reminiscent of diamonds: the gleam of truth, granted to all who belonged to the Commander. A black, curly beard bushed from the Wynaerian's chin down nearly to his waist. Mismatched clothes were haphazardly thrown over him, green and red. He was barefoot, as always. He carried a basket full of bread and rocked on his heels.

"Papa, I caught Nuncle Suri!" Mena exclaimed, hanging on me. She had dubbed me "Nuncle" before learning to pronounce her u's and had yet to drop the title.

I grinned at Juris. "What brings you all hailing?" asked I, stepping up to him.

Juris held out the basket, beaming. "I'm on a commission from the missus," he announced in a deep voice that rumbled from his belly. "She packed a basket of bread as an offering and temptation."

I raised my eyebrows, glancing at the freshly baked

bread. "Temptation to what?"

Mena dropped from my arm to hang on her father. "Papa, ask him!" She looked at me from between Juris' legs. "I let you up if you said yes," she added seriously in reminder.

Juris' face wreathed in a smile that engulfed his cheeks and made his eyes disappear. "Ah, now you've made a promise to the princess, you ought to keep your word," he said sagely. "Lili wants you over to sup with us tonight."

"Aye, I reckon I can come for that. I wouldn't miss Lili's food for the world." I winked. "Let me put away my knife, and then we can go."

Juris took a shuffling step into my hut, nearly knocking his head on a crossbeam in the ceiling. I followed with Mena and Poil.

My simple wooden hut was dark inside from the dimming starlight. In the far left corner stood my bed, at the end of which was a bare table with spindly legs, and a chair awaiting use. Above the table, a window overlooked the mountains in the north. The only other window hung opposite, looking out on my outdoor kitchen. My doorway, merely an arch to pass through, stood alone on the eastern wall.

I strode to the table, unsheathing my knife. With a practiced motion, I strapped my blade to the table's underside in a hidden catch. Its sheath I unbuckled from my belt and tossed on the tabletop.

Mena and Poil watched in fascination.

Juris set the basket of bread on my table and took a step back, folding his hands in front of him.

I turned to Mena. "I said yes," I told her. "Will you lead the way?"

She cocked her head up at me and studied my features. "No. I want to ride!" she said decidedly. Reaching her hands up to me, she gave a little jump of anticipation.

I laughed and reached down to swing her onto my shoulders.

"I wanna wide!" Poil demanded. He tackled my legs and

settled down on one foot.

"Go!" Mena ordered.

Juris laughed, a great booming roll that could scare small children and put birds to flight in the tops of trees. "I'd say you have a following," he chortled.

I grinned. "If they don't knock me over, it will be a miracle."

Juris waved a hand and stepped from my hut into the dirt street. "Come, Lili will wonder where we are. We can't be late for the Light Dancing."

In a slow, awkward manner, I shuffled along the streets beside Juris, who shortened his stride to walk with me. Mena continued to chatter to herself and Poil, while her brother remained content merely to hang on for the ride.

"You haven't visited for some time," Juris commented.

"Aye," I agreed. "I've been meaning to visit."

His rumbling voice gentled to a purr. "I know, lad. Things've never been quite the same, 'ave they? Your assignment changed you in many ways."

"No." I looked ahead, shifting my grip on Mena's legs.

Juris raised his eyebrows. "Oh. It's a lassie's got your heart, is it? What's her name?"

I looked at him in disbelief. Still, I answered. "Her Earth-name is inconsequential, if the Commander allows ..." Realizing what I was saying, I shut my mouth and shook my head witheringly.

Juris put a hand over his heart, face open with honesty. "As your own dear friend, am I not entitled to such knowledge as who holds your heart?"

I grinned now at the mock injury in his voice. "The Commander holds my heart." I spotted Juris and Lili's cottage up ahead and jerked my head toward it. "The home is holding up well. Will it fit another new baby?"

Juris' eyes smothered again in a grin, this time proud. "Aye, we've made accommodations in the back. He'll stay with Lili and me until he's grown some. Then we'll put him in with

Poil. They can share for a while."

"You know it's a boy?"

Juris shrugged. "I'm hoping. Lili wants a girl." He rolled his eyes. "I guess we'll see when the time comes."

I studied the house. "Yes, they'll be fine here for a while," I said. "Until they become young men and guardians."

Juris waved that away. "As the Commander's, no real harm can come to 'em. I hope they get along well."

I snorted. "I know about brothers."

"Mommy!" Mena cried. She bounced on my shoulders, kicking her heels lightly against my collarbones.

Ahead, Lili stood just outside the door of their cottage, leaning back against the door frame. Slight and comely, she looked fragile beside Juris. Her hazel eyes were encased in that same diamond-like covering from the light of truth. Long, blonde hair brushed to her waist, held out of her face with a wide white band. Her arms were crossed, but she smiled when she saw us. "Welcome!" she called.

"Look at Nuncle Suri!" Mena called back. She proceeded to grab my hair in little fists and neigh like a horse, kicking my collarbones again. "He's my noble steed!"

I laughed outright, wondering where she'd learned such a phrase. "I found a little princess wandering alone. Art thou her mother? Thy resemblance is so great, she must be thine!"

Lili laughed. "Oh, noble steed, it is fortunate that thou hast stumbled upon my little lost daughter! How great and kind thou must be! In thanks, I beg thee, accept a small morsel from my table."

"Small morsel accepted!" I affirmed. I reached under Mena's arms and lowered her to the ground. "Go on, little princess." Disentangling myself from Poil's grasp around my leg, I set him down and gave a bow to Lili.

She curtsied back and stepped aside, motioning me into their home. "Thank you for accepting our invitation," she said warmly, following me.

Unlike my home, Lili and Juris' cottage had four rooms –

three bedrooms and an open living area, with a kitchen, table and chairs, and a sitting area. Avid readers, Lili and Juris had a luxury of bookshelves, complete with writing utensils. Juris was a shipmaster, an Earth-term we adopted to describe Wynaerians who taught tunnel-traveling. His gatherings from around the universe were displayed throughout the home, many strange and wondrous things.

I surveyed the cottage with a small smile, perfectly at home. Lili and Juris had practically adopted me into their house as their son. My own parents had died when I was a lad, cut down by Embers. Since, Lili and Juris filled their places as well as they could.

"Come with us," Lili invited, motioning to the table, which stood beneath an open window. It was filled with food. "The Light Dancing will not wait."

I grinned and took a seat at the table. Mena and Poil fought over sitting next to me, which only ended when they each had a seat beside me. We lifted our thanks to the Commander, and began our meal.

"Nuncle Suri," Mena began as she watched Juris ladle smoked meat and fresh tomatoes onto her plate. "Where have you been?"

I reached for the basket of bread and retrieved a roll before turning to her. "I went to Earth on an assignment. The Commander sent me away." I held the roll out to her in offering.

She shook her head in refusal of the bread and looked up at me. Her face scrunched into confusion. "Why would he do that?"

I smiled. "He wanted me to lead an Earthling to him." I raised the roll to my mouth to take a bite.

"No!" Mena protested, eyes wide. She reached for the roll and snatched it back. "You can't eat yet!"

I gave her a confused expression. "Why not?"

"You haven't juttled!"

I glanced at Lili. "Juttled?"

Hiding a smile, Lili gave me a prim look and said, "You've

gotten them into a bad habit of expecting a show before eating. She wants you to juggle."

"Yes!" Poil exclaimed, bouncing in his seat. "Jull, jull!"

Juris' shoulders shook in a suppressed chuckle.

With a resigned sigh, I reached for the basket of rolls and selected four more. Lili watched me with a disapproving expression.

"You want me to juggle?" I asked, weighing the rolls in my hands and glancing between Poil and Mena.

"Yes, yes!" they cried together.

Stepping away from the table, I tossed the first roll into the air, followed closely by the second. The third, fourth, and fifth joined the first two in a circle. Once I got into a rhythm, I started throwing harder, lengthening the space between two rolls. My audience gasped and applauded. Mena squealed with delight.

"Catch!" I said. With a quick flick of the wrist, which almost cost me losing one, I tossed a roll to Mena. She caught it.

I returned to a rhythm of juggling four. "Ready, Poil?" I glanced at him.

He nodded eagerly.

The second roll went to Poil, who fumbled his catch and dropped it. The bread bounced on the table and he leaned over to retrieve it.

Once I threw the third roll to Lili, I reverted to juggling the final two in my right hand. After a moment, I tossed one to Juris, keeping the last for myself.

Mena laughed and clapped excitedly. "Now you can eat!" she pronounced.

I dipped my head in acknowledgement, retaking my seat. "Thank you." Turning to Poil, I continued, "I see I need to come over more. You haven't quite learned to catch yet."

He blushed.

"You only need practice, laddie," Juris said, returning to his plate of meat and vegetables. "Suri'll have you catching 'em faster than he can throw soon."

Lili smiled. "Now, however, we need to eat. It is nearly time to gather for the Light Dancing." She took a bite of tomato, looking at me.

With that reprimand, I bowed my head to my plate and began to eat. The children and Juris followed suit, and soon silence reigned in the cottage as we supped together.

When the meal was finished and the dishes washed, we left the cottage behind. Striding quickly along the path, Mena and Poil rushing ahead and running back, we headed toward the double valley. Other Wynaerians passed us and were passed by us as we walked. At each encounter, we exchanged greetings.

By the time we reached the lower valley, the sun had set. Together all Wynaerians, save those who were unrepentant, sleeping, or caring for the young, gathered in a circle. Mena and Poil, as at the supper table, claimed either side of me.

Silence reigned over the planet, unbroken save for the nocturnal insects and the sound of our breathing.

Once in a circle, I slowly reached my hands out to Mena and Poil, who also reached for mine. My wrists faced skyward. There, on my left wrist, engraved in the skin where my veins showed through, was the Commander's mark: a white circlet of thorns. I had only time to glimpse Mena and Poil's identical marks before we clasped wrists and our marks were covered. Around the group, the others did the same, man to woman, woman to child, until all were connected. Once joined, we stilled, as only our kind can do: halting movements and breaths.

We waited.

The darkness grew deep around us. Stars plotted constellations in Open Space. Slowly, the moons began to rise. Wynaeria has three moons and each rises from a different direction – north, south, and east. One is blue, one golden, and one green. When all were at their peaks, their light converged to create waving beams in the air surrounding us.

Still, we waited.

As the dancing lights began to fade, there came a spark from the mountains. Brilliant light flew down a mountainside and crossed the plain with tremendous speed. Within seconds, it entered our circle and rose into a wall before us.

The Beam of Light had come.

We bowed to the ground in reverence.

"Commune with me," his voice boomed.

"Come, and welcome," we replied in unison. Poil's hand trembled in mine.

The Beam expanded outward, washing over each of us until we were all encircled in his glorious light. Fully engulfed in his whiteness, we could distinguish his Wynaerian form at the center of our company. He was taller than any, with hair glowing white and fiery ruby eyes sparkling. His skin glowed bronze and a smile stretched across his strong and kind face.

As one, we began to turn around the Beam, slowly at first, and then gathering speed. Soon, we were whirling tirelessly around our Commander. Worship sprang to our lips, unbidden, as the Commander began to dance.

We once lived in deep-set darkness
inept to see the light for fear.
Our chains imprisoned us alone
underneath the terrain so drear.

Wasting away, as ones unloved
we waited for someone to come.
Our enemies had broken us
seeking to make us succumb.

Then, in the nightening, he came
as one to avenge the broken.
He tore off our chains wrathfully;
merely a word was spoken.

In outrage and justice he killed
the Unruly that caged his own.

Those who survived were put to flight,
in fear of his deathly tone.

From prison to freedom that day,
as one we worshiped our Saviour:
the one who had rescued our lives.
His name is the Commander.

When the starlight faded completely our revelry ended. We bid each other quiet farewells and returned to our own homes for the remainder of the night. There were no words in any language to describe the wonder we had taken part in. Some Wynaerians wandered away in pairs or threes, in an effort to prolong the community we had experienced. Lili and Juris gathered Mena and Poil and walked away together toward their cottage, the children nearly fainting on their feet.

I meandered away alone, skirting the others and walking along the edge of the forest to my hut. Open Space was at its darkest point on our planet and made my way nearly indistinguishable. Ahead, I could only just perceive the edge of the village.

Suddenly, a voice spoke in my mind. *Suri.*

I stopped walking. "Yes, Commander."

I have an assignment for you. Are you willing to go?

Excitement rose in me. "Yes, Commander."

There is destruction to be faced first, he informed me. *The adventure has not yet arrived.*

"When will it?"

The Commander did not answer.

I continued on my way without questioning him further. Soon, I reached my hut and stepped inside.

Moseying over to my bed, I lay down on my back, smiling in anticipation. My eyes sought the rugged ceiling.

~ ~ ~

Dawn came and I remained lying in my bed. The night had passed peaceably, though I had not slept. For a Wynaerian, sleep is only needed once every couple of weeks: a pattern only broken while tunnel-traveling, when it is required more often. I hated the nights when I had to sleep and could not think or just lie quietly.

Turning my gaze to the side, I looked out the window of my wooden hut to the open horizon. To the west the double valley reached up; beyond, the forest stretched out to the mountains. Directly ahead was part of my village, huts dotted among the hills. At the further end lay the harbor on the sea, where tunnels were created to traverse Open Space. That was where Juris would be now, teaching others to create and sustain tunnels. Soon, Poil and Mena would be old enough to learn.

I got up from my bed and stretched, yawning. Shuffling over to the doorway, I looked out.

Not many Wynaerians were stirring yet – it was still early. Starlight filtered down, creating dappled shadows and golden drops on the huts and streets. Morning mist settled over the tranquil village, the only conscious beings the working restless, and animals. Soon, I would be leaving to go to the forest, where guardians trained in combat with each other.

As I stared out, a dark splotch rose on the horizon, like that of a black hole. It began spreading, slowly overtaking the harbor and coming toward the village. Unnerving screams accompanied it.

A shudder ran through me.

Embers.

I reached for the knife strapped to the underside of my table.

Wynaerian mothers were gathering at hut entrances, holding back their small children, and watching the darkness on the horizon, the origin of the screams. Throughout the village, men hurried to collect weapons, preparing for battle. Some already raced to combat the enemies.

Entering thoughts and hearts and spirits, the darkness became tangible. It reached me at the entrance to my hut. Gloom shrouded the village, making every shape indistinct. With the black came an overbearing terror that filled me. All desire to join the fray disappeared in its presence. My heart pounded.

The Commander's words, *Devastation is coming against Wynaeria,* re-entered my mind. I shuddered.

Embers dispersed through the streets, bringing their darkness with them. Villagers began to flee from their huts, carrying what goods they could manage. They made for the harbor, where they could escape Wynaeria for another planet. Small children screamed and cried in the Embers' night, separated from their parents.

Chaos, a leader among the Embers, led a dance through the streets, laughing and mocking the terrified villagers. In his wake, horses and cats and dogs shrieked and screamed and barked. His followers wreaked havoc, setting fire to gardens and tearing down what they could of the huts.

They were destroying my country.

Anger rose in me like an undertow from the sea, pulling me toward the battleground; but fear had taken a much deeper root and ordered me to stay. I crouched down in the darkness beside my hut, unseen, and watched, trembling.

Nearby, an old Wynaerian, tired and worn, hobbled away from the village. He stumbled toward me in the shadows, but didn't see me. His eyes were shining and fearful. His crutch nearly fell from his fingers. I recognized him: a friend, Firen.

A streak of compassion entered me. "Let me help you," I said quietly, drawing up beside him and reaching out a hand to steady his faltering steps.

"Commander," the man muttered, apparently oblivious to my touch. "Yes, Commander. Yes, I will obey you."

"What?" asked I, unsure I had heard him correctly. I supported him as we headed away from the burning village. The

Embers had yet to reach my house.

Firen didn't answer.

When we stepped in the shade beyond my hut, I turned back.

Many villagers had already fled, through tunnels or to hide in the forests. Some still rushed away, out of the village, toward the harbor to Open Space. Others were fleeing past the old man and me, out of the village into the fields beyond. All screamed. "Get out!" they screamed. "Get out! Get out! The night is never ending!"

I followed their example, my heart leaping in my throat, dragging the old man with me toward the fields.

Behind us, the Embers had done their work. They had made way for their leader: the Burning Ember, who arrived in the form of an orange glow on the edge of the harbor. He now came directly toward us. Soon, his presence would enter our homeland and consume it.

When we reached a hill overlooking the village, the old man pulled away from me. He stood tall, straightened, and lifted his face toward the burning village.

"What are you doing?" I shouted angrily.

"I will go," whispered Firen, ignoring me.

"No," I protested. "No, you can't return!" I stood still, torn between escape and preventing his return. He would be killed!

The old man didn't hear me. His face turned to the Burning Ember, and his eyes brightened. "Yes, my Lord," he murmured. "Yes, I will go on the adventure."

"No!" I shouted to him. "You can't go back! You'll burn!"

The old man heard me then. He turned to face me, eyes determined, shining with the light of truth. "Then I will burn," he said.

His words pierced me to the quick. I could not run toward the sea, where I would safely exit the planet through a tunnel. I stayed to watch.

Our village was being destroyed by the Burning Ember.

Wynaerians who had not escaped screamed as his fire consumed their huts. His shadow was lit up like flames. Out of the smoke, his body materialized, shrouded and wispy, a darkness deeper than that of the others. They had all deserted at his arrival.

Suri, the Commander whispered in my mind. *Go with him.*

Realization doused me. *This* was the adventure. I shoved the Commander from my mind. "No!" I told him fiercely. "No, I will not go with him. I will not die with him!"

Firen laughed, his back now completely straightened. His crutch lay on the ground, illumined by firelight.

"Come to me," the man taunted the Burning Ember. Then I saw that he was no longer old, but young. His back no longer hunched and his knees were steady. He was healthy again. With another laugh, he raised his hands to stop the inferno before him.

"*No!*" I yelled, desperate. "Run!"

But Firen didn't acknowledge me. He opened his arms wide and lifted his face to the firelight. "Embrace me," he said. "I sacrifice myself for my village."

The Burning Ember had to obey. He engulfed the Wynaerian, who disappeared into his blazing inferno and night. His work accomplished as allowed by the Commander, the Burning Ember could go no further.

He stopped there at the edge of the village, snarling and looking up into the sky in rage. His hands were in the form of swords, dancing with flame. Then he left as quickly as he had come. A trail of fire in the sky showed the dark tunnel he used to depart.

The Embers had done their work well. The huts were destroyed, the gardens burned, the animals scattered. Very few Wynaerians remained. Those who did now crept from their hiding places, sooty and scorched. They knelt in the rubble of the town, devastated. Some cried and wailed over their lost loved ones; others were stone-faced and saddened.

I stared in shock and horror. When had Wynaeria ever been desecrated? As I sank to my knees in the ashes, the Commander's voice penetrated my mind.

You lied to me, Suri. As punishment for your cowardice and deception, you are hereby exiled from Wynaeria until redemption is explained to you. Your life will go on, and you will remain scarred with shame because of your fear.

~ ~ ~

"Well done," the Commander's voice boomed throughout Open Space. "Well done, my faithful servant. Now enter into paradise."

From the tunnel exiting Wynaeria's atmosphere, I looked back. A piercing regret cut me deeply at the Commander's words. It was only then, staring back at my destroyed homeland, that I remembered his question from the previous morning.

Will you?

Fury and disappointment swallowed me. I turned away from Wynaeria; my cheeks were wet with tears.

Chapter 2
The Grip of Darkness

I had been wandering aimlessly for weeks. After my banishment from Wynaeria, I had traversed several different planets, always run off again by Embers or others who did not desire my company. Now I was on Earth, to complete the assignment the Commander had commissioned. He had finally revealed to me the Earthling he wanted me to guard.

I was half-heartedly obeying, still angered at him for exiling me and ashamed that I had let an old man better me. I had no real desire to disobey the Commander, but I did not like his harsh demands.

I had adapted into a human form from my own Wynaerian one. It was confining, something I'd forgotten from my last assignment. My Wynaerian body was lighter and more durable. An Earthling body is less pliable, more easily damaged, dull, and opaque. In addition, it is less substantial, crafted more of matter than the essence of life in spirituality. It was this difference, more than any other, that made me gripe. While I still retained the ability to slide through doors and walls as needed, albeit only on Earth, I trod heavier and could not withstand the pressures of the universe as well when traveling this way. Perhaps the greatest difference was my lack of appetite – in Earth's atmosphere, my body did not need food or drink for several days running. This, I took to be the Commander's doing, since guardianship would be made more difficult if I had to nourish my body as frequently as Earthlings and yet still retain my vigilance.

Through a tenebrous forest in eastern America I now walked, the Earth's star dipping down below the horizon. The gloom made no difference to me, as I could see clearly through the darkness. Nimbly dodging trees and stepping over underbrush, I made my way toward a clearing, where the silhouette of a small log hut could be made out. Around me I heard crickets and cicadas performing their choruses, though I could not perceive their forms. The pleasant summer night surrounded me, wrapping me in its gentle embrace.

Stepping out of the forest into the clearing, I silently sidled up to the hut and peered through the doorway. Inside, there was a single room – kitchen and bedroom in one.

A boy and his mother lay together on a feather tick on the floor, sleeping peacefully. The boy could not have been much more than eight years old, by Earth's time. He was curled into his mother, who had an arm over his shoulders. She murmured softly in her sleep and shifted. Brilliant light shone from her heart, the reflection of her soul. She belonged to the Commander. The boy beside her also had a glowing radiance, though his was not as bright. He had not yet accepted the Commander as his master. This light came from his simple faith in what he knew about the Commander.

Shifting my gaze from the Earthlings, I scanned the crude home. Two straight-backed chairs were pushed under a worn wooden table directly in front of a small iron cook stove. In the corner their single mattress lay. The hut was not insulated and it appeared they were covered with the only three blankets they possessed, made of wool.

How do they keep warm in winter? I wondered. I shook my head in disbelief and took a step forward. Kneeling beside the two Earthlings, I placed a hand on each of their foreheads and breathed over them.

"I give you warmth and love." My exhalation created a golden circle of heat that permeated and surrounded them: a shield.

Proud of my success, I stood back and looked down at them. They still slept peacefully, though blushes of pink spotted their cheeks. Grinning, I turned to leave. They would be comfortable through the night.

A picture flashed in my mind.

Bright white blinded me at first, but then shadows appeared and slowly hardened to show two humans. As the mist cleared, I saw the two Earthlings behind me, in exactly the same position as they were currently. Suddenly, the mother tensed and arched her back, screaming silently. The boy flinched in his sleep, but did not wake. The woman relaxed again and exhaled, a soft smile appearing on her lips.

The vision faded.

Startled, I stumbled backward a step. I shook my head slowly, trying to clear my mind. Never before had I seen the future of an Earthling so clearly.

I spun back to look at the boy and his mother. A shudder went through me. She was going to die.

~ ~ ~

Throughout the Earth-night, I walked the perimeter of the wooden hut, seeking the cause of the woman's death. No threats appeared, but I knew one would come. All the futures I'd seen so far had transpired.

I tramped around the clearing, sometimes going a few paces into the forest as I watched. As I did not need sleep – and rather detested the practice – I was glad of the movement. Every hour, I looked in on the Earthlings, to strengthen the shield of warmth and make sure they continued to sleep unperturbed.

When the night was at its darkest, a change occurred in

the atmosphere. I stood still outside the Earthling hut, alert. Something deep inside me shifted. A heavy burden entered my chest and weighed on me, pressing against my heart. I bent over with the pain. A lump filled my throat and love flowed into me.

This was the Commander's work.

When I was so full of the agonizing weight and burden of love that I could hardly draw breath, it eased.

Lead your charge well, the Commander murmured in my mind. *Be my light to him.*

Once before I had experienced this transfusion of love for an Earthling from the Commander. It was a forging of a bond between myself and the boy in the Earthling hut, my new charge. The bond could only be broken at the death of my charge, or the termination of my guardianship.

The heavy weight on my chest lifted slowly. I breathed easier. The future of my charge's mother once more entered my consciousness and I continued my vigilance.

When the sky began to lighten, another change rent the atmosphere. My spirit became troubled, similar to when the Embers invaded Wynaeria. Scanning my environs, I could perceive no such threat, yet I was experienced enough to know that didn't mean that one was not there.

With greater vigilance, I continued my round. Circling the hut for the final time, I saw the reason for the disturbance. A dark shadow plastered itself against the outer wall, barely perceptible in the early morning light. I stilled to watch, without revealing my position to the Ember.

Sidling along without a sound, the Ember crept to the door of the hut. He was only shadows, exuding black mist. There were no flames. He opened the door and slipped inside. I heard an angered growl and knew he saw my protective circle of warmth. A smirk flicked across my lips.

Before I could triumph over him, though, a sharp pain pierced my chest. I arched my back and opened my mouth in a silent scream. Somehow, I knew, this was also happening to the woman in the hut. For several long seconds I remained in the torturous position.

Suddenly, I was released.

Breathing hard, I unsheathed the knife concealed in my silver tunic and made my way stealthily to the hut. I wanted to remain hidden from the Ember as long as possible.

Above, a brilliant light darted into Open Space from the roof of the hut. I knew then the woman had gone to the Master.

In the doorway of the home, I peeked in at the Ember.

He stood over the boy and my shield, breathing curses. His form shuddered and I knew he concentrated intensely on breaking the protection. He was not strong enough.

With an angry shriek, he transformed his hands into blades and punctured a hole in the top of the circle.

As if I had been the brunt of his attack, I felt a stab in my back and bent double, gasping.

The Ember chuckled. "You did not think I knew nothing of you?" He turned to face me, his eyes violet slits in his face. His success in burrowing a hole in my shield of warmth had greatly weakened him. His voice came out strained.

I straightened and looked him full on, carefully avoiding any provocative motions. The Commander had restrained the Embers when his blood was spilled, so I could not be attacked first. As soon as I made the slightest threat, however, he would leap on me.

"Chaos," I greeted with a slight jerk of my head.

His smile was cruel and taunting. "You are Suri," he sneered. "Guardian of the Earthlings." Almost imperceptibly, he began rocking side to side, as though preparing to lunge.

I took a step toward the boy, now lying with a troubled look on his face. The hole Chaos had made in the shield was beginning to give him nightmares. He would soon start feeling the Ember's presence, and before long he would begin to see him. I could not let that happen. Walking past Chaos, my knife lowered to my side, I stepped to the shield. With a gentle motion, I pressed the hole closed.

I was only stalling. The boy would awaken and Chaos would attack. Somehow, I had to be able to escape with the Earthling. For now, my strength was sufficient to protect him. Yet if Chaos overpowered me in a duel, the boy would be killed and I would bear the consequences of a failed assignment.

Mind whirling, I let none of my fears show and turned slowly to face the Ember.

He yearned to battle. His eyes gleamed with hunger for the sight of my dead body. A look of detest crossed his face.

"You cannot fight me," I taunted. "I have not provoked you."

Chaos sneered. "I could break the agreement," he hissed. "However, there are greater ways to attack you." A twisted look of pleasure etched his face. He motioned to the still-sleeping boy. "Do you know who he is?"

"My charge," I answered unwaveringly, eyes steadily boring into his.

Chaos laughed, a low, ruthless sound that rebounded around the small hut. "He is one I used to know."

I stared at him, taken aback, and recovered quickly to prevent him from seeing my momentary shock. "Enough speech," I snapped. "If you cannot attack me, depart."

"We will not battle today, young warrior," he responded angrily, curving his back as though pained. At his words, I knew a messenger restrained him, though I could not see it.

He continued, "Your master has forbidden it; but be assured, inexperienced one: there comes a day when he will turn his back. Then, I will destroy you." He spat at my feet.

"I welcome it," I lied.

Chaos retracted his blades. "Be ready." Then he was gone.

Relief surged through me. For an unknown reason, the Commander had forbidden Chaos to attack. The knowledge was enough for the moment. Turning to the boy, still sleeping beside the corpse of his mother, I felt anger rise in me.

Yes, I vowed, *There will be a day when I will battle Chaos; and I will steal his life away for the pain he caused this boy.*

Suppressing my rage, I sheathed my blade. Then, silently, I crouched against the wall to wait for my new charge to awaken. An unpleasant surprise awaited him.

As though he heard me, the boy turned over in his sleep and sighed deeply. His eyelids fluttered open, but he didn't see me. I was invisible to human eyes, traveling in the guise of the universe. To those who could see me, I appeared as a shabbily-dressed human-like being, with a form suited to tunneling between stars.

The boy sat up sleepily, yawned and rubbed his eyes, and looked down at his mother. "I'll be right back, Mommy. I want to get you something."

Without waiting for a response, he jumped from the bed and scampered out of the hut. In moments he returned, clutching a bouquet of wildflowers in one hand. A wide grin spread across his face. He bounded over to his mother and held the flowers out in front of her blanched face.

"Look," he said. "Wake up, Mommy. Look what I've brought you." When she didn't respond, he placed them in her hand. A confused look crossed his face at her cold skin. "Mommy?" he asked worriedly. He put a finger beneath her eye and then lifted her eyelid. "Mommy!" A note of panic filled his voice.

I stepped toward him. "She can't hear you."

The boy couldn't hear me, either, but my words could be felt, an idea in his mind. He began to tremble and I shielded him in my arms as sobs broke from his little chest. He knew she was dead.

For a long time we stayed there as the boy grieved. He didn't understand what had happened, but he was quickly comprehending the burden of death. Soon, we would have to rise and leave his mother, but for the moment, I let him rest and be comforted.

I waited for his grief to abate, looking up at the ceiling of the rugged hut. I imagined Open Space beyond. My mind wandered to my home planet and a small smile curved my lips as I imagined my return.

Stars would streak past as the planet loomed before me. Gradually it would grow as I drew nearer, until I broke through the atmosphere and landed. A harsh aura would enter me. Something deep and terrifying.

For several minutes I would lay prostrate on the ground: shuddering, still, shuddering – in a cycle only broken when the Commander invaded my presence.

A thrill went down my spine and I chuckled softly, gripping the boy's shoulder.

The air of Wynaeria would reach into my skin, overtake the atoms that held my body together. Prickling ice would douse me, seeping through every pore of my spirit until I grew numb.

Then the Commander would come. His presence would raise me into life once more. His breath would strengthen me until I could feel in Wynaeria's atmosphere. He would speak until my lungs were filled only with his words.

My first steps on Wynaeria's landscape would be trembling, faltering. The Commander's gentle hand would guide me into the brightness of the meadow. His touch would at first be fire, searing until my skin fairly burned; but as it lingered and intensified, my back would straighten, my knees bend, my head would rise. When I could step alone, the Commander's touch would have so consumed me that I would be the flame of the burning.

For several moments, my body would glow golden with the fire, then slowly it would fade, leaving a harsh casing of protection on my skin. When that happened, the atmosphere would feel normal again. Strengthened so, I would no longer need the Commander's steadying presence, though I'd never be outside it, for then my body would be Wynaerian again.

Fully Wynaerian.

Satisfaction filled me at the prospect. I had only to finish my assignment. Brought back to Earth by my thoughts, I glanced again at the boy, dragging my eyes down to his.

Waves of terror and sorrow rolled off him to equally overwhelm me. I dealt with them by degrees, slowly, calming the combusted atmosphere in the room.

With my comfort, he stopped shuddering so fiercely and lay rather quiet, gazing at his mother with red eyes. He was bewildered, afraid, alone, wondering what darkness had come over his world.

"Come away now," I finally said, standing and pulling away from him.

He lifted his tear-stained cheeks with determination, obeying my words which were simply an impulse to him.

"What do I do now?" His voice was quiet, stricken. He looked out of the door of his hut into the beautiful day that had heralded such darkness.

"Say goodbye."

My charge stood and looked down at his mother's body. For several moments, he stood still, conflicted. He was only a boy, facing a decision that would change his life, but it had to be made. The boy raised his chin in defiance of the grief. Then, in a much older voice, in obedience to me, he whispered, "Goodbye, Mommy."

It was unfortunate that such a young human had to experience this pain, but I knew there was no other way for him to complete that for which I had been sent to help him. So I only eased his pain for the time. One day he would have to return to what was now his present, resolve his emotions, understand. He would have to reconcile his mother's death as he would one day have to reconcile his father's departure. The thoughts brought me sorrow.

But for now.

We would be leaving soon: as soon as he realized there was nothing left for him in this hut. With the preparation I had been performing on his heart, there was only a final surge of strength to give him before departure.

"I love you." The phrase released the boy's claim on his

mother.

His words swirled slowly around his mother's body, a brilliant golden light. They could no longer warm her as they once did, but none could contend with the offering. The light slowly seeped into her skin, fluidly coursing its way through her. It wrapped around her heart in a golden case, perfectly beautiful.

Now go, the Commander murmured. *Leave her to me.*

I wrapped an unfelt arm around the boy's shoulders. Gently, I led him from the hut, reassuring him through my presence. He needn't return to this hut – not for years – so I kept all thoughts of Earthly matters at bay. Though I did not yet know where we were going, I knew he would need nothing. I would provide for him.

As we walked into the forest, he began to sing.

> *Goodbye, Daddy*
> *Goodbye, Daddy*
> *I'll see you*
> *Some other time*
>
> *Goodbye, Mommy*
> *Goodbye, Mommy*
> *I'll see you*
> *Later on*

It was his father's departure, his mother's death, his own beginning of a journey. These were what brought him to the despair of goodbye.

His sorrow flooded into me, as part of the bond between guardian and charge. Filled with his sadness, I dwelt with him through the pain, strengthening his trust in me.

As we walked out of sight and sound from the hut, I looked back. A tendril of soft, white flame curled into the sky. There was no smoke from the fire, and it did not burn very long.

In a few moments, it drifted away on the air, as though it had never existed, but I knew what trace it had left. That of an empty clearing. The Commander's fire had consumed the hut and the body inside.

~ ~ ~

As the day waned, I grew increasingly weary. We had traveled west through the forest since leaving the hut behind. Lost and scared, the boy had wavered from fear to sorrow to anger with each step that we took. His altering mind created tension and confusion in me, which caused my protection to weaken.

Disgruntled and agitated, I began to weary of this assignment. With my rumpled spirit, I quickened my pace and attempted to focus solely on our progress.

The evening darkened into night, and the Commander had not revealed where I was to escort my charge. Since he needed protection through an Earth-night, I started pondering where to place him.

Trees would be unwise, as he wasn't a proficient climber. He was far too afraid of being in the air. The ground would be dangerous, for there were many Embers around and on the ground we were more easily hunted. Yet the boy had no relatives, and there were no friendly humans nearby who would receive him.

Save for one.

I shuddered at the idea of taking him there. Surely elsewhere would be better, safe from danger and temptation.

The Commander thought differently.

Take him to your girl.

Anger sparked in me at the order. The day had been long and hard, and now the Commander demanded this from me? Bitterness pricked me.

No, I argued, carefully concealing my anger and defiance from my charge. *I cannot return to her. My guardianship is finished.*

He needs shelter, the Commander persisted. *She will welcome him.*

And destroy me! I retaliated, incensed. Everything in me rebelled at the thought of returning to her.

This assignment is not for your *sake,* returned the Commander. *You are here to protect the boy and guide him in truth. Do not mistake your purpose on Earth. Obey me.*

I clenched my teeth and did not answer. He had stripped away a carefully placed protection in my heart and mind, a shield that locked away my previous guardianship in forgetfulness. I would not allow him to order me until my guard had been replaced.

Halting my charge, I instilled him with the idea of sleeping on the ground. I gave him the thought of excitement and adventure to dispel his fears.

It wasn't difficult, as he had grown to trust me.

As I encircled him in sleep, increasing drowsiness in his body, the thought of safety returned to me. I lifted my head and searched the forest for any unnatural shadows. None arrived, and so I settled down with my charge and he fell asleep.

~ ~ ~

"Come to me," a hissing voice beckoned from before him. *"I can give you all that you desire."*

The boy jerked his eyes in the direction of the eerie voice, but saw only the outlines of the trees. *"Who are you?"* he asked in trepidation. He stood alone in the midst of a dark forest, trembling with fear.

"No one of consequence," the voice soothed, changing from grating sharpness to silky comfort. *"I want to help you. You are so lost and alone. I wish only to bring you joy and peace."* This time the words came from behind him.

The boy spun to find the speaker, but again saw nothing. He clenched his fists and waited. All was silent for a moment.

"Listen to me," the voice continued, suddenly against his ear. "I will lead you in the right way. You will be loved, and wanted."

Evil chuckles rose from the underbrush.

Despite his crippling terror, the boy raised his head in curiosity. "How?" His query was only a whisper.

Something cold swept across his cheek and sent a fiery chill down his spine. He shuddered and darted his eyes back and forth between the trees, searching for the source of the voice. He could see nothing in the darkness.

"You need not fear," remarked the voice. "I find you worthy of protection. There is nothing that could harm you against my protection. I will lead you in safety."

"Why are you saying this?" Cold sweat beaded the boy's forehead and trickled down his back. "Why do you think I want something from you?"

Again that cackling laughter that made him shiver. "Everyone wants something from me," came the response. "I can tell you who killed your mother. I can help you find your father. I can make you victorious over your enemies. Is that not what you want?"

Penetrating through his fear, the words began to persuade him. He looked down at the ground for a moment. Yes, he wanted those things. More than anything, he wanted to know who killed his mother and where his father might be found. Could he really trust this mysterious voice?

"Why do you want to help me?"

The voice responded pleasantly, "You are very valuable to me. There is so much I can give you, so much I can make you. Those who would harm you can be silenced and stopped. I can help you achieve victory over all."

The promises swirled in the boy's head, fogging his thoughts and rousing desire in him. His heart thumped in anticipation of believing the voice, but with some effort he checked his eagerness.

"How do I know I can trust you?"

This time, the laughter was quieter and gentler. "There are none who would not trust me. What could I gain by lying to you?"

Taking a step, the boy moved toward the irresistible voice. "I don't know," he answered honestly.

"Then look at me and listen." Two eyes, one violet, the other red, appeared before him. A silhouette detached from the shadows of the trees and stepped before the boy. It stood in the shape of a man, but appeared murky and indistinguishable. Gliding closer, hardly seeming to touch the ground, it moved until it was directly in front of the boy, a mere foot away. A white glow showed a crooked smile beneath the mismatched eyes.

The boy took an involuntary step back. What stood before him didn't seem to have any substance, only shadow. It had a kind face, in spite of the eerie eyes, and an agile, nearly fluid, body.

The shadow held out a hand to the boy. "I am tangible," it said softly. Its eyes gleamed. "You can trust me. I will not hurt you. Do not be afraid of my appearance; it is merely a form I take."

"What are you?" the boy breathed in fascination. Suddenly his fear was extinguished. With burning curiosity he seemed unable to control, he reached out a finger to the silhouette's hand. It was cold as ice and firm beneath his touch. Swirling dark mist enveloped his finger and concealed it from sight. It felt like cold wind, leaving a tingling fire over his skin.

When his finger was encompassed, a surge of electricity coursed through the boy's arm up to pierce his heart. His recently dispelled terror returned full-fledged. He gasped in surprise and looked up at the shadowy figure, wide-eyed. Try as he might, though, he was unable to break the suddenly relentless grasp it had on his hand.

Again, the silhouette's smile flashed brilliantly in the night. "I am an Ember."

~ ~ ~

I jerked out of the boy's thoughts, drained. In the quiet of darkness, I regained my breath. Beside me, the boy flinched in his sleep, but didn't wake. He began drawing in heavy breaths and clenched his fists, curling into a tighter ball on the ground where he lay. A shiver ran through me because of his fear.

Scanning the forest around us, I looked for the intruder who caused the dream. There was nothing. Disquieted, I turned back to the boy. How did an Ember enter his dreams?

What disturbed me more, however, was the boy's lack of terror. He didn't seem as afraid as he should. Embers were dangerous enemies, but even more dangerous allies. They could not be trusted and if the boy did not have a healthy respect for them, he could be ruined.

With these troubled thoughts in my mind, I resumed my vigilance, more alert now than I had been. If the boy allowed the Embers to influence him, I would be rendered powerless, and my assignment would be a failure.

I attempted changing his mind about me, but discovered he no longer listened to me.

I knew why and anger overtook me, but I did not have the mental energy to begin regaining my charge's trust. For now, I looked up into Open Space and exhaled slowly.

~ ~ ~

Near the middle of the night, I noticed the difference. Apart from my knowledge, a shred of my anger had entered the boy's heart when I had disobeyed the Commander. It now fueled his thoughts and entered my consciousness through his disturbing dreams.

These he had the remainder of the night, causing him restless slumber and, in turn, charging fear and vengeance in me. The Ember knew his work well, slowly weakening the connection between my charge and me. My strength was not enough on its own to withstand the barrage, so when the boy finally awakened, I was as drained as he.

The boy opened his eyes and stretched, yawning. He shivered in the cool morning of the summer day, wet with dew.

I frowned. For the first time in my existence, weariness overtook me so that it was hard to think clearly. Even so, I knew the boy should not be cold so close to me. I was created with the abilities to provide him warmth, shelter, and courage; none of these remained in the boy from the day before.

"Commander," I muttered disconsolately. "What is this?"

His words, *Take him to your girl,* made me shiver. If I obeyed, could I stand against the temptation to Reveal? I must. Another night like this, and I would be destroyed; my charge would be in the clutches of the Burning Ember.

Wrathfully, I stood. "Get up," I told the boy sharply. Through no fault of his own, I was resentful toward him.

He seemed to understand something had changed in the night. Fear no longer assailed him; he scoffed at the nightmares that had overwhelmed him only moments before.

Standing, the boy turned around, searching for the best way to proceed. Already he seemed like an arrogant young man rather than a frightened boy.

I began walking east, toward my girl's house. "This way," I called over my shoulder. At the moment, I didn't care if he followed or not. I, for one, had decided to obey the Commander.

The boy proved to be as irritable as I. He scuffled along in the underbrush, kicking pine cones and twigs and muttering under his breath. His fear dissipated with the rising sun and pride took its place, urging him to avenge his mother's death.

Whatever the Ember had changed in him, he was no longer the charge I'd had the day before. Where light had been in his heart, there now spread a shadow. Wispy, but nonetheless substantial.

The Ember's tilling went deep.

Raw fury burst from me. Almost without my consent, I

shot a Channel of light into the boy, as fiercely as I could manage.

He did not respond.

Again and again, I assaulted my charge with light, attempting to break the darkness that surrounded him. Each time, my effort was ignored, and my wrath grew.

Concealing my rage from the boy, I ranted inwardly to the Commander. *Must we find her? I will Reveal and you will banish me from Wynaeria forever. The boy has already turned to darkness. His light has faded. Why didn't you warn me that this would happen?*

You disobeyed me, Suri. These are the consequences of your decision. The Commander's voice was firm. *The boy needs your girl. You must take him to her.*

It is a difficult thing to return to a previous charge, I grated to him. *What if I Reveal?*

It is forbidden, he answered. *You will not Reveal.*

His words were an order as much as a warning. If I Revealed against his command, the result would be far worse than the evil already infiltrating my Earthling charge. He was on the brink between total chaos and rescue, where I could still draw him back to the Commander. Should I disobey my master, the boy would fall to destruction and suffer the consequences – darkness wrought in him, perhaps to the point of becoming an Ember.

I shuddered in revulsion at the thought.

Regardless, the result depended on my obedience to the Commander. I looked up to Open Space in disgust and angrily shook my head. I had no choice. I would obey the Commander.

Chapter 3
Failed Guardianship

I knew it was my own anger coursing through the boy that continued to feed his ravenous hunger for revenge for his mother. Even so, I could not control myself. The knowledge that my rage could destroy my charge did not daunt me. Were I to perish in this assignment, another would take my place. Still, I did not relish the idea of failure, especially in light of my previous excursion to Earth years before.

Then, I had obeyed the Commander immaculately, remaining in my girl's presence only until she began to suspect me. I had begun materializing and hardening into an Earthling's body. I had begun to Reveal. Then I'd had no choice but to leave. If I had Revealed, she would have been persuaded to keep me with her. The Embers would have discovered my traitorous deed and attempted to bring me down with them. Moreover, by order of the Commander, I would be banished from Wynaeria as a renegade and no more allowed to set foot on my beloved planet. Had I Revealed, I would have secured my own demise.

Now, I was returning to my girl with a new charge, and the Commander expected me to uphold my integrity and not Reveal.

"Come this way," I told the boy, changing our course slightly. We had wavered in our direction because of my distracted thoughts. Muttering fiercely under my breath, I exerted my mind to concentrate solely on the boy.

The sunrise brightened the sky with brilliance, bringing hope. Streaks from the Earth's star stretched across the blue expanse – salmon pink, deep purple, and blood red. Colorful and warming, the sun's appearance brought the first softening to my charge's features.

Gradually, the day grew hotter as we continued to walk. My charge was hungry, but afraid of eating something harmful, he ignored my suggestions of edible plants.

Too preoccupied with my own troubles, I ignored his hunger, convincing myself it would soon be set to rights when we reached my girl. For once, I was very glad to be abandoned on Earth. In my rebellion against the Commander, I was able to follow my own desires without the conviction he would have undoubtedly brought had I been on Wynaeria.

The sun was high and my charge's stomach was complaining loudly when I first spotted my girl's cottage through the trees. Intense relief and fear flooded through me. Relief, that my charge would have a different guardian besides myself, even if only for a time. Fear, that I would soon be gripped in temptation and unable to resist it.

Commander, give me strength, I griped cheerlessly.

I was uncomfortable around all Earthlings, save children. Little ones were easy to get along with and love, but adults were pure trouble. Unfortunately, my girl was now an adult. She had also been the only being in my existence to ease my insecurity, and now returning to her would be dangerous. When she had been my charge, she was merely a child, not much younger than the boy. To face her as a maiden would be precarious; yet I had no other option.

I did not anticipate our reunion.

My charge and I walked toward the house until he could

see it. Then he broke into a run, scrambling forward. For the first time since the Ember's nightmares, he was no longer angry, but excited. His happiness brimmed over to me, and for a moment, the shadow shrouding his heart dimmed.

Running to the cottage door, the boy banged against it with his fist. "Please!" he cried. "Please, let me in!"

I restrained myself from going forward, staying far away for the initial greeting. Beneath a tree thirty paces from her door, I awaited my girl's arrival.

She opened the door.

Her light-skinned face was beautiful – young, yet weathered with wisdom. It was no longer wreathed in smiles as it had once been, but held a blissful contentment that gratified me. Her figure was trim and slight, beaten by the sun and acquainted with work. On her wrist, invisible to the Earthlings, there was engraved a circlet of thorns, identical to mine. Her eyes sparkled, framed by hair that brushed to her waist. Love that I'd given her long ago still encased her heart in a shield. She was well protected.

Above all else, though, a light shone from her eyes. It looked like gemstones were reflected in the deep pools of blue. The effect was that of glassy eyes, as though teary. The intensity of their brightness gave me pause. Though I knew many who possessed this light of truth, granted only by the Commander, I had never seen it so vibrant.

I bowed before my girl in respect, though she could no longer sense my presence.

"Oh, my dear young boy," said she softly at the sight of my charge. Her features wrinkled in concern and she knelt before him, reaching out a motherly hand to cup his cheek. "Are you all right? What happened?"

The boy stared at her dully for a moment. Then the overwhelming terror of being alone washed through him. He ran into her open arms and buried his face in her stomach. For a long time, he could only sob into her while she stroked his head and murmured comforting words.

Momentarily, her goodness disarmed me and my anger disappeared. I took a step forward before a sliver of grudgingness toward the Commander returned and my obstinance held me back.

"There, there, dear," my girl soothed the boy, brushing his hair away from his tear-stained cheeks. "It's all right. Come inside now, and eat. There's time later for you to tell me." She knew there was a story, and, like all good mothers, she knew to wait until the boy had eaten before discovering it. My girl put her arm around my charge and led him into her home, leaving the door standing open.

I stood behind, outside, looking in.

The kitchen was small but effective, open to the outdoors in front and back. Three cupboards, a workstation, and a cast iron stove took up the space. A doorway to the left opened to a small but comfortable parlor, furnished with a single table, a small wood-burning stove, and four chairs. On the far wall stood my girl's bed, covered by a feather tick. Behind the house stood beehives which provided my girl's livelihood.

The walls were made of cedar logs, the floor of dirt. The furniture had been bought or traded for with honey and beeswax in town, several miles' walk away. In summer, the doors and windows remained open; in winter they were shut tightly and sealed to keep out drafts. The dwelling was humble and simple, but comfortable and welcoming. My girl loved it.

Now, she led my charge to the worn wooden table. While he seated himself, she prepared two plates of food: fruit, biscuits with honey, and a small piece of cheese. When she joined the boy at the table for the meal, she bowed her head to pray.

As I listened, a strange longing filled me. Her words, sincere and filled with love, reminded me of the time not so long ago when I had been close to the Commander. I wanted reconciliation between myself and my master, but I didn't yet want to let go of my anger toward him. Unable to have it both ways, I retained my arrogance and became indifferent. Later,

51

when there was time for such, I would ask forgiveness and be reconciled to the Commander. Now was not that time.

When my charge had eaten and was calm once more, he told my girl of his troubles.

"Now I'm an orphan," he finished listlessly.

My girl had tears in her eyes, and love flowed from them into the boy's.

"You poor boy," she said.

The boy resented the word, but allowed her to wrap him in her arms. At her touch he thought of his mother, which bothered him. He wanted to be strong, so he restrained his sadness that was barely at bay.

Despite his determination not to show weakness, I noticed his fatigue. With a word, I prompted my girl to put him to bed, and she obeyed.

Standing, she took him into her arms and carried him to her bed in the corner. There she tucked him in with care and said a quiet prayer over him.

"Sleep well," she whispered.

The boy's eyes closed. Sleep was taking him quickly into its embrace. "Goodnight," he murmured sleepily.

My girl gave a radiant smile that shortened my breath.

Carefully wrapping into myself, I stifled my desire to Reveal. For only a moment, I had nearly become visible, disarmed by her overt purity.

Unable to bear her presence, I left the cottage and leaned against the outer wall, breathing deeply. Anger swept through me at my glaring inability to remain inconspicuous.

"Commander," I muttered, looking up into Open Space littered with his glory, "is this another test?"

My Commander didn't answer me that day, or for many days to come.

From where I stood, I heard my girl exit the house to attend to her bees. A few minutes later, I returned to my charge's side, where I belonged.

~ ~ ~

For several hours the boy slept, due in part to my presence and his own bodily comfort on the bed. This time, there were no Embers creating nightmares in his mind. His face was soft and sweet in the tranquility, and I easily remembered how I loved children.

The sun was slanting in through the windows when my girl entered the house, her daily chores of weeding, harvesting, and watering the garden, and caring for the bees completed. She smiled at my sleeping charge and quietly stepped to his bed. Looking down at him, her face filled with compassion. She brushed the hair away from his eyes.

At her touch, the boy stirred and exhaled deeply in sleep.

"Sweet boy," my girl murmured. She turned away and began preparing a meal. She set bread dough to rise, brewed tea, and made a rabbit stew for my charge. Then she sat at her table and waited for him to wake, drinking her own mug of tea.

As I stood against the wall, watching over the Earthlings, I discovered there still lingered a connection between my girl and me. I could still see into her heart and thoughts, could still glimpse parts of her future. The realization made me glad. I could have more than one charge at a time. A part of me wondered if that was the Commander's design in sending me here; the other part of me squelched that hope.

The boy stirred again on his bed, and I returned my full attention to him. Whether my girl was to be my charge again did not matter compared to him. He was far more important than any other human now – including her.

She turned her beautiful green eyes to him and her entire face lit up with joy. "Oh, good," she said. "I'm glad you're awake. Did you sleep well?" She stood and knelt beside him.

I chuckled wryly. Of course she couldn't know the dreams of peace that he'd been having, but the idea that he was discontent in her cottage was ludicrous.

My charge sat up in bed, yawning and rubbing his eyes.

"Yes," sighed he. Grinning, he bounded out of bed. "Thank you." A shadow crossed his face and I could feel his anxiety again. His mother once more surfaced in his thoughts and his smile vanished.

"Oh, dear," my girl said softly, kneeling and taking him into her arms. "It's going to be all right."

He shook free from her embrace, straightened his shoulders, and hardened his expression. The look on his face pierced me with anguish. He was consciously listening to the Ember's voice in his mind, drawing on anger and hatred to fuel him rather than love.

I frowned.

"Are you hungry?" my girl asked, interrupting my thoughts. She seemed not to have seen the disturbing conclusion in the boy's expression. "I've made stew and bread."

My charge nodded. "Yes." Then, remembering his manners, "please."

My girl laughed lightly, returning to the kitchen. She ladled the stew into a bowl and set it in front of the boy with a slice of bread toasted on the stove. "Here you are."

"Thanks." As he dug into his meal, my girl poured a cup of tea for him. He looked up in surprise, which quickly turned to a grin.

"Now," my girl said, taking her place across the table with her own meal. "What's your name?."

His grin widened. "I'm Robert."

"Robert," she repeated, eyes bright. "That's a nice name." After taking a bite of bread, she continued, "Where do you live, Robert? How did you find me?"

The boy's eyes tightened. "When Mommy died, I ran away." He gave her a beseeching look. "Don't send me back."

"Why ever not?" my girl asked, surprised. "You should return to your home and live with your family. Do you have any brothers or sisters?"

Robert's expression darkened into mutiny. "No."

"What about your father, then?"

"I don't have one. He left."

My girl was silent for a moment after this pronouncement.

Robert continued eating. He wasn't going to divulge information easily. He wanted her to work for it. Though the thoughts didn't cross his mind so blatantly, he liked being paid so much attention.

"How did you find me?" she repeated finally.

"I don't know."

Shrugging away the unsettledness that filled me at the boy's complacency, I spoke to them. "I led you here."

"I think someone led me here," continued the boy, paying heed to my words. He cocked his head slightly as though listening for more, a much older look than there should have been crossing his features.

I gazed at him. As he spoke, the shadow that had punctured his heart noticeably swelled to extinguish more of the light in him. Plagued by this, I attempted to Channel more light into him – created by the Commander's love. As I worked, the Earthlings continued their conversation.

My girl's eyebrows shot up. Her face filled with knowing. "You think someone led you here?" she probed. "What makes you think so? No one accompanied you. Did you see someone?"

"No." Robert shrugged. "I guess I imagined it."

My girl studied him pensively for several moments, a crease in her forehead, a finger to her lips. When she spoke again, it was in a different tone. "I don't think you imagined it, Robert. I'm sure someone led you here."

I narrowed my eyes at her words. She couldn't possibly be referring to me.

"Who?" Robert scoffed, already dismissing the feeling of my presence he'd had as we traveled.

My girl tilted her head slightly, gazing at him unblinkingly. After a moment, she shook her head infinitesimally and spoke in a quieter voice.

"I think perhaps we should save that conversation for

later. There are still many things for which we must first prepare." Her expression brightened. "For instance, what are you going to do?"

Robert scowled. "Am I going to live with you?" His voice, like his look, was quickly losing its boyishness. Perhaps the shadow over his heart was more invasive than I had thought.

"I can't turn you out. Would you like to stay here?" my girl countered. That same pensive expression remained, as though she too could see the darkness surrounding him.

"Yes. I like it here." Pointedly, he made a spectacle of gazing around the cottage. He smiled. "Where will I sleep?" His mien returned to the impishness of an eight-year-old boy.

My girl laughed. "I have extra bedding beneath my bed. I never use it, so you can have it. I'll set up a cot on the floor for now. After some time, maybe I can purchase a bed frame for you."

~ ~ ~

Despite her kind intentions, my girl never was able to buy a bed frame for Robert. That night, as they slept peacefully and I watched over them, a shadow began to creep toward the house.

I slid from my watch post by Robert's cot to the window and glanced out into the night. Nothing seemed out of the ordinary, but the heaviness that weighed down on me could have only come from an Ember. Though I could not see it, I knew one was there.

After several moments of inactivity, I relaxed my posture. My mind was far from at ease, but whatever threat loomed outside the cottage was biding its time – probably hoping for me to leave my station.

Just as I was beginning to think I'd imagined the creeping darkness, my girl stirred in her bed and mumbled.

"Please." Her voice was merely a breath, strangled and terrified.

I shifted to look at her, opening my mind to look into

hers. Until this moment, after discovering I could still see into her mind and heart, I had carefully avoided any mental contact with her, knowing she could easily detect my presence. Now, however, I had to know what terrible dream was causing her discomfort. If I did not, both she and the boy could be harmed.

I was not disappointed.

She ran from the hut into darkness. Wordless screams broke through her lips, a reflection of her agony. Her back was striped and bled from the whipping she'd just received. Still, her mental torment exceeded her physical.

"Oh, God," she gasped, the words torn from her lips in a desperate whimper. "Please."

Tears rushed from her eyes and dripped from her chin to the ground, as step by pounding step she left them behind her. She headed for the forest, where there was cover from the terror behind her. Unspeakable pain filled her.

As the shadows engulfed her, something built up in her chest and spilled over. A strangled cry slid through her teeth. She tripped and fell into the underbrush, but unable to bear stillness, she pushed up again and continued.

She had to get away.

Suddenly, she stumbled into a clearing. On the far side, rather than returning to unending trees, a cliff dropped down into a gushing river.

The Cliff.

She had not meant to return to this place of torture. There were hidden memories here that she suffocated in the recesses of her mind. Drawn to the edge of the stable ground, she halted and stared down into the blackness. From this height, she couldn't see the water, but she could hear it. It was thunderous.

She looked down the 200-foot drop ending in a river below. Only a second passed, showing her the times she'd tried and failed, the times she'd dreamed of something more. She jumped.

Wind whistled through her hair, calming her. Dreams

*sprang to her mind: thoughts long forgotten, hurt that killed ...
all drawing up, surfacing in her mind. Her life flashed before her
in only a second. A life of secrecy, pain, hurt, horror. A life that
would now end.*

*An incomprehensible scream broke from her lips as wind
pricked her eyes cruelly, provoking tears. The ground came closer,
haunting in the back of her mind, rushing forward to meet her,
when suddenly ...*

It was over.

She shuddered, flinching back from the Cliff. Despite her desperate
plight, she could not bring herself to throw her body over the edge.
Sweat poured from her body as she listened to the sudden
rhythmic beating of death drums, pounding through the forest
around her.

This is it, *she thought.* The end has come.

*Another minute and everything would be over. If only she
had escaped before it had come to this. If only she had realized the
truth before it happened. Only then could she have been freed.
Now there was no other way.*

The drums beat louder.

She turned. A man, like a mist, materialized out of the
shadows around her, hardly substantial. His eyes burned like fire,
a disconcerting violet glare. He clutched a knife in his fingers.

"Remember my promise," he whispered maliciously. He
hefted the knife lightly, springing toward her to hold it to her
throat. As she looked, though, she realized the blade was not held
in his hand – it *was* his hand.

She nodded slowly, resigned to her fate, fear wrapping her
in its cold embrace. "I remember."

A wicked gleam entered his eyes and his lips pulled back in
a snarling smile. "Now die," he breathed. He thrust the knife into
her neck, an action that would cause any human to die.

She was no mere human. Something much stronger than
mere bodily stamina upheld her. She had a light in her soul.

Returning the man's gaze, she stared into his eyes, stared into the depths of his ravaged spirit, illuminated by his features. Defiance radiated from her face. Blood flowed from the new wound in her neck. The battle was not yet over.

As the man watched, blood slowly trickled down her throat. Horror drew across his face – terror beyond imagination. Soon there would be nothing that could help her.

The invisible drums beat faster.

She drew up, oblivious to the pain. Drawing up a hand, she caused the man to fly backwards. He crashed into the trees behind her. Some form of power deep within her had arisen and overtaken her. Laughing, she watched as the man slumped, neck broken. Then she turned and ran through the forest, her feet light as a breeze, fairly flying through the air.

She did not know how long it was before she collapsed. The passage of time was meaningless. She only knew the days grew rougher; the pain grew harsher. Her limbs numbed and her mouth dried. Soon she would be unable to continue. The vultures would come and feed on her flesh, tearing her apart, piece by piece.

Staggering forward, she used her hands to claw her way further through the dry desert. She could not remain in the path of the sun when it rose. The night engulfed her now and she was safe. Soon, however, that would change and she would be ravaged by vultures.

The sun rose slowly ... too slowly. By the time it reached its peak, the birds had already begun circling above her. One by one they dove and then drew up again, slightly lower than before, until it would be too late.

Her head filled with chaos. The night came back to her: the night when this had all begun. The night that had forced her destiny upon her. The night when her father had betrayed her.

The vultures circled closer.

He loved her. Surely, he loved her.

The vultures could feel her body heat.

How could he have done this to her? Couldn't he see how

he had hurt her?

The first vulture swooped low and landed on the ground, inches from her face.

Her eyes opened and she stared into the bird's hideous features. "If I must die, I'm taking you with me," she whispered fiercely.

The vulture drew back his head and, quick as lightning, struck her forehead. Blood trickled down into her eye so she couldn't see. Down across her face it streamed, until it dripped off the end of her chin, making a small pool beneath her.

The vulture struck again and screamed.

She had no energy to resist. She could not live; the scars were too deep. All she wanted was to sleep. She couldn't breathe. Slowly she dropped into a black abyss in the depths of her mind.

Above, the rest of the vultures blocked out the sunlight and swooped to join their leader.

I flinched, pulling out of my girl's nightmare. It was not merely a dream I had observed, but a memory. Or, at least, a distortion of a memory: far more painful. I drew a shuddering breath. Though I had only observed, and not experienced it from her point of view, the depths of her slumbering terror overwhelmed me. I blinked my eyes rapidly to extinguish the visions in my head.

My girl twitched in her bed and gathered her hands into fists.

She had indeed seen an Ember. Whether with her physical eyes or merely in dreams, the shadowed being had invaded her. Still, the light with which the Commander had infused her refused to be tinged by something sinister.

Guilt washed through me. Her memory was my most tormenting regret of failure. It was only because I had disobeyed the Commander and left my girl defenseless, that she had been hurt that night. I had been tortured by it ever since.

I swallowed. How could I defeat this overbearing

remorse?

Shaking my head in incredulity at my girl's resilience and my own failed attempts at repentance, I once more gazed out the window.

At the edge of the forest, I saw the reason for the unnerving disturbance in the Earth-night. An Ember waited in the gloom, as my girl's premonitory dream had suggested. Or perhaps the dream had come because of the enemy. Regardless, it was his tilling that caused this tide of horror between myself and the humans.

I glanced back at the boy sleeping soundly and my girl struggling to stand firm in her nightmare. Neither of them could withstand an Ember at close quarters. Even at this distance, their minds were being steeped with dread.

I would have to remove them from the confrontation that was surely coming. Another failure was not permissible. I could not disappoint the humans. Or my master.

"Commander, help me," I muttered, finally releasing all my previous anger toward him. Squaring my shoulders and murmuring quick words of comfort to the Earthlings, I stepped to the door of the hut and looked out.

"Suri," a grating voice breathed, confirming my suspicions. "How I've longed to meet you before now. I would have, but the Enemy would not allow me."

"He is no enemy to me," I retorted, finding the Ember's eyes in the shade of the trees.

A harsh laugh resounded. "Yes," he sneered. "I forget the commitment you have to such a tyrannical entity." A flicker of fire penetrated the atmosphere. "Do not try to escape the onslaught," my taunter continued. "You will not live out your purpose."

I felt the wave of mist and fire before I saw it. In that moment of preparation, I was allowed to step aside from the attack and create a barrier.

Like sunlight in the middle of night, a wave of light filled the distance between myself and the attacker. Just as I had encased my girl and Robert's hearts, I now immured the hut and myself in a shield of clear gold. An overflow of the Commander's love bled from my heart to make the crystal-like barrier.

It was beautiful. Impish delight laced with shock filled me and spilled over into a laugh. The Commander was audacious. How had I withstood that magnitude of love concealed inside me? Did I really contain that power without knowing?

The Ember moved into view, a look of utter disbelief twisting his face. At my look, he snarled in disgust and his eyes flooded with hatred. Quicker than my eyes could follow, he stood outside the glowing shield, hands formed into blades, scraping against the indestructible gold.

I couldn't restrain a pronounced smirk from claiming my features.

"You are safe tonight, Suri," the Ember hissed grudgingly. "Do not grow lazy in your vigilance, or I *will* kill you."

Behind the Commander's protection, I did not feel the cold breath that exuded from his mouth, nor the invasive dread that surely accompanied it. I could see, however, the expanse of evil with which he attempted to overcome the shield.

Another smirk at his failure sparked across my lips.

"A warning to you," he growled. "Do not forget the extent of our power."

Completely protected from him, to me his words were empty.

I gave a mock bow. "Consider your message delivered," I snarled.

With unusual deftness, the Ember departed.

Despite my brave words, I was glad when he disappeared. A sigh of relief escaped my lips. I had not wanted to fight him and the Commander had, amazingly, granted that request.

Around me, the incredible shield continued to glow

golden, shimmering of its own accord.

I shook my head in awe, closing my eyes. "Forgive me," I murmured to the Commander. Grieved by my arrogance toward him, I bowed to my knees and lowered my head. "I do not deserve your goodness, nor the power you have granted me. Let me never presume on your presence again."

Chapter 4
Dueling With Shadows

I rose quietly from my kneeling position. For a moment, I remained stationary, resting in the Commander's presence and conviction. Looking up to Open Space and marveling over the stars, I returned to the hut.

I glanced at my girl from the doorway.

Her features were pleasant now, no longer tortured by the nightmare brought by the Ember. Her fingers relaxed from their fists and she exhaled softly, deep in sleep. For the first time that night, her dreams were free of fear.

Robert, likewise, now slept peacefully, utterly unaware of the near fight that had transpired. His mind was unperturbed.

In relief, I leaned back against the door frame and exhaled. So long as the Earthlings were safe, there was nothing to be anxious about. Closing my eyes and lifting my face to the ceiling, I breathed a prayer of thanks to the Commander.

Tranquility ruled over the remainder of the night, and when morning came, the fear in the darkness had all but abated. Robert and my girl rose well-rested and refreshed, dreams nearly forgotten.

As they breakfasted together, an aura of content settled between them, and the meal was companionable. I only wished to join them in their discussion.

"Do you believe in angels?" Robert asked, his voice satisfactorily boyish again.

My girl glanced up at him in surprise. "Yes," she answered. A small smile began to curve her lips. "Do you?"

Robert shrugged, looking down at the biscuit he held. For a moment, he stalled his answer, chewing. "I guess so," he answered finally; then, under his breath, "It makes sense."

"Why do you ask?" Curiosity instilled her voice. She looked at the boy, attempting to discern his thoughts.

Robert snorted quietly. "I just don't understand. If there are angels, why didn't they stop my father from leaving? Why didn't they save my mother?"

Comprehension filled my girl's features, and compassion, her heart. "It is not for us to question God's design," said she. "We know He is always right. Who's to say what wrong would have been had your mother lived?"

Robert glared at her, anger and resentment burning in his chest, building up to an outburst. "If He wanted her so badly, why did He give her to me?" He set his jaw and looked down again, as though his eyes could bore a hole into the table.

My girl was silent for a moment, an ache filling her face. "I cannot say, Robert," she answered. "She was a gift to you, to be enjoyed while you had her." Heaviness clouded her mind. "Why do you think angels could have saved her?"

A hint of a smile touched Robert's lips. "They can do anything."

"I don't know," my girl cautioned gently. "They are God's messengers, and can do whatever He allows them. I don't know that they can do anything, though."

Now Robert lifted his chin in defiance. "Of course they can! They can go anywhere and help anyone! They can fly!"

I couldn't help a small laugh at his indignation at my girl's ignorance. My outburst cleared some of the tension from the air.

"Have you ever seen an angel?" my girl challenged

teasingly. "How do you know they can fly?"

Robert shook his head. "No," he admitted, "but that doesn't mean they can't. How else would they get around? Mother said they could fly," he grumbled.

My girl looked at him for a moment, took a bite of her own biscuit, and chewed thoughtfully. "I guess that makes sense," she agreed finally. "It would take a long time for them to walk everywhere." She laughed.

Robert wasn't finished with his questioning, though. "Have you ever seen an angel?"

That question took my girl off guard. For a moment, her composure twisted into a most extraordinary expression. She looked sorrowful. Then she smiled and said, "No. Of course not. Only very special people see angels, and not very often." Briskly, she continued, "However, they do help us. God sends them to protect us and tell us His messages."

Robert mulled that over. "Have they given *you* a message?"

Now she laughed, all trace of her sadness gone. "Yes. At least, I think so." Finished with her breakfast, she stood. "Come, there is work to do in the garden."

Robert followed my girl out of the back door to the hut and into her small yard. I went with them, still pondering their discussion, as they meandered over to the garden.

My girl knelt and began pulling out weeds from among the vegetable plants. "Help me, Robert, and it will go faster."

Obediently, the boy crouched down and began to help. He was pensive as they worked, thinking about angels and why his mother had to die. At every thought of her, he winced and a shred of anger took over more of his heart. The shadows the Ember had planted in him began to spread, commanding more of him.

I kept a wary watch on the boy, afraid of the swiftness of evil in him.

"Am I special?" he suddenly asked. His eyebrows were

drawn together in concentration, as he watched his dirt-stained hands.

A quick smile crossed my girl's face. "Of course," she answered lightly, lifting the leaves of her tomato plants to check for worms. She shot a glance at Robert and continued, "Everyone is special. That's the way God made us."

Robert snorted derisively. "If everyone's special, why can't everyone see angels?"

Understanding lit my girl's eyes. "Ah." She moved to the next tomato plant, contemplating her response.

Robert had already forgotten his question by the time she replied, his mind on the praying mantis strutting between the cucumber vines.

"It has to be a very important matter for angels to show themselves. Only those people who are particularly chosen by God to do something very special are able to see them." The same sorrowful expression returned to her face.

I wondered at it, unsure why angels made her sad.

"So I'm not very special," Robert concluded. "Because I've never seen an angel."

His brusque tone brought my girl from her sudden dejection and made her laugh. She began harvesting the ripe tomatoes and cucumbers, lighthearted once more.

"Who's to say how special you are, Robert? Only God knows what you will do." She continued, "but seeing angels isn't very important – not overall." She bent to look under the leaves of the squash plants for any ripe produce. "See, what's important is that you do what God wants. Compared to His approval, seeing angels is nothing." She ruffled his hair with her free hand, the ripe vegetables held in the folds of her apron.

Robert nodded. "I suppose."

My girl jerked her head toward the hut door. "Come, now. Our work here is finished. Help me carry the vegetables in, and then let's look for honey."

Eyes wide, Robert reached out to take some of the produce. "Honey?" he breathed, mouth open as he stared at the vegetables in his hands. Skipping to keep pace with my girl as she headed toward the house, he gasped, "You have bees?"

~ ~ ~

Days passed quickly as Robert and my girl settled into a comfortable way of life. In the mornings over breakfast, my girl read some pages from the Tome of Essence, and they prayed together. Afterward, they weeded the garden, harvested the honey, and cleaned house. From lunchtime till supper, Robert played in the forest around their hut as my girl did small jobs and read aloud in the autumnal afternoons. When the need arose, we traveled to a nearby village where my girl sold or traded her honey for wares and meat. When the need arose, I left them to forage for my own food, which I ate without letting them out of my sight.

I was content to merely watch the Earthlings relate to each other. Though there were times when the Commander's orders seemed harsh and unnecessary, when I reminded myself to heed them, I quickly grew happy again.

Only once did the subject of angels come up again. It was late one rainy night before bed. The supper table was cleared and Robert was snuggling into his cot on the floor. My girl leaned over him to kiss him goodnight, and he rolled to look up at her.

"Do you think it was an angel who led me here?"

Startled, my girl drew back to gaze into his earnest face. "It could have been," she conceded quietly. After a pause, she murmured, "I think an angel led me once."

At her words, I straightened at my post beside the door. Confusion swept through me.

"What happened?" Robert breathed.

"Once, a long time ago," she began softly, her eyes lost to a memory, "I ran away. My mother had died several years earlier, and my father was very mean to me. I didn't like living with him, so I left." Her voice grew wistful.

"It was dark and raining outside, like now, and I was frightened. I didn't like the night. The thunder was so loud it hurt my ears. I was more afraid of my father, though, so I started toward the town only a few miles from our home. Something began chasing me – I could hear it behind me when I stopped. I was so afraid, I began to run.

"I was in the forest around our house and there was a log across my path. Because of the storm and the darkness, I didn't see it. I ran right into it and tripped." A smirk lifted her lips for a second. "When I stood up, I was cold and dirty and wet. Yet there was still noise behind me and I was terrified. I started running again and it wasn't long before I fell.

"This time, I couldn't get back up. I sprained my ankle and I was hurting. As the night got darker and the storm worsened, I lay there crying and screaming. I begged God to protect me."

Robert was staring at her wide-eyed, his own story etched clearly in his mind.

"It seemed like demons were attacking me," my girl shivered at the memory, "but I couldn't see anything. I felt hands and claws on my arms and legs, scratching me," her voice dropped to a whisper, "but there was nothing there." A tremor of her old fear slivered into her, but she continued undaunted. "I prayed and asked God to take away the demons." She was quiet.

"What happened then?" Robert's voice was awed.

My girl absentmindedly began twisting and untwisting her fingers in a long-forgotten nervous habit. "A new hand touched me," she marveled. "It wasn't cold and scary like the others, but warm and comforting. As soon as I felt the touch, I felt safe."

I listened, intrigued by her version of that night.

"Courage swept through me and I was no longer afraid. I stood up in the forest and continued on my way, suddenly bold as a lion." She chuckled. "It took several days, but with the gentle hand guiding me, I made my way to my aunt's house."

"You think the hand was an angel?" Robert breathed, impressed.

My girl shrugged, embarrassed at the idea. "I don't know." She looked down at the enchanted boy and smiled. "Now, it's time for you to go to sleep. There's plenty of time tomorrow to talk some more." She leaned over and kissed his forehead, smoothed his hair, and tucked the blanket up to his chin.

Robert curled into his blankets and closed his eyes. "Goodnight," he murmured.

"Sleep well." After singing a hymn to the boy, my girl stood and crossed to her bed. Shuddering slightly at reliving her nightmarish past, she slid beneath her own blankets and pulled them to her chin.

It was the first time in a long while that she had a bout with fear. Unable to sleep, tossing and turning, wide-eyed, my girl finally got up from her bed and sat at the table. There she sat, poring over the worn pages of her Bible by candlelight, trying to soothe her rumpled spirits.

I stood over her, attempting to comfort her, but incapable of taking away her panic. "Commander," I murmured in the dimly lit room. "Restore her peace."

Gradually, my girl grew sleepy enough to brave returning to bed. Barefoot and weary, she stepped across the dirt floor and snuggled under her quilt. Reciting verses to herself, she was finally able to drift into a dreamless sleep.

I stood beside her bed for a time, looking down at her, bringing comfort. After a while, I turned to Robert.

As before, the golden case around his heart was fading. Soon there would be no more protection for him and Embers would assail him from every side.

Inwardly groaning, eyes watchful, I knelt beside his bed. For a long time I only stared at his blackening heart. If the rate of the encroaching shadows could not be checked, havoc would break out in him. Hate would gnaw at him until it sprang at my girl and hurt them both. Terror and evil would be his allies. He would shun goodness and embrace the Embers.

I could not let that happen.

"Commander, let me reach him," I entreated. I reached a hand to touch Robert's chest and Channeled my love into him. At first, it appeared to work, fighting back the gloom that threatened to destroy him. Then, as I watched with growing anxiety, the shadows resisted and retaliated. As though it lived, the dimness in my charge's heart swallowed his golden shield of innocence.

I knew then what I had failed to recognize earlier. The boy had already embraced the Ember who visited his dream. He had entertained and encouraged it, hastening his own destruction. Without intervention from the Commander, resistance was futile.

"Strengthen me," I muttered aloud. "I cannot win this war on my own." Shaking my head in resignation, I settled back into a cross-legged position and stared down at the obstinate Earthling.

It would be a long, hard fight.

~ ~ ~

The Earth-night passed far too slowly for my contentment. I was disgruntled and unsettled. Robert's allowance of the Embers' nature to spread through him proved to be harrowing.

Exhausted, I remained cross-legged beside him throughout the darkened hours, often speaking to the Commander on Robert's behalf, and pleading for a change in his heart. The Commander, as usual, remained silent through my appeals.

When the sun rose the following morning, I was haggard. My girl likewise was unrested, due in great part to her sleep deprivation the previous evening. Robert alone remained unchanged by the passing night. He was quickly growing more like an Ember.

My girl left the cottage for a time, wandering alone

through the forest for a little way. I knew without needing to eavesdrop that she was speaking with the Commander. If my assumptions were accurate, she would be thanking him for his strength through another terrifying night.

Robert stayed in the hut, sitting up in his bed and staring out of the window. He was the calmest I'd seen him, thinking about his mother and missing her. He seemed overly content to merely stay there, motionless.

Taking advantage of his stillness, I turned from him to seek out my girl. While it was unnecessary for me to protect her anymore, I liked the idea of her being my charge again.

Striding through the door of the hut, I stepped into the trees to observe her. She stood quietly, head bowed, beneath the overhanging branches. Her lips moved and only a gentle whisper escaped them.

"Father, help me lead him."

I realized she was praying for Robert. Had she seen the evil creeping in on the boy? Did she feel the evil at work, attempting to destroy what little good I could accomplish?

Wondering made me peer into her thoughts to see. They were tumultuous and bewildered, but an undercurrent of peace filled her mind. She was anxious over the boy, begging the Commander to save him. Overwhelming sorrow filled her as she prayed on Robert's behalf.

"There is so much anger and revenge in him. I need you to intervene. Lead him to you, Father," she murmured aloud. She clasped her hands and placed them under her chin, swaying gently. Eyes still closed, she reverted to silent prayers, no longer able to form comprehensible sentences as she groaned to the Commander.

Shocked by the strength and depth of feeling in her words, I stared at her in amazement. Where did her devotion to the boy come from? Yes, he'd been living with her for many days now, but that she should have become so attached that easily was startling. Sometime during our stay, she had begun to love Robert.

A sudden urge to Reveal swept through me. I fought it back testily, outraged at the very thought of such a desire. My head cleared of confusion, I waited for my girl to finish her lone wandering. Leaning against the trunk of a tree, arms crossed over my chest, I glared at her in impatience. I was unsure of the safety of leaving her in the forest, and I did not desire to do so. Robert, alone in the hut, was more secure now than either my girl or myself. I did not worry about him.

Finally, my girl lifted her eyes and smiled. In a childlike spirit, she spread her arms wide and looked up into the brilliantly blue sky. For a moment she held her position, breathing deeply. Then her arms dropped back to her side and she turned toward her house. A peace was etched comfortably into her posture which unsettled me.

I followed uneasily as she led the way back to Robert.

We had not traveled far before I realized something was wrong. Tendrils of black smoke curled up into the sky from the position of my girl's house. Chagrin gripped me.

"Wait," I told her. She had yet to see the smoke and I knew if she did I would be unable to stop her from running toward the house. If I could retain her, however, it would be simpler for me to find and save Robert.

My girl paused, and glanced around wonderingly.

"Don't go back to the house yet," I continued quietly, trying to keep the note of panic out of my voice. It worked.

Relaxed, peace lingering from her communion with the Commander, she slowed her meandering walk and stood still. She quickly became preoccupied with observing a butterfly and I took the opportunity to scamper.

Berating myself at my foolishness, I bounded to the cottage, sprang through the open door, and skidded to a halt in the entrance of the kitchen.

Robert was in the same position as when I'd left, sitting calmly on his cot, hands folded under his chin. His eyes looked straight forward, completely oblivious. Beside him on the dirt floor, a fire had been kindled. It was quickly surging toward the boy's bed.

A corner of the quilt draped onto the floor, a mere inch from the licking flames. I leapt for it and flicked it up onto the bed.

"Get out," I grated to Robert. His posture explained the scenario and anger rippled through me. It was not an Ember who had spawned this attack; merely the shadow encompassing the boy's heart. He wanted to burn.

Robert didn't listen to me, ignoring the small part of his consciousness that acknowledged my warning that his actions were dangerous. He was absorbed with his black thoughts. As he was so inattentive to my voice, there was nothing I could do to prevent his desires from occurring.

I was forbidden to touch him and I knew I could not break that rule. Instead, I leapt to the quickly-growing fire. Kneeling, I removed my traveling cloak and beat at the flames to suffocate them.

The task was weary and burdensome when I would much rather beat sense into the boy, but proved an acceptable outlet for my anger and served a productive use. The fire died down. When only smoke remained, I turned to the boy in disgust.

"You are recidivous," I spat.

Robert looked around for the first time, seemingly bewildered. With tantalizing slowness, he rose from his bed and stretched, yawning.

"Hello?" he called into the empty house. His eyes alighted on the fire's ashes and soot-blackened floor. He raised his eyebrows and an impish grin spread across his features.

I wanted to strangle him for his insolence. Instead, I clenched my fists and teeth and bored my eyes into him.

"What happened?" he muttered aloud. A playful look came into his eyes and he glanced around guiltily, as though he were looking for my girl. When he realized he was alone, he let loose a terrific shriek. Pumping his fist in the air with delight, he danced around wildly.

Concern touched me for a moment at his strange

behavior. Then my wrath returned, and all compassion for him fled.

"How do I protect an idiot?" I muttered scornfully. My question was somewhat directed at the Commander, but mostly a release of my anger.

My girl entered the hut then, still tranquil. When she saw the scorched dirt and smelled the remains of the fire, she looked at Robert in disbelief. A touch of concern reached her eyes, but she spoke calmly.

"What happened?" she asked quietly. Her eyes burned.

Robert grinned mischievously. "I was playing."

My girl raised her eyebrows. "With fire?"

There wasn't a hint of remorse in Robert's features. "Yes." He motioned to the spot on the ground where the flames had been. "I put it out. Nothing was ruined."

I scoffed. Though it was true my presence went undetected, particularly now that the shadow had completely ensconced him, Robert's version of events was preposterous.

My girl was quiet as she studied the boy, a finger to her chin. Evidently, she was wondering what to do.

I helped her. "He needs to be punished."

My girl glanced in my direction as though she'd heard me. For just a brief instant, her eyes narrowed and gleamed. Something flickered over her countenance before she turned back to Robert.

"Come with me," she said, turning on her heel. "It's time for breakfast."

I stared at her back indignantly. Would she really forgo discipline? Another thought quickly crowded my mind, though; one far more serious.

Had she seen me?

~ ~ ~

Sobered by Robert's dangerous nature, I watched far more closely over him and my girl. The knowledge that the boy could never be left alone was torturous, for there were often times when I wished to leave. Only at night, when he was safely sleeping, was my desire fulfilled. Then, I would escape outdoors to commune with the Commander and scout around the house.

On one such night, I discovered a disturbance in the atmosphere outside the cottage. Having only just shoved away from the wall to circle the property, I was immediately on guard. The moon shone down brightly, illuminating the clearing around my girl's house. I trod lightly over to the shadows beneath the trees. It took a moment, but searching with my eyes, I found the Ember.

"What are you doing here?" I demanded.

"Suri," the voice came back, lulling and surprisingly gentle for such a caliginous creature. "I thought we were past pretenses."

"I pretend nothing."

A low chuckle reached my ears. "Indeed." The Ember stepped into my view, violet eyes gleaming eerily. "Do you really believe you can protect the Earthling?" A rumor of superior disdain underlined the question.

I clenched my jaw. "As the Commander allows, I am able."

The Ember stepped closer, his vapory murkiness spreading out to envelop me. He was several inches taller, and much stronger. A sneer curled his lips.

"What message have you this time?" I mocked. As he had not attacked immediately, I was sure I would escape unscathed once more. As would the Earthlings.

"Have you not noticed?" he taunted, suddenly leaning into a crouch, preparing to spring. "Your charge, the dear boy –" his words were deriding "– has welcomed us readily in his midst. Do you really believe one such as you can stop that?" He grinned. "You will not defeat us, guardian. You will fall."

"Is that your only warning?"

His eyes narrowed. "Be watchful. The boy has welcomed us and we are free. Already he invites us into more alluring waters than before. As his strength grows, so, too, will his defiance of you and your master. Do not be misled. You will be destroyed."

With a final exhalation, the Ember disappeared.

I was beginning to wonder about their arrivals. This was the second time I had only been warned, and not attacked, by an Ember. Why were they refraining from a fight?

Shaking my head, I turned back to the cottage. It took only a moment for me to realize the extent of the Ember's message and revulsion licked through me.

The cottage roof was on fire.

As I started back toward the house, realization crashed in on me. The Ember had not been here to warn me. He was merely distracting me while allies wreaked havoc. Fueled by anger, I darted inside. "Get up!" I hissed, striking panic into my girl and Robert.

Immediately, they were both alert. My girl jumped from her bed and knelt by Robert to gather him in her arms protectively as smoldering debris fell from the burning ceiling into her bed and caught the blankets on fire.

Robert shrieked in surprise and wrapped tighter into her.

"Get out," I ordered, stepping to them. I placed my hand on my girl's elbow, strengthening her.

She rose obediently, raising Robert up with her. Their lungs filled with smoke, causing them to cough. My girl blinked her eyes in pain and Robert clenched his fists against his eyelids.

"We have to leave," I muttered. I stayed with them, gently guiding them through the hazy room.

My girl scampered back to her bed, where she fumbled in the blankets, yanking her hand back when a spark burned her. Just as quickly as she got there, she returned to Robert's side, clutching her Tome of Essence.

The flames were beginning to spread from the ceiling down the walls. Robert and my girl began coughing from the smoke, their chests congested. I shielded them as best I could, urging them on through my words and touch.

We broke out into the calm night air. Stars twinkled dimly above, outshone by the crescent moon. My girl and Robert huddled together in shock by the well-tended garden. Sparks flew out from the fire to the grass, but had yet to spread further than the hut.

Now that the Earthlings were out of danger, I thought of where to station them for the night. I knew another place where we we could go, but I was loath to take them there. Glaring up at the night sky, as if he would reach down to talk with me, I muttered my complaints to the Commander.

"It will be too difficult for me if I take them there. Wouldn't it be safer in the forest?"

Even without the Commander's response, I knew. No. The forest was unquestionably out, as the Embers could still be milling around. We would only be safe with those who belonged to my master. I could no longer protect the Earthlings on my own. I needed others. Those others, however, were not those I desired.

As I debated internally, I watched the Earthlings comforting one another. My girl kissed Robert's hair and murmured soothingly. The boy's arms were around her, his former impudence nearly forgotten.

"Come on, then," I said dully, succumbing to the logic that fought back against my jealousy. "We're going to Eversen's."

My girl's eyes lit up as the thought occurred to her for the first time. "I know where we can go," she murmured. "I know someone who will take us in."

Robert pulled away from her and looked up earnestly into her face. "Who?"

She smiled. "He's an old friend of mine, who lives not far from here. His name is Eversen." She took the boy's hand and began leading the way from the house.

At the edge of the forest, Robert pulled away from her touch and turned back. By the light of the fire I saw a grin pull across his face, and a shiver ran through me. What should have killed this boy was making him smile.

"Come on, Robert," my girl said, thinking his pause was from sorrow, unable to see his expression from her position. She steered him away. "We'll be at Eversen's soon."

Shaking my head in disbelief, I followed the Earthlings. As we walked, I strengthened and encouraged their resolve. They were both exhausted, but still able to draw courage from me. They pressed on through the forest with me for quite a ways.

Only once did my girl trip and she caught herself before falling. Robert looked at her with wide eyes, but, at her silent persistence to continue, he said nothing.

It was not long before we came upon the dreaded clearing. Immediately, I was cautious and resentful. Robert broke into a run toward the hut that stood out in the darkness, illuminated by the moonlight. My girl followed, breathing a sigh of relief.

Robert pounded on the door. "Help!" he cried, much as he had when arriving at my girl's. "Help! Please, let us in!"

Ruefully, I thought of the alleged terror he had perfected. His ability to rally so quickly against his circumstances was unnerving. I wondered if it was an Earthling trait, or merely because of the shadows encroaching on him.

It was several agonizing moments before the door opened. A young man looked out. He was tall, with dark skin and dark eyes. His broad shoulders were brushed by brown hair, disheveled from sleep.

I looked him over carefully and discovered his mind and heart were shrouded from my sight. It was understandable, as he was not my charge. Still, the thought was disconcerting. I glanced at his wrist, and saw the Commander's mark engraved on his skin. In his eyes shone the light of truth. He was trustworthy.

Eversen did not speak when he saw Robert and my girl. His eyes widened, but he stepped back and allowed them to enter, cordial. I stepped in as he closed the door.

"I'm sorry, Eversen," my girl murmured, as they stopped just inside his door. "I don't mean to intrude. My hut was burned while we slept and I didn't know where else to go. May we sleep here for the night? In the morning, I'll find another place for us to go."

Eversen's face transformed with a huge grin as he nodded eagerly, motioning for them to follow, and led the way down a dim hallway to a spare bedroom. Flinging open the door, he ushered my girl and Robert inside.

It was a small room, furnished only with a bed and wash stand, but cozy and welcoming. My girl smiled slightly, some of the weariness leaving her features.

"Thank you, Eversen."

He nodded and tapped Robert on the shoulder, jerking his head to leave the room. We left my girl to sleep and Eversen settled Robert on the floor by the wood stove in the kitchen.

When all the Earthlings had gone to bed, I left the house to sleep outdoors. It had been too long since I'd last slept, nearly three weeks rather than the usual two, and I was drained. It took a few minutes to find a suitable spot where neither Embers would assail me, nor cries from the Earthlings would go undetected. I decided on a sturdy oak tree, and swung myself up into the highest branches, which also conveniently provided an ample lookout.

Only after ascertaining that there was no danger did I lean my head back against the trunk and close my eyes. Within moments, I slumbered.

~ ~ ~

When I awoke, burning sunlight shone in my face. Groaning, I lowered my head and shifted forward into a more comfortable sitting position. I yawned. It was already well after morning – the sun directly overhead. Blinking to adjust my eyes, I thought of my charges and remembered the reason I hated sleep so intensely. Those first few waking moments are full of confusion and grogginess, very unsuited for guardianship.

Swinging agilely from the tree's branches and landing in a crouch on the ground, I rose alert. Now that I could evade sleep for several weeks, I sauntered happily to the house.

My contentment lasted only until I reached the open door and saw Eversen lunching with Robert and my girl. They were gathered at the kitchen table, sitting comfortably. Eversen had a thoughtful look on his face as my girl spoke.

"You don't expect us to stay here for a long time, do you?" She appeared hesitant to accept that much welcome from him.

If they were discussing future plans, surely the past had already been discussed. Then Eversen must know about Robert's mother and the fire. Perhaps they'd even returned to my girl's hut to see what remained. I was disgusted with my need for respite. It seemed there were many discussions I'd missed.

Eversen studied first Robert and then my girl. He smiled and nodded.

"Eversen." My girl's voice was reproachful. "You can't possibly be able to provide for us both. Are you sure we won't be a burden to you?"

Eversen raised his eyebrows in what appeared to be astonishment. He vehemently shook his head.

My girl watched him for a time and finally nodded. "All right. If you really think we won't be too burdensome."

Eversen snorted and shook his head, rolling his eyes.

"Thank you." My girl blushed becomingly, lowering her eyes.

I glanced sideways at Robert, gauging his demeanor. He was staring pensively between Eversen and my girl, absorbing each word. His expression left an aura of guile about him, reminding me of the Ember who'd accosted us. I frowned warily.

"How long will we stay?" the boy inquired, his voice aloof.

I gazed at his heart, which was now completely obscured

from my sight. Only grey swirls showed, all previous light extinguished. I had no insight to his intentions and could only guess as to what his question meant.

Eversen shrugged indifferently. His eyes were bright.

They had finished their meal now, and rose from the table. Robert's eyes darted around the small kitchen before boyishness entered his expression once more. Throwing a smile at my girl, he cavorted outside.

Eversen cleared the table of dishes to wash.

Apprehensive about Robert, I left my girl alone in the kitchen to follow him. As expected, he frolicked nearby, waving sticks in the air as swords. From outward appearances, he was a normal boy. I leaned against the outer wall of the hut to watch him.

Robert made slashing noises with each thrust of the pretended weapon, prancing in circles and lunging occasionally at imaginary foes. A sly grin turned up one side of his mouth, but otherwise he seemed perfectly at ease. His mind was focused solely on his game.

I crossed my arms in frustration, practically glaring at the Earthling. If only I could lift the veil over his heart and see what was happening in him.

I muttered aloud. "Commander, he's shielded from me. How can I fight something I don't understand?"

As expected, the Commander's answer was silence.

After brooding for several more moments, I had an idea. Pushing off from the wall, I strode over to the boy and placed my hand on his head. Nothing changed.

Pursing my lips in slight exasperation, I touched his chest. This time, Robert seemed to feel me. He jerked away from my hand and looked around in bewilderment. A slight look of pain crossed his face, as though he had been burned.

Intrigued, I took a step back and Channeled the Commander's love into the boy. Though his heart did not open to me, the smoky veil faltered marginally. I repeated the action more forcefully.

Robert gasped and stumbled backward. He steadied himself before falling, but the sticks he held dropped to the ground. A tortured expression flooded his features. It held for a moment, prolonging his shortness of breath, before fading completely.

This was unusual. The Earthling didn't respond to my touch or my voice, but when I impaled him with the Commander's love, he acted hurt. While the discovery was welcome, it did little to impede the Ember's work.

Robert returned to his game.

I wasn't finished with him, though. Again, I Channeled love into him, with the same results as before. Over and over I punctured the shadows surrounding him and gradually they began to fade.

My strength waned long before I had eradicated the veil. Before I stopped, however, a brief glimpse of his golden belief peeked through. It was enough to encourage me. Surely if he was too far gone, there would be nothing but blackness all the way through. As that wasn't the case, I had hope.

The prospect looked bleak, but I began to contemplate how to destroy the Ember's influence in the boy. I would need help from the Commander, as well as another Wynaerian. The darkness would not break by my own power. Would that I could summon another, I mused to myself.

I left the boy to play and rambled to the back of the hut, still deep in thought. There, Eversen was working hard. He stood by a chopping block, cutting logs for firewood and stacking the newly cut wood against the house. Already the pile was large, and growing with each new piece. My girl sat on a stump nearby, reading her Tome of Essence she had rescued from the fire. Behind them, a small stream sliced through the landscape, giving off a faint trickling noise.

Suddenly, my girl looked up. "It's such a comfort to be welcomed here, Eversen. I woke up last night from my nightmare and felt glad that I wasn't alone."

I tensed at her words. She'd had another nightmare?

Again, I grumbled to myself about the necessity of sleep.

Eversen looked up to give her a warm smile, wiping the sweat from his forehead with his free hand, then returned to his work.

Encouraged, she continued. "I thought of this while I lay in bed," she murmured, turning back a page in the Tome of Essence. "I was thinking of my father, and being alone, unwanted." Her voice tightened marginally. "It comforted me."

She took a moment to find the verse and then read aloud softly, "'He brought them out of darkness and out of the shadow of death, and brake their bands asunder.'" A soft expression came over her face as she fingered the page lovingly. "It has always been hard, remembering my parents. Reading this makes it easier. To *know* I'm not alone anymore, that I have someone ..." her voice trailed off.

Eversen stopped his work and looked at her, his forehead creased in sympathetic understanding. He reached out a hand to pat her shoulder comfortingly. When she glanced at him, he raised his eyebrows.

"I slept well after that," she affirmed and grinned.

Fierce jealousy struck me at the look that passed between them. I ground my teeth and turned away.

In the past, I had been the one to comfort her, and now I was unable. Unintelligible mumbles filled my mind at the injustice of the Commander's demands. Wasn't it enough that I had to battle with the boy's insolence? Must I struggle, too, with my girl's unattainable status?

I scrambled away from the Earthlings, desperate for peace and silence in my own mind.

Once beneath the shading arbor of the trees, I slowed my pace and seethed inwardly, giving full vent to my bitterness.

Suri, the Commander's voice reproved me.

I grimaced, but my fear of him was not enough to discount my resentment. *Yes, Commander,* I rumbled.

It is not only for Robert that I commissioned you here. You, too, must grow and change. His words soothed, with only an undercurrent of reprimand.

I know, I retorted.

Do you?

The question was not rhetorical, but I didn't answer. A rebuke deserved, I was rightfully cowed. Still, my bitterness was not completely repelled.

Yes, I do know, I answered. *That doesn't mean I have to like it.* I could almost hear the Commander's chuckle, but knew it was only my imagination. He would never laugh over my disobedience.

I wandered through the trees, trying to grasp the origin of my ire. Though I did not discern when, my anger gradually faded. Weariness took its place and I remembered my purpose as guardian.

The Commander would never charge me to do something of which I was incapable, I reminded myself. Turning my thoughts to better channels, I meditated in disgust on my selfishness.

I'm sorry, I finally repented.

It was the first time since the Commander's rescue outside my girl's hut that I acknowledged my inadequacy. Sorrow at my own weakness and pride stung me.

Change me to be like you.

I am.

Chapter 5
Malice and Zar

The night drew on and the Earthlings all remained inert in their beds. I entered the house from my outdoor round to confirm their safety and calm. All remained silent.

I gazed down at Robert on the floor, his makeshift cedar bed slightly sturdier than the night before, made by Eversen. He was curled into a ball, breathing steadily. Once more, I pierced his heart with the Commander's love, just to ascertain that my earlier assessment was correct.

As I did so, the atmosphere changed. I delved into his thoughts and immediately drowned in terror.

Fire rose all around, mingled with tangible darkness. Hissing and snarling surrounded him. He was alone except for the voices – those dreaded beings with the maniacal eyes.

He screamed, but no sound came. His throat was so hoarse, desiccated. He could not close his mouth to clench his teeth. Terror swept up his spine. Frantically, he tried to force his mouth closed. His inability to perform the irrational desire fueled his fear.

"You cannot disobey," a cruel voice murmured from somewhere to his left. "You must do what we command."

"Leave me," the boy gasped, able finally to move his lips.

"Please." Tears rose from his chest, congesting his breaths. "Please."

His supplication fell on deaf ears. "You cannot escape us," the voice intoned dryly. "You beckoned us to come, and so we have."

"Leave me alone!" the boy shrieked, leaping back frantically.

Harsh laughter sounded in his ears, close and breathy, rolling up from a deep chest. "Ah, but now you are too late. It is only out of fear that you beg us to leave. Once you discover what we can grant you, your opinion about us will change." The voice turned soothing.

The boy shuddered. "I don't want you," he reiterated softly. Dread froze his legs so he could not run. His mind clouded with gloom until he could no longer see where he stood.

A soft touch reached his consciousness. At first gentle and comforting, it quickly turned hot until it seared into his skin. He felt like he was flaming. The heat traveled from his forehead where it originated, down into his chest, through his arms and legs, until it completely enveloped him.

Blinded and burning, the boy stumbled forward, striving to escape the torture. He shuffled his feet mere inches before the pain paralyzed him. It was no longer just on the surface of his body, but crawling deeper into his flesh, delving under his skin down into his bones.

"You see the penalty of your feeble endeavor to escape," the voice crooned. "Now burn."

I gasped as I pulled away from Robert's dream and staggered backward a step. Drawing a shuddering breath, I ran my fingers through my light brown hair and noticed light sweat beaded on my forehead. The terror of the dream had not vanished with awakening. I looked down at the boy, heaved a deep breath, and tried to regain my composure.

"Commander," I murmured, holding a shaky hand out to

touch Robert's chest. "Steal away the despair."

The Earthling's face was passive in the gloom. His breathing was almost imperceptibly ragged and his hair was damp with sweat. At my words he sighed deeply and shifted in his sleep. For the moment, calmness claimed him.

Now wary, I left to determine Eversen's and my girl's condition. Making my way into the spare bedroom, I paused outside the door for a moment, listening. She breathed deeply, so I walked in and stood over her.

Her features were beautiful in the gloom, softened by slumber. I was taken off guard for a moment, reminded of the last time I had been sent on an assignment – when she had been my charge. Then, she had been much more cognizant of my presence and I could easily dispel her fear.

My girl gasped in her sleep.

The noise was loud in the silent night and peculiar for her peaceful countenance. Remembering her worst night, I closed my eyes and eavesdropped on her dream.

"Father, please!" she begged. She knelt before him beseechingly, arms upraised to protect her face. "Don't put me in here! Please!"

Her father held a riding crop in one hand, raised to strike her. His other hand grasped a bottle, which he raised to his lips. He swayed unsteadily, but regained his balance. "Hold still," he ordered, glaring at his daughter. His voice was low and raspy, words slurred from drink. The riding crop came down, striking her across the wrists.

My girl scampered backward as far as she could into the wood shed, trying to escape from her father's wrath. "Please," she begged, eyes wide, arms stinging and weary from being upheld so long.

Laughing, her father struck her again. He didn't respond to the fear and pain in her eyes. The punishment was justly deserved in his mind and he would discipline her severely for her disobedience. Anger crossed his face, eyes narrowing on the cages along the wall over her shoulder.

"Father," she pleaded, seeing where his gaze had gone. Terror lurched through her. "Please, stop it! I'm sorry! I'm sorry!" she gasped the words breathlessly, hoping to escape from his rage.

My girl's father swept her aside and reached to unlatch the first cage.

My girl screamed and scrabbled to the open shed door, desperate to escape. Her fingers grappled with the handle, but she was apprehended before the door swung open.

"Get away from there!" her father bellowed, thrusting her backward into the opened cages.

Bloodcurdling shrieks burst from her, but her father paid her no heed. He abandoned her to the imprisonment. She heard the lock click on the outside of the shed door and her hopes plummeted, replaced by utter dread.

She heard the scratching as the birds flew from their cages, startled by her outbursts. Unable to contain her horror, she cowered to the ground, covering her head with her arms and sobbing wretchedly.

The birds flew around her frantically, beating their wings against her arms and face as they tried to flee. They screeched, sending chills down her spine.

She closed her eyes, yearning for the end, rocking back and forth on the ground. Her body shook with sobs.

Breathless, I jerked out of my girl's consciousness. Something was wrong. The Earthlings should not be all having nightmares at the same time. Someone was orchestrating them.

I gazed at my girl in sorrow. Breathing a word over her and commending her to the Commander, I skipped from her room for Eversen. If both my girl and Robert had dreams, he was sure to have one also.

I entered his room without pause and darted to his bedside. He tossed and turned, a groan emitting from him. Immediately, I immersed myself in his mind as well as I could.

He was alone, shrouded in mist. The ground on which he stood was brown with mud. He turned around, absorbing his surroundings. Nothing could be discerned through the overbearing fog. Shapes and shadows flickered into being as he moved, but quickly vanished again as he paused. Cold trickles crept along his body.

He took a step forward and his foot sank deep into the muddy ground. When he attempted to raise it again, it stuck fast. Unreasonable frenzy made him try again and again. With each tug his leg only grew more firmly fixed.

He opened his mouth wide to call for help, but no sound protruded. His skin crawled, as though someone were watching him, but when he spun his head to look, there was no one there.

Who are you? *He wanted to shriek.* What do you want with me?

The only answer he received was silence, combined with the pounding of blood in his ears. Standing alone in a miry bog devoid of life, he summoned strength to withstand the torture by envisioning rescue. But as time went on and nothing changed, his breathing grew more ragged. He began to wonder if he would ever escape.

Bubbling, crippling panic rose in his throat and he again opened his mouth to scream. He was mute, as always. He looked in all directions, swiveling his head to glance over his shoulder.

Words began crowding his mind, taunting and true. Unwanted. Unloved. Abandoned. Defective. *They sprang from his own deep-seated beliefs, born from his mother's strong disapproval of him. They ravaged his mind, overtaking all reasoning thought.*

Alone, powerless, he bowed his head in defeat. Fear reared up and overwhelmed him, tingling coldly along his skin. As the despair engulfed him, he spread his arms wide and threw his head back, screaming silently to the heavens for mercy.

When I pulled out of Eversen's dream, I was more drained than I had been in Robert's or my girl's. It had taken more effort to penetrate his mind, as he was not my charge. I was better able to understand him, however. The same wrenching loneliness that Eversen's dream had magnified was my exiled experience. Pity washed through me.

I murmured soothingly over the Earthling, giving him what comfort I could. My protection completed, I wandered to the front door of the house. Daunted at the power the Embers had gained over the humans, I surveyed the area for the one creating the distress.

As before, I saw no one. The night was calm and peaceful. Crickets and cicadas chirped in harmony in the forest. Frogs chorused by the stream. An owl swooped across the clearing, casting a shadow over the ground. The moonlight illuminated nothing I could not already distinguish, yet it was still a comfort. The stars twinkled above in the summer evening.

A biting whim that it was Robert's doing entered my consciousness. After exploring the option inwardly, I discarded it. It was impossible that the boy could exert such powerful emotions over his companions. He had not been shadowed by Embers for more than a few weeks. Yet I knew the force of the Embers was growing stronger in him.

Frustrated at my ineptitude, I leaned back against the wall of the house, arms crossed.

"Commander," I adjured softly. "Give me adequacy." Encouraged by the sound of my own voice, I continued. "The Earthlings are unaware of the power of the Embers, but no less affected. I am insufficient to protect them. Guide me." I let my request hang in the pregnant air for a moment and then murmured, "As your will requires."

For some time I stayed outside the Earthlings' hut and listened in silence to the night passing. Because of my vigilance, I knew when the atmosphere changed. Suddenly charged with electricity and tension, I knew another had arrived.

Cold seeped through the air from the forest, nearly

visible,   prickling like ice. The temperature dropped dramatically within several seconds and the animals no longer serenaded the sky.

"Which are you?" asked I, moving out from the shadow of the house and into the moonlight.

I barely saw the flicker before the flame was whistling through the air toward me. I flung myself to the side, unsheathing my knife. It had been a long time since I'd used the weapon and I felt gratified at the familiarity of wielding it. Crouching, I scanned the area, unable to detect any movement.

"You will not *see* me, Suri."

"Did you bring the nightmares?" The question was unnecessary, a vague attempt at discovering the intruder's position.

A barking laugh served for confirmation.

The sound came from my right and I shifted slightly to face it head-on. "You are not in form?"

This time a scoff. "In form?" he mocked. "There are no pleasures worthwhile to justify such tedious misery."

Against my will, his words brought a snicker from me. It was true that traveling in form was not a luxury. The guise of the universe was restraining and inconvenient.

"Do you travel in form?" the Ember inquired.

He was bantering, which meant he was alone. Had there been others, they would have converged to slay me. However, the fact that he was being overt was dangerous. One reason for his flippancy could be inexperience: perhaps he was wondering how best to attack a more formidable foe. The other reason, however, was more likely. He could be bored, toying before he struck. The implications of that scenario were that he was a much more powerful opponent, a cat playing with a mouse.

I answered his question. "Yes." I still did not relax my stance, tensed to spring at the first sign of my enemy.

He sighed, disappointed. "You are not supposed to answer my goading. That only serves to displace your concentration." His voice came from behind me now. He was Reverberating, a way of rebounding his voice from different directions to unsettle an opponent.

I refused to let the new whereabouts of his words disorient me, and kept the same posture. "You want me to be focused?" I couldn't keep the slight incredulity from entering my voice, nor could I control the lift of my eyebrow.

He chuckled, the sound before me again, and for the first time I saw the glint of eyes in the night. "Good," he complimented me, his voice now coming from my right. "You are at least informed of Reverberation. Perhaps that will work to your advantage. Yet perhaps that is asking too much from a cowardly guardian."

I tensed and stilled at his insult.

"Entirely," he whispered off to my left, in response to my earlier question. "I am much stronger than you, Suri. It will be far too easy to dispatch you once I attack. I'd prefer you were roused to anger and wholly intent on killing me, rather than distracted by meaningless babble."

"The chill is distracting," I commented wryly.

"An unfortunate effect of my presence," the Ember responded vapidly from behind me. "As is the fear. I do not bring them intentionally. They are merely a part of my existence."

"I understand," I assured him, staring steadily forward.

His teeth flashed among the trees. "I thought you would."

"You could control your Reverberating, however," I mentioned. "It serves to be unnerving."

His laugh was black. Evidently he had finished baiting me.

I could finally see his movement in the forest as he leaned into a crouch, matching my posture.

"You may want to run now," he warned softly, an evil undercurrent in his voice. "Or at least attempt to protect your precious Earthlings. They needn't be harmed by our fray."

"They are satisfied." Even as I spoke, I sent what

protection I had to the three slumbering forms in the house behind me. Beseeching the Commander to see to their safety, I returned all thoughts to the Ember before me.

"Are they?" Though the retort was mocking, a true note of amusement underlaid it. His eyes widened.

The strange new tone made me turn. It was a mistake.

Robert stood in the open doorway of the house, staring out into the night wide-eyed. His knees were trembling and his mouth parted in horror. He was frozen with fear.

In the instant it took me to glance back, the Ember was already in midair leaping toward me. I managed to sidestep the attack, but not completely. As he hurtled past, the Ember's craggy sword clipped my shoulder.

I clenched my teeth in pain and resisted the urge to apply pressure to the wound. Instead, I spun quickly and jabbed my knife. The Ember was quicker. He had already anticipated my move and stood slightly to the left.

I heard a scream pierce the night air.

As one, the Ember and I glanced toward the hut. My girl stood with Robert, arms around the boy, looking directly at the Ember. With a rakish grin, he turned to me.

I only managed to gasp out, "Commander, *no*," before I was tangled back into the fight. My mind whirled. She could *see* him? He was *Revealed*?

Both of the Ember's swords were exposed now. He swung them at me, scissoring through the air. I evaded the attack by back-stepping and ducking in one fluid movement.

Dropping into a squat, I leaned on my left leg and struck out my right to trip the Ember. The momentum of my kick made me fall sideways. The Ember flailed a blade at me as he, too, fell heavily to the ground.

For a moment, we were both breathless. In the brief lull, I heard my girl sobbing and Robert whispering words to her. Then the Ember sprang to his feet and stabbed downward.

I was too preoccupied with rolling over in avoidance to

pay any further attention to the Earthlings. I reached to trip my enemy again, but he expected it and leaped lightly over my arm.

"What is it?" my girl whimpered.

Fury at her trepidation fueled my attack. I leapt to a stand and lunged for the Ember. He parried, forcing me into a circling pattern.

"Give up, Suri," he admonished, swords lowered. "You know you cannot defeat me."

"I don't recall knowing which one you were," I retorted coolly.

He snarled, but didn't lunge as I expected. Remarkably benign for an Ember, he gave a short, flourishing bow. "Malice at your acquaintance," he Reverberated from all around me, giving a dramatic impression to his introduction.

"So you're the famed Malice," I jeered, "come to put an end to a 'cowardly guardian.'" I reiterated his description of me. "Am I proving too difficult for you?"

Perhaps it was unwise to taunt such a fierce enemy, but it was instinctual, as he had frightened my girl and shadowed Robert. Now, were I to be given another chance to live that night, I would not change what I did. The proceedings were catastrophic, but the result was worth it.

Malice attacked. Swords ringing so quickly I only just managed to dodge them, he leaped and feinted, parried and lunged. Tremendous strength accompanied his onslaught, forcing me back into defensive positions. I didn't have time to charge him. I could only block his blows.

I was wearying fast, and I knew I could not withstand the attack much longer. It took all my concentration to stay out of his reach. If something didn't change in the situation soon, I would be killed.

Malice's fierce chill grew colder as the time passed. He never seemed to tire, despite his ferocity. Shadows wafted through the air, clouding out the moonlight and surrounding me. Gradually, the frigidity combined with darkness began to slow me. It was growing more difficult to penetrate the shadows surrounding me.

Then I made a mistake. Malice feinted and I fell for it, allowing him to sweep a sword beneath me, slicing open my leg. I collapsed to the ground and raised my knife in defense.

Malice sneered, but he was panting. "You put up a good front," he admitted. The admiration in his voice was unmistakable. "I didn't expect you to hold out so long. Congratulations." He dipped his head in a token of respect. "Now, however, I weary of dueling you. It has been enjoyable." He raised a sword almost quicker than I could see.

I exhaled shakily. "You will not prevail." Unlike others, I wanted to watch my execution. I kept my eyes fixed on Malice's, waiting for the fatal downward swing.

His eyes flickered angrily and he swung.

A blinding light bounded between the sword tip and my body just before impact. The weapon rebounded with a resounding *ping!* and Malice was thrown backward. He managed to keep his balance, but only just.

A shield converged around me, formed perfectly to the shape of my body. I staggered to my feet and looked down, breathing hard. Golden light, reminiscent of the Commander's shield at my girl's hut, glistened from me. I raised my hands to examine them, wondering at the phenomenon.

A chuckle sounded to my right. "Don't look so shocked," a very familiar voice advised.

Reeling toward the sound, mouth wide with disbelief, I faced the newcomer.

A spindly young man, of medium height and remarkably strong stood before me. He, too, was wreathed in a protective light. His features were weathered and calloused, used to the weather of the universe. Now they stretched into a mischievously lopsided grin. Thick, dark eyebrows raised over deep brown eyes, shining in the reflection of my golden shield. He raised a hand, wrist up and stepped toward me.

"Zar."

My older brother laughed again and clasped my forearm in greeting. "Yes, it's been a long time," he agreed. "We'll catch up later," he continued, turning away from me to face Malice, who stood warily watching us. "The fight is uneven now," Zar cautioned. "Do you still intend to finish your work here?"

I was rendered speechless for a moment, watching the exchange.

Malice snarled angrily. When he spoke, his words were mild, voice slick with persuasion. "I concede that my power is insufficient to destroy you both at present. Let me roam. Otherwise," he held out two fingers pointed at Robert, "I will have a new apprentice. If you bind me now, I will only resurface. Then I will find this boy and complete the work I began in him. My followers will be stronger than any you can conjure. If you let me go free, however, I will leave you alone for the present. Perhaps by my return you will have received ample training and resources to war with me."

Zar grinned. "You don't really expect me to believe you?" His voice was patronizing. He took a cheeky step forward, casually brandishing an over-sized dagger.

I smothered a snicker.

Malice stood his ground, but he could not disguise the pronounced lift of despair from the atmosphere.

"I can dispatch you quickly or slowly," Zar offered debonairly. "Which would you prefer?"

I enjoyed watching him bait our common enemy. A grin sprang to my lips. The uncertainty of my recent battle with Malice seemed inconsequential and unfounded. How had I imagined we could not defeat him?

Malice's eyes narrowed. His answer was a hissing exhale. "Quickly."

"So be it." Zar gave a mocking bow. As he straightened, his blade was already twirling, faster and faster. As it spun, a beam of light shot from his fingers and surrounded the blade. He plunged it swiftly into Malice's chest. There was a loud tearing noise as the Ember disappeared in a flash of sparks. All the remaining cold and darkness dissipated with his departure.

Zar turned to me, motioning with a jerk of his head to the humans huddled together at the door to the hut. "You ought to settle them down again. We can talk when you're done."

I looked at the Earthlings. They were shivering with fear. How much of the encounter they had witnessed was a mystery, but it was obvious they had seen and heard enough to know it was an uncommon night. I sighed. Back to the drudgery of protection again.

Zar flipped his dagger into the air and caught it smoothly as I turned away. "I'll wait for you," he said conversationally, eyes on his blade. "Take your time."

"Make yourself useful and find something to eat. It's been several days since I've had anything." I shook my head as he saluted jestingly. "At ease, soldier," I muttered. I heard Zar's soft chuckle as I reached the trio of Earthlings, still trembling with fright.

"Commander, restore your peace with them."

I stopped before the humans to look them over. My desperate attempt at protection had worked. Faint outlines of golden shields identical to the ones around Zar and me surrounded each of them. Robert's was the weakest, beaten back by the murkiness inside him. I frowned. At a glance, I could see Eversen's and my girl's protections remained ample.

"Come inside, then," I beckoned. "The danger is over." I waited for the humans to listen and believe my Channeled comfort before following them into Eversen's hut.

"What happened?" Robert asked. He, of the three, knew the answer best. He had felt the confrontation and, to some small extent, understood the battle between good and evil that had taken place. His question was acerbic to me.

My girl shivered. "I don't know. I woke up from a nightmare and felt like I was burning." Her voice was soft, trembling.

Interesting. The ice of the Embers felt like fire to Earthlings? Intriguing, but unimportant. They had been frightened and now needed comfort.

Eversen grasped my relief before the others. He placed a soothing arm around my girl and squeezed lightly. With his other hand, he rubbed Robert's shoulder.

My girl leaned into him and sighed heavily. "Are you all right?" she asked Robert.

The boy nodded. As I watched, the light surrounding him flickered and faded completely, squelched from the inside out. "I want to go back to bed." His voice was unnaturally calm for the anxiety he had just endured. Without waiting for a response, he ducked out from under Eversen's touch and scampered to his bed.

Unease filled me. Rather than disturbed at what had happened, he was almost … happy about it. I turned to Eversen and my girl. "Get some sleep as well. It's been a long night."

Inwardly, I petitioned the Commander. *Let them sleep unmolested.*

~ ~ ~

When the hut had grown quiet once more, I sought out my brother. Zar sat languidly in the clearing, still twirling his dagger between his fingers. He didn't look up as I approached, but a smirk stretched across his features. I was gratified to see a small bundle on the ground beside him.

"Welcome back," he greeted me.

"What are you doing here?" Though I was pleased to see him, I couldn't suppress the tinge of aggro that seeped into my voice. Dropping to the ground beside him, I reached for the bundle: a loaf of bread, strips of dried venison, and a small canteen of coffee wrapped in a thick green cloth. Undoubtedly, Lili had sent this.

Zar was unperturbed by my question. He sheathed his dagger and laid back in the grass, staring up at Open Space, and still wearing his lopsided grin. "You didn't think I'd leave you to your fate? The Commander sent me to protect you." He glanced askance at me. "You might be dead if not for me."

I snorted. "Without a doubt. Even on my best day I'm no match for Malice alone." I tore into the bread, washing it down with the coffee.

"Ah, the fate of the wee brother. Unable to cope with a single Ember in the superior ways of his elders. Poor lamb." His eyelids fluttered to half-mast.

I shot him a look and changed my tone. "What are you really doing here?" Turning my attention to the venison, I only half-listened to Zar's response.

"I wasn't lying," he protested, feigning grievance. He fingered the hilt of his dagger, and completely closed his eyes. "The Commander has orders for us."

I waited, content with being nourished again.

"We have to remove the Earthlings. Eversen will be granted his speech. Robert will be changed. We're going to Corant."

"What about my girl?"

"She's coming too, Suri," he assured me. "We have to travel by your tunnel to get there. Just in case you've been hiding under a rock, the Embers are converging on Robert. We have to remove him to a safer planet."

"The Commander ordered this?" I checked, finished with my meal and brushing my hands free of crumbs.

Zar nodded. "He sent me to find you," – he stifled a yawn – "and I obeyed, naturally. I wouldn't lie to you. How else do you think I managed to escape Wynaeria and make it here without a detachment of armed guardians apprehending and imprisoning me?" His tone held an innocent air.

I chuckled. "Easily. You blinded the guardians observing the atmosphere, perhaps involving several of them with covert bribes. Then you escaped in a tunnel and landed on Earth before it shattered from lack of energy."

"Simply because you are unable to maintain a tunnel, you think I cannot? I have learned things you will never know."

Zar pounced before I could recognize his intentions. He tackled my legs and knocked me to the ground. Before I could catch my breath, he pinned my legs with his knee and pushed into a mount, straddling my stomach.

I swung my fist at his face.

Zar jerked his head back and pushed my arm further into my swing so it wrapped around my neck in a choke hold. His face pressed into my forearm.

I wrapped a leg around one of Zar's and curled my arm further around my neck, grasping the ground with my fingers. In one swift motion, I rolled around him and broke his choking grip. I landed on my knees, hands holding down Zar's chest.

My brother reacted automatically. His leg came up and kicked out my right knee. Simultaneously, he grabbed my wrist and threw us both to the side.

Instinctively, I threw out an arm to catch myself.

Zar used the momentum to push out from under me. He swung a leg over mine and twisted over my side. I pushed myself up to my knees. Zar snaked a hand under my right armpit and up behind my neck. With his other hand, he fisted my tunic and tugged it to choke me, effectively putting me in another hold.

Zar chuckled breathlessly.

No weapons allowed, I muttered to myself, though it was unlikely I could have drawn my knife in my inert state.

"No weapons," Zar confirmed as if he could read my thoughts. "Think." He tightened his grip to add emphasis.

An impish grin spread across my face at the gambit I contrived. Bracing my knees into the ground, I threw myself forward with as much strength as I could muster.

Zar tumbled over me with the momentum and released his grip to keep from hurting either of us. He landed on his back, laughing. "Much better," he approved as he stood to his feet. Dizzy from the flip, he staggered and fell before he could regain his balance. The drop knocked out his breath and he lay spread-eagle on the ground, dazed.

I laughed at his gracelessness, still attempting to regain my own breath from the lark. The merriment cost me my breath and I clutched my stomach as it began aching.

"Be my guest. Laugh at the incapacitated brother," Zar moaned, rolling over. He struggled to his knees.

Bridling my amusement, I went to help him. He knocked my hand away and stood unsteadily on his own, provoking more mirth.

He shook his head at me. "Charlatan." His eyes were bright.

"You initiated it," I reminded him, finally conquering my humor. "I was perfectly within the rules. No weapons." I spread my hands in surrender and grinned innocently.

"Yes, weapons," Zar said, eyes searching the ground. He stalked past me and retrieved his dagger from where it'd fallen when I'd thrown him. Straightening, he sheathed it once more. "The night is drawing late," he said, turning back to me, "and I am overdue on sleep." He yawned in confirmation of his words. "Where is there a safe place to sleep for the night?"

I pointed to the forest. "The best refuge I've found is in trees when wandering on Earth. Embers are much easier to avoid when they don't immediately see you above them."

Zar dipped his head in acknowledgement. "Until the sunrise, then," he said and strode away into the trees.

I watched him go, still grinning, and then turned back to the house to check on the Earthlings, my laughter resurfacing. For once, I had bested my brother.

Chapter 6
Revealed

Despite the turmoils in the middle of the night, the Earthlings woke well-rested. They attributed Malice's attack and whatever they had seen of it to delusions fashioned by nightmares. Aside from fatigue, there seemed to be in them no lasting repercussions of the midnight encounter.

The day progressed as usual. Zar remained exhausted from his recent tunnel-traveling and it was around the noonday meal before he elected to awaken, and joined us.

"Welcome to the living," I greeted him. I stood in my favorite posture, leaning my back against the wall with my arms crossed. The Earthlings sat around Eversen's kitchen table, having just prepared their second meal.

"Thanks." He gave no indication of recognizing my sarcasm. Instead, his gaze flitted to the Earthlings as he studied them for the first time, his brow wrinkling as his eyes fixed on my girl. "Does she see you?" asked he.

I shrugged. "There was once when it seemed that she did. She's ignored me since, though. They can all feel my presence and Channeling, but don't recognize me as another being."

Zar nodded, glancing at my girl again with a thoughtful

expression. Then he shrugged too and looked back at me. "When are you going to rouse them to depart?"

"When does the Commander say?"

Zar cracked a smile. "Immediately, I suppose. There wasn't a specific time limit, but we have no reason to delay."

I pushed away from the wall, dropping my arms and turned to the Earthlings. "We have to go," I said.

"We should leave," my girl ventured to Eversen. "There's something oppressive in the atmosphere here. I don't want to pass another night like that." She shuddered.

Eversen nodded in agreement. Robert looked up at her with a mixture of disbelief and disappointment. "We don't have to go? Surely we can stay?" His voice had a note of wheedling in it.

My girl shook her head. "No. We need to leave. The village is not far from here – only a few miles. We can travel there. I would feel better if we were around other people."

Robert made a face.

She turned to Eversen, ignoring Robert's displeasure. "You buy and sell in Bedwin, don't you?"

Eversen nodded. They had all finished eating by this time, so he pushed back from the table and gathered the dishes to wash. My girl followed him and they began the preparations for a journey.

I turned to Zar. "Simple."

He snorted. "Simple until they realize they'll never make it to the village Bedwin. How have you decided to travel through a tunnel with them? Do you have any special powers the Commander neglected to impart to me?"

I grinned. "No. I guess we'll figure that out when we get there. You don't know how to make them travel-worthy, do you?"

Zar thought for a moment. "I have an idea," he said finally, a calculating expression on his face. "I'm not sure if it would work, but I don't see why we shouldn't try. Traveling with humans can't be much different from Wynaerians ..." He looked up at me. "What do you think?"

I chuckled. "I think we're going to need to Reveal."

Zar immediately shook his head. "No. It's forbidden on Earth. You're already in exile. Do you want to add more to your discipline?"

I sighed, turning away to look at Robert, who was still seated sullenly at the table. "No," I answered grudgingly. Then a thought occurred to me. "Is it only forbidden to Reveal on Earth? What about on Corant?"

Zar shrugged and furrowed his brow, also baffled. "I don't know. The Commander didn't specify. Do you know how to tunnel-travel *without* Revealing?"

I scoffed, waving my hand in superiority, as though I'd done it before. I answered truthfully, however. "Of course not."

Zar sighed. "Neither do I. I suppose we'll have to Reveal, then." He glanced up at the ceiling, as though he expected to see the Commander. He looked slightly fearful.

"He'll provide an answer or we'll Reveal," I said, not fully trusting the plan. I jerked my head in the Earthlings' direction and returned to our original subject. "We'll have to change their structure. Do you have the strength to do that?"

Zar flexed. "Of course!"

~ ~ ~

It was several hours later before we left Eversen's hut. The unpremeditated departure had sent my girl and Eversen into a flurry of cleaning, cooking, and packing supplies. Their activities seemed to indicate that they didn't plan to return for several months. This perception was understandable, as it would more nearly be years before they returned – if ever. The one thing Eversen and my girl did not predict was Robert's reaction.

"No!" he shouted angrily when my girl told him it was time to leave. He had been crouched down outside in the grass watching ants parade their food in a line. Now he stood, red-faced with set jaw, glaring at my girl. "I don't want to go anywhere!"

My girl was taken aback, recoiling as though Robert had slapped her. "We have to go," she said softly. Her eyes glistened with sadness, but she didn't cry. "We'll be safe in Bedwin. There are many other villages nearby and nothing sinister will find us."

Robert's eyes were fiery. "You can go," he suggested darkly. "I'll stay here. I don't want to go to Bedwin."

My girl looked at him thoughtfully. "You can stay," she allowed quietly. "Eversen and I will go alone. You will have to take care of the house, weed and water the garden, and make sure there's enough firewood for each night. Don't forget to go hunting for rabbit and deer for your meals, and cook wholesome bread. You can harvest vegetables and fruit from the garden to eat with your meals. Keep the house in good repair until we return."

She sighed and shook her head before continuing in that same soft, directive voice. "When it rains, you'll have to shutter the windows and make sure all the cracks in the walls are sealed well. If there are leaks, it will flood the dirt floors and create a mess." She touched Robert's head. "We'll miss you in Bedwin, but I suppose you're right in staying here. It will be nice to have a warm home when we return." She started back to the house, thought better of it, and returned to Robert. "Oh, one more thing. If there are any other creatures outside at night, Eversen keeps his bow beneath his bed."

Robert looked shocked.

I sniggered at her genius.

My girl turned without another word for the house. As she and Eversen fastened their packs, Robert walked in. His face and voice were brooding.

"I'll come," he announced, as though the idea were his. "It will be safer with you than here alone." He shot my girl a dirty look. "Besides," he continued, turning to Eversen, "I like Bedwin."

Zar, snickering where he stood safely out of the way, glanced up to meet my gaze. "The only virtue of Bedwin is the small size. Unfortunate, really, that such wonderful people and intriguing wares must be peddled in a dinky town."

"What a shame," I assented.

Zar sighed sadly. "I need to change their form."

"Enjoy yourself," I wished, giving him a swift, mocking bow. "I defer to your wise judgment. You, who practiced so freely on our dear friends on Wynaeria."

Zar shot me a look. "Tough work," he groaned. "Earthlings are different from gnomes and mermaids. More substantial, in some ways, and airier in others. It's hard to perfect the art."

I grinned cheekily. "You volunteered."

"Go away," he muttered, turning to the Earthlings, who were still gathered in the kitchen. He closed his eyes and concentrated.

Muttering words under his breath that even I couldn't hear, he began to Channel. In the air around us, lights like those of rainbows began to glow, drifting lazily from Zar's mouth. They swirled together, each color distinct, and traveled slowly toward the Earthlings. One by one, the bright colors faded into the Earthlings' skins, down into their hearts, where they swirled together. Gradually, the dancing rainbows faded into a hard crust around each of the Earthlings' hearts. Light pulsed over the bronze-colored shields, washing over organs, blood, bones, exuding outward to the skin. The pulses grew faster and faster for several minutes and then finally stopped.

Each Earthling glowed brightly from the shields for a while before the lights faded from them, leaving their appearances much the same as they were before. Only those who could see into hearts were able to perceive the distinct difference – the strong, firm look of those in the guise of the universe.

Zar opened his eyes, breathing heavily. Small drops of perspiration dotted his brow, and he wavered backward slightly before regaining his balance. Smugness filled his eyes.

"Bravo, bravo," I approved. "Though I would have quickened the pace a bit."

Zar rolled his eyes. "You would be unconscious if you'd exerted that amount of energy on the Earthlings."

"I would not!" I protested indignantly.

Grinning, Zar continued, "Come now, we have work to do. We need to depart."

"And why should *you* not inform them of this?" I continued in that same indignant tone.

Zar chuckled, clapping my shoulder. "It is the right of guardianship. I defer to your exceptional rapport with them. Consider it a token of respect; something I *do* have for you."

"Sure you do," I muttered, turning also to the Earthlings. "Well, come on then," I said to them. "We have a long way to travel before nightfall. No time for chatting." I turned to Zar. "Firm enough?"

He nodded seriously, a hint of humor twitching his lips. "I reckon it'll do."

The Earthlings, oblivious to our banter, looked around the small house once more to be sure of everything. Almost simultaneously, they hoisted the sacks of provisions they'd packed over their shoulders. After assuring them of their decision, Zar and I led them out into the yard. Eversen turned back to close and bar the door and then we were all treading into the forest.

Sunlight speckled the underbrush, bright and hot. There were no clouds in the deep blue sky, either white or otherwise. A gentle breeze whiffled through the trees. It was a very pleasant day to be traveling. The only downfall was the reason for the journey.

"Don't be so dour," Zar reprimanded me. "There's nothing abhorrent about Corant. The inhabitants are kindly enough, their dwellings comfortable ... and don't forget the rainbow prisms."

I scoffed lightly. "Yes, the grandest planet in Open Space."

Zar smirked. "Better than Jaada," he pointed out.

"Is there any ulterior motive for our traveling to Corant?" Despite my raillery with Zar, leaving Earth was an exciting prospect. It had been three months since I'd arrived, confined inside this atmosphere until further orders from the Commander. I was eager to adapt into the firmness of the guise of the universe again. My substantialness had lessened from the lack of hardness in Earth's atmosphere. I was becoming languid.

"Why do you think I know? I don't question the Commander."

"Indeed." My voice was disbelieving.

"I don't know," Zar clarified. "Knowing our Master, however, yes, he has ulterior motives – and no, there's nothing to be done about them."

"Then we'll be ready when the orders come." I kicked the brush at my feet and muttered, "What is he doing?"

Out of the corner of my eye I saw Zar glance up at Open Space. "At the moment?" he asked. "No idea." He was silent for a moment and then continued in a different tone, almost serious. "I do know one thing you don't," he said.

"Hilarious."

"I'm not jesting," he insisted. "I thought I'd warn you before you discovered it yourself."

Intrigued, I listened, though I couldn't squelch my impish expression.

"Your tunnel is ... different." Reverence colored his words. "It's astonishing. Rather than connecting solely between two planets – Wynaeria and Earth – it leads to every planet we've charted."

"*What?*" I was stunned.

Zar nodded. "It's split between different fields in the atmosphere of Open Space. Think about that."

"Believe me, I will. I didn't know that was possible."

"Did anyone? I believe the Commander was the only one who thought of something like this." Zar couldn't contain his grin.

~ ~ ~

The sun was just dipping over the horizon, spreading brilliant colors across the sky, when we arrived at the tunnel. We came out of the forest into an open meadow which overlooked a cliff face that dropped down into a ravine. A river rushed wildly through the gorge, somewhere miles away dropping down into falls. The meadow was filled with wildflowers and long grasses, blowing in the humid wind. In the center, where I had entered Earth's atmosphere three months ago, stood my tunnel.

It was a prism of sparkling lights – gold, silver, blue, green – rising upward into Open Space, where it disappeared. Even a Wynaerian's eyesight couldn't follow its tremendous path. The tunnel's opening was nearly fifteen feet in diameter – plenty wide enough to hold two Wynaerians and three Earthlings. Where the edges of the giant circle touched the ground flamed a blood-red light. From previous experience, I knew that once the tunnel was destroyed that red light would char the ground where it touched.

I grinned. The tunnel exuded an aura of inexplicable joy and comfort. Even the Earthlings, who were blind to the tunnel, could feel the difference it made in the air around them.

"Glad to be leaving?" Zar asked.

"Absolutely," I answered, stepping toward the tunnel. I had forgotten where we were until my girl gasped. "Oh," I grunted, turning toward her.

Sure enough, she remained at the edge of the forest, staring wide-eyed at the cliff. She was trembling with fear and sorrow, remembering her nightmare. This was where she had run on the worst night of her life, when she had contemplated ending her life.

"Of course," I grumbled to myself. I lifted my hand to

send her comfort, but Zar intercepted me.

He skipped to my girl's side, standing before her and opening his hands out to her. He didn't touch her, but closed his eyes and breathed words of comfort. "Don't be afraid," I heard him murmur. "You don't have to be afraid to come here again."

I lowered my arm and waited.

Eversen and Robert were both looking at my girl with concern. Eversen took a step nearer and held out his hand to rub her shoulder, seeming to understand her reaction. Robert, however, quickly recovered and turned away.

Troublemaker as always, he scampered to the cliff's edge and looked down toward the river below. "Look!" he shouted. "It's a long way down!"

"Robert!" my girl exclaimed, terror flooding her.

"Robert," I groaned. "Get away from there before you fall."

The boy, as usual, didn't listen to either of us. Rather, he raised his arms and laughed. "It's beautiful here!" he called back. "Can we stay? Look at the sunset!" He pointed and leaned into the wind slightly. The pack over his shoulder seemed unusually heavy. "It's so nice," he breathed. If he fell, he would die.

As his guardian, I couldn't let him fall. I started toward him.

"Robert!" my girl screamed again.

Zar remained with her, concentrated on Channeling.

Eversen left my girl's side, shaking his head vigorously. He sprinted to Robert's side and yanked him away from the edge. His eyes were dark with fury and he tightened his grip on Robert's arm.

I shook my head disbelievingly, standing in front of the boy. "Idiot," I whispered. "Are you trying to be killed?"

"We should leave quickly," Zar called from across the meadow. "She's not going to calm down here."

"Get to the tunnel," I said shortly to everyone present.

Eversen dragged Robert away from the cliff toward the

middle of the clearing where stood the tunnel. They didn't enter it, however, only stood at its edge.

I joined them and Zar coaxed my girl over to us.

"They won't be any calmer on Corant," I warned him, looking up at the exterior of the glistening prism. "Ready?"

"Always." Zar placed a hand on my girl's arm.

I gripped Robert's and Eversen's shoulders. "Help us travel safely," I murmured to the Commander, and as one we all stepped into the tunnel.

Immediately we were transported.

Light streamed past, too blurred for us to distinguish the colors. We could not control the speed at which we traveled, and for only a second I wondered if the Earthlings could endure it. Then the pleasure of being once more in a tunnel through space blocked all thoughts of them. There was no wind, no discernible movement, the way we were flying. Stars – planets – meteors – flew by. Out in Open Space, the aroma of the atmosphere changed from that of Earth. It was clean and fresh, devoid of any singular smell.

I closed my eyes briefly, reveling in the experience.

As we neared Corant, our speed slowed by degrees until we were hardly moving. The purplish planet grew larger and larger before us until we were too close to see the curvature. Still, we could not distinguish the landscape, as we were too high in the atmosphere. I had only time to note that Corant was in the midst of its night before the lights of the tunnel grew brighter. They blocked out sight of any surroundings and blinded our eyes.

Finally, the tunnel deposited us.

As we were familiar with tunnel-traveling, Zar and I landed lightly on our feet, letting our knees absorb the impact. I sighed happily, straightening and running my fingers through my disheveled hair. Zar stretched his arms out and exhaled loudly, as though the journey had wearied him.

We shared one brief, wordless smile before my girl and Robert screamed.

I glanced at Zar and then turned to face them directly. Eversen had a look of horror on his face, mouth open in his silent version of a scream.

"Not so loud," I said over their shrieks. "We're not going to harm you." I Channeled comfort to them and soothed their overwhelming fear.

Zar stifled a chuckle at their petrified faces.

"Who are you? Where are we?" my girl demanded. Her voice was weaker than she'd intended it to be. She was trembling with fear again, clutching Eversen's shoulder with one hand. Her fingernails dug into his skin, but he didn't seem to notice. "What happened?" she continued breathlessly.

All three Earthlings stared at Zar and me, wordless and apparently oblivious to the fact that they were several light-years away from Earth. Perhaps it was too dark for them to see. I also noted that they looked older – only slightly, but enough to make a difference.

I took a breath of the subtly sweet peach scent of Corant before answering. "My name is Suri," I said in a more gentle tone. Now that they were no longer screaming, perhaps I could explain things. "This is my brother, Zar." My curiosity got the better of me and I asked, "Can you see?"

"Suri," rebuked Zar, also breathing deeply. "Not so direct. They're terrified." He, too, spoke in a much softer voice. I'd never heard him so gentle. He gave a debonair bow to the Earthlings. "Forgive us," he requested. "We are used to tunnel-traveling and being Revealed. I know it must be overwhelming for you."

I stifled a laugh at his formality, but followed his lead and bowed before he could see the humor on my face.

"Who are you?" repeated my girl tremulously.

"We are called Wynaerians," I interjected as Zar opened his mouth to answer. "We're very similar to humans, though slightly different. Before we explain everything, there is an empty seor nearby we can rest in."

"Why should we trust you?" My girl's voice was shrill.

113

This was more difficult than I'd thought. I looked at Zar for direction, but he was as clueless as I. Neither of us had Revealed to Earthlings before. How did we establish trust?

"Er," I began. "Well ..." no brilliant words were coming to mind. "Commander," I implored under my breath. "A little help?"

Zar took a step toward the humans. "We won't harm you," he repeated my earlier words. "Please, follow us to shelter. We can explain anything you ask."

I gave him a warning look, Channeling all the while.

Zar shrugged and held out his hand to the Earthlings.

Robert ignored him and looked at me. His fear had been replaced with wonder. "I know you," he said.

I raised my eyebrows, surprised. "You know me?" I repeated, unable to hide the incredulity in my voice. I knew, of course, my charge could sense my presence, but I didn't know he'd recognize me when I was Revealed.

Robert cocked his head to the side, puzzling over the conundrum. "How do I know you? I've never met you before."

I grinned, bending down before him and placing a hand on his shoulder. "That, I can answer easily," I informed him. "I am a Wynaerian. We are a race of living beings the Commander commissions to protect Earth – humans." I raised my eyes jauntily.

Zar coughed, suppressing his chortling. "You think he understood all that?"

Robert turned to look at him, taking a step forward. "I understood," he asserted proudly. "He's my guardian angel."

I shifted my weight uncomfortably. "No, not exactly."

Zar didn't try to hide his laughter this time. He let it out loud and almost bent over double with his amusement, clutching his stomach. "Guardian angel," he snickered.

The Earthlings stared at him in a mixture of confusion, amusement, and concern.

I shook my head. "I don't know why it's funny, either," I told them. "I'm not an angel," I continued to Robert. "I'm a

Wynaerian. We're the race of another planet." I looked to Zar for help, but he was useless.

"Come," I said to the Earthlings. "There's a seor not far from here where we can stay for the night and explain everything. I know you are tired. It's been a long day for all of you and you need to rest." I held out my hand to Robert.

The boy looked at it dubiously for a minute and then took it, smiling up into my face. "I believe you," he said.

I hadn't meant for him to take my hand, but to give me his sack of supplies. With my free hand, I relieved him of the burden and slung it over my shoulder. I began leading him in a westerly direction, in search of the seor I knew was nearby. As we walked, I glanced behind us. My girl and Eversen still looked doubtful, but they couldn't let Robert walk off with me alone. With a dark look, my girl stepped forward. Eversen and Zar followed.

"How long have you been on Earth?" Robert asked me as we walked. Amazingly, he was content to let me hold his hand.

"About three months," I answered.

He tallied that in his head and then stopped short. "You were there when my mom died."

"Yes," I replied slowly, as we began walking again. I wished he'd waited to figure this out until we were all gathered in the seor. I didn't enjoy the thought of retelling my story. "I gave you courage to leave your mother's hut."

Robert looked down at his feet as they scuffed the purple ground of Corant. He suddenly noticed the color and pulled his hand away to lean down and touch it. "What is this?" he breathed, eyes wide, as he pushed his fingers into the ground. The spongy earth was soft and flexible. It sprang back into place when Robert lifted his fingers away.

"It's the ground of Corant," I explained. "We're not on Earth anymore. We're on another planet. I was wondering when you would notice." I couldn't hide my smile. "Can you see anything else around us?"

Not far in the distance on every side, there were giant,

crooked sticks jutting into the air. Some were green, some brown, the rest pink or blue. They had no leaves or fruit, only branches, like skeletons of what once was. Rough, jagged bark peeled off many of them, drooping to the ground to provide ample shade during the sweltering Coranta days.

Robert strained his eyes to see what I saw, but he shook his head. "No." He started to listen. "I don't hear any animals," he realized. "There are no frogs or crickets. Are there animals here?"

I shrugged. "Yes. There are a couple types of animals around here. Much of the Corantas' sustenance, however, comes from the plants they gather and the fish they hunt. There are bodies of water nearby where Corantas swim, and bathe."

"Will I get to see them?" Robert's eyes sparkled with excitement.

"Yes, I'm sure." I espied the seor I was looking for and motioned to it. "Can you see the seor? That's where we're going for the night. It's empty. The Coranta that used to live there has long since been dead."

"I don't see anything," related Robert. "How can you see in the dark? Are your eyes better?"

I laughed. "No. They're only different. Wynaerians can see much further in the dark than Earthlings. We also have other ... talents. I'll tell you when we are all together, though. I don't want to repeat everything."

Robert was satisfied with that answer and continued to squint his eyes to see the seor as we approached. Finally, he gave a shriek of delight and pointed. "Is that it? The big lump?"

"Yes."

If he saw what it really looked like, he would not describe it as a 'lump.' Seors are some of the prettiest dwellings of any creature I have encountered. They are fashioned of yellow and gold marble, mined from gorges on the surface of Corant. In the light of day, they glisten and give the impression of being fluid. They are solid, but easily manipulated into different shapes, to fit the needs of whoever finds them.

The one before us was little more than a hovel by Coranta standards. It was rather spacious, though, and with help from Zar, I could easily change the shape to accommodate the Earthlings. As it had been standing alone and untended for so long, it was rather dilapidated, but well away from any other, which just suited our needs.

I paused with Robert outside the opening, a wide, dark mouth. Steps led down into the seor, curving out of sight into the main area. There was no door.

"Zar," I said as he came alongside me, leading Eversen and my girl, both of whom stopped short at sight of the seor. "Can we manage the current shape for the night? It's rather …" I looked over the abandoned dwelling.

"Pathetic," he supplied, grinning. "I think it will work for the night. No need to keep the Earthlings awake longer than necessary. We'd better make sure it's empty, first, though. There could be vagrants or vermin."

"Well, then, lead the way." I stepped back from the cavernous opening to make room for Zar.

Muttering, "That's right, send the fearless older brother," Zar ducked inside and down the stairs. Almost immediately he called back, "Come on! It's quite safe and completely empty!" He stood at the bottom of the stairs, looking up. "Rather dilapidated," he agreed with my earlier assessment.

I stepped back and waved the Earthlings in. "Go on, there's nothing to fear," I reassured them.

My girl shot me a distrusting look, and gingerly placed a foot in the seor. Zar helped her down and out of sight, then returned for Robert and Eversen. I glanced around outside quickly before entering last.

The stairs sloped gently downward with only a slight curve. I descended swiftly to the bottom.

"Well it's definitely spacious enough," Zar commented. He stood alone in the middle of an open room. The walls were made of the same gold and yellow marble as outside, with similar fluidity and brilliance. The ceiling rose close to twelve feet high. On either side of the main area two openings presumably led to more rooms. The room in which we stood was perhaps twenty feet wide. The floor was made of just the same substance, only more solid. The aroma was that of lilacs. In the middle, at the Earthlings' feet, rested Eversen's and my girl's packs; the room was otherwise empty.

Everyone turned to look at me as I entered. I stepped into the room, surveying it, and lowered Robert's pack from my shoulder. "Yes, it will do nicely with a few renovations." I grinned.

My girl looked at me aghast. Eversen and Robert were not much more composed. "Where are we?" my girl demanded. "What are you doing with us?"

I exchanged a pensive look with Zar. He shrugged. "We're not trying to harm you," I said gently, trying to calm her. As I spoke, Zar Channeled comfort to them. "We are here to protect you and lead you to the Commander. Ordinarily, we would not have Revealed, but tunnel-traveling is impossible without doing so. We had no choice."

"Where are we?" my girl continued. She was fierce with anger.

I sat on the bottom step of the stairwell and clasped my hands in front of me, looking at her seriously. "We're in a seor, a dwelling place on Corant."

"Corant?" Now her voice was disbelieving. "What is Corant?"

Zar answered for me. "It's the planet we're on. The Commander sent us here." He stretched out his hands to the seor's walls and manipulated the marble into a bench, then stepped away and motioned for my girl to sit. "Please. We will explain all you wish to know. Would you allow a night's worth of sleep between now and then?"

My girl looked sullenly at Robert and Eversen. Eversen gave the slightest lift of his shoulders. Robert nodded vigorously, obviously ready to sleep.

My girl sighed. "I suppose explanations can wait for the

morning."

"Sleep, then," Zar beckoned. "There is room aplenty for all of us. Come with me. I'll lead you to the separate bedroom so you can have privacy." He held out his hand to my girl.

She looked warily from his hand to his eyes and then took his hand. Zar led her through the opening to the left.

"Well, then," I said, standing. "I suppose we'd better prepare beds for you as well." I stepped to the wall where Zar had already changed the shape of the room and stretched out my hand.

Concentrating intently, I willed the shape of the wall to move. Outward, down, further back, not so narrow ... the marble obeyed my whims and soon there was a bed, not very soft, but at the perfect height and size for one of the Earthlings. The effort expended more energy than I had reckoned and I had to rest for a minute before creating the second bed.

Eversen and Robert stared at me in astonishment.

"How did you do that?" Robert breathed, awed.

I grinned sheepishly. "We have talents," I said lightly, shrugging. "The Commander allows us." I gestured to the beds I'd made. "Please, lie down and sleep. Zar and I will stand guard outside. Rest while you may."

I gave a short, respectful bow, and departed up the stairs. The night was peaceful. Croaking could be heard, deeper than that of frogs and drawn out much longer. Those sounds are only made by Coranta trees when the warmth of daylight leaves them. The magnitude of the choruses indicated a forest of them nearby. I listened, but heard no nocturnal animals. Perhaps we were in an uninhabited region. A gentle breeze wafted against me, with the scent of ripe peaches native to Corant.

I leaned back against the soft exterior of the seor and pulled out my knife to throw while I awaited Zar's appearance. He wasn't long in joining me.

"She seems to like you more than me," I commented casually, keeping my eyes on the blade I held. I glanced up at Open Space, glad for the clear night.

Zar scoffed. "She doesn't know you yet," he said, "and I wouldn't trust you either if you kidnapped me, transported me to another planet, and then proclaimed you were protecting me." He snickered. "It does sound far-fetched."

"Is she sleeping?" asked I, idly twirling the knife around my fingers. I was concentrating more on the night air and Zar's response than what my hands did.

"Yes. I –" he cleared his throat "– may have made her drowsy. You're not offended, are you?" He sounded cocky.

"Not in the least," I said dryly. "Do you think they'll be able to sleep? Those beds didn't look exactly comfortable. There don't appear to be many hours left of the night, either."

"They're all sleeping, Suri," he reported cheerily. "So long as no nightmares or Embers happen along, I expect a quiet, peaceful night. I may even catch up on more sleep myself."

I stared at him, agape. "How can you possibly enjoy sleeping? It's an utter inconvenience, and most dangerous."

Zar bounced his eyebrows. "It's so *restful*," he sighed. "Most unlike any other experience afforded us. One doesn't have to plan and plot, or be afraid of attacks. It's perfectly blissful."

I snorted, bringing him out of his reverie. "Indeed." I laid my head back against the wall. "How much should we tell them? If it sounds ludicrous for us to be their guardians, how much more so the rest of our story."

"Ah, well. We tell the truth and then prove it."

I closed my eyes. "Easily spoken. It won't be so easy to convince them. "I don't think they'll quickly believe us. We are strange and unknown to them, as well as everywhere we take them. How will they see with the eyes of a Wynaerian and know we are their helpers? What fear they will have."

"They'll overcome it." Zar spoke confidently.

Chapter 7

Corantas and Yures

The night on Corant passed quietly. Zar and I were lax in our vigilance, confident there were no Embers nearby. When the star that served as Corant's sun rose, the Earthlings still slept peacefully.

Zar and I had spent the night talking and laughing, catching up on the months we hadn't seen each other. The starlight rose and brightened the landscape of Corant as we waited for the Earthlings to wake.

"If they're not up soon, they'll never see what Corant really looks like," Zar said, feigning impatience. "Had this been *my* first day on a new planet, I would not be spending it sleeping."

"Yet that is precisely what you wanted to do last night," I pointed out. "Sleep your life away. That's how you miss everything of importance."

He gave me a repulsed look. "I've been to Corant before," he said haughtily. "There was no need to spend the entire night awake. Nothing new to see."

I rolled my eyes. "Forgive me. I forget. You've explored every region in the universe, all fields, each planet, even the suns!"

Zar sniggered. "Well you should know it, too!" he retorted playfully. "At least one of us is well-traversed in the universe." Abruptly, he stiffened, lowering into a defensive position.

His posture silenced me. I listened intently for what he had heard. Then he straightened again, smiling broadly.

"I believe our charges have awakened."

Movements in the seor reached my ears. "So they have." Gesticulating to the seor's opening with a mock smile, I continued, "Shall we?"

Zar chortled, ducked his head, and disappeared inside. I followed after him.

Robert bounded from his bed, stretching his arms and grinning widely. For the first time since his mother's death, the shadow around his heart was diminished. Eversen was bright-eyed, though still sleepy, rubbing his eyes. My girl was as joyous and energetic as Robert, though she concealed it better.

"Do you have ideas for breakfast?" I murmured to Zar as the thought occurred to me. It would have been easy to find food for them on Corant, but it was unlikely they would accept it for fear of their safety.

"They did pack provisions," he pointed out. "No need to spoil all our secrets when they provided perfectly well for themselves." He gestured to their packs, which no one had moved the night before.

I gazed down at them. "I do believe we're the best guardians the Commander's commissioned yet," I said seriously.

"Who is the Commander?" Robert said.

I looked up and met his gaze, raising my eyebrows. Eversen and my girl were also watching Zar and me. "He's our master and lord. He created us and sends us on assignments to protect humans. On Earth, you call him Jesus."

My girl gave a small gasp. "He speaks to you personally? Have you seen him?"

I grinned. "Yes."

Irritation quickly colored her features at my monosyllabic response.

"Suri," admonished Zar. "We promised answers last night. It is only right to answer truthfully and completely."

"Yes, yes." I waved a hand in his direction and stepped to the center of the room, toward the food sacks. "They need to eat first," I added, crouching. I didn't bother moving the packs, but molded the golden marble around them into a table. Within moments, I finished and stepped back, satisfied.

The table stood on a single, wide leg that fanned out into the rest of the floor. The tabletop was circular and sturdy, perfectly balanced on the single leg, and bearing the sacks I had neglected to move.

I glanced at Zar.

He gave me a disapproving, yet amused, shake of the head.

"Chairs will be a bit more difficult," I mused, circling the table. "Yet I think I can manage them."

Zar came to my side and helped. Soon, there were five chairs erected from the ground. They stood evenly spaced around the table, one for each of us.

"Please, be seated," I invited the Earthlings.

My girl gave me a wary look, but Eversen and Robert immediately obeyed, and after a moment, she followed. Zar and I took the remaining seats.

As they rummaged through the packs, I leaned forward and absently drummed my fingers on the tabletop. Zar reclined in his chair, arms folded behind his head.

Suddenly, my girl gasped.

We all jerked our heads to look at her.

She stared down at something in her hand and turned to face me. "What is this?" she asked in a low voice, lifting her arm to show me.

Engraved on her wrist, as I had already noticed, was the Commander's mark. It hadn't occurred to me that they would become visible to the Earthlings once we'd left their homeland.

Zar smirked, allowing me the explanation.

"I have one too," I told her, lifting my wrist to show her. "It is the Commander's mark – a circlet of thorns. It represents his death and how we can live with him because of it."

My girl lowered her eyes to the mark, and studied it intently.

"Eversen has one as well," Zar said conversationally, gazing toward him placidly.

"Why don't I have one?" Robert whined.

I gave him a cold look. "You do not yet belong to the Commander."

My girl looked darkly at me. "You have much to explain." She dropped her arm and returned to the food sacks, and removed bread, dried fruit, and dried venison for their breakfast.

When each of the Earthlings were eating comfortably, they began their questioning.

"Where do you live?" my girl asked.

"Wynaeria," I answered promptly. "It's a planet much like Earth in many respects." I hesitated. "There are plenty of differences, but you could survive there. There is a single island on the planet, surrounded by sea. Though we can all swim, most of us don't, due to the many large, and often fearsome, sea creatures that dwell there. On the island live many of the beings that gave birth to human legends." I glanced at Zar. "There are gnomes, mermaids, fairies, and dragons."

My girl gasped softly.

"Long ago," Zar continued, "there were many tunnels that led from Wynaeria to Earth. The beings passed through these tunnels to Earth, where they appeared to humans. Earthlings were often terrified or fascinated by the Revealed creatures. Over time, tunnel-traveling grew too rampant to be sustained. The tunnels were too numerous and died too quickly to return living ones to Wynaeria. Finally, the Commander permitted only guardians to continue traveling to Earth, as they were invisible. The decline in travels helped protect the atmosphere of Earth, and gradually the reality of living beings dwindled to mere myth."

The Earthlings were stunned.

Finally, Robert ventured, "what is tunnel-traveling?"

"It's the way we journey through the universe," I explained. "To leave a planet, we create a tunnel made of light," I hesitated, "or darkness," I amended. "The tunnel creates a pathway from one planet to another. Only the person who fashioned it can travel through it – unless they invite another to join them. The tunnel diminishes the space between planets, making the journey much faster than any other form of transportation."

They had to digest that for a moment.

"Did we tunnel-travel to get here?" My girl looked amazed.

Zar barked a laugh, which made the rest of us jump. "Sorry," he apologized, amused. "It was the thought of being able to travel between planets *without* a tunnel. It's impossible. There is no other way to go between two places in the universe."

"Yes," I answered my girl's query. "We traveled through a tunnel to get here. What was it like for you?" I added, curiosity overcoming me.

Eversen grinned and gestured wildly in enthusiasm.

"It was very short," Robert considered. "I thought we were standing still, but the air was different." He scrunched his forehead thoughtfully. "It was much warmer than it had been, and then all the sunlight disappeared."

"Strange," I murmured, enthralled.

"Any other questions?" Zar asked, ignoring me.

"Why did you come to Earth?"

Ah, I thought, wincing, *the crux of the conversation.* I took a breath, all lightheartedness gone. "I was sent to watch over Robert." I eyed him as I spoke. "The Commander wants me to lead you to him," I told him bluntly.

This simple statement brought fire to the boy's eyes. Defiance immediately overtook him and the shadow darkened considerably around his heart. He opened his mouth to retort, but was evidently too angry to speak. He pressed his lips into a fine line.

My girl noticed and wondered at his attitude, perplexed.

I tore my eyes away from Robert and looked between her and Eversen. I continued in a lower voice, "I failed to obey the Commander while I was on Wynaeria. He sent me to Earth. Here, he commissioned me to watch over Robert and guide him to himself."

"What does he want with me?" Robert snapped.

"He wants your heart." Zar spoke softly, his eyes on the edge of the tabletop where he ran his fingers over the surface. He raised his eyes to meet Robert's. "It's a serious thing to reject the Commander," he added gravely.

"You have a role to play as much as we do," said I.

"He's only a boy!" my girl defended him.

I gave her a pitying look. She loved him as a son and disliked our need to confront him. A bit of fire entered her features. "His role is just as important," I rebuked her softly. "Only the Commander knows the fullness of our respective parts. That doesn't make one of us more or less vital."

Eversen flicked his eyes from Zar to me. Somber lines carved his expression.

Zar passed a hand over his eyes wearily and I realized he was Channeling. I paid closer attention to the aura of the room. The boy was very near sparking fire again as he had in the hut on Earth. Instantly, I joined my brother in his work, easing the tension in Robert.

The boy stared balefully at me. He hardly blinked, so intense was his glare. When he spoke, his voice was dark and carried a much older air to it. "I do not want your interference." He stood and crossed the room, hands clenched into fists at his side. He reached the staircase, visibly trembling with his wrath. "Do not follow me." He darted up the steps.

My girl half-stood, then sank back into her chair. She looked much the same as Zar, uneasy and exhausted.

I could hear Robert sit down outside and begin poking the ground angrily.

There was silence in the seor for several weighty moments. I gazed down at my hands unseeingly, lost in thought at my own rebellion toward the Commander. I grimaced.

Finally, Zar spoke. "There are many more questions you have for us. We can continue to explain if you wish. Robert won't be returning for a while. He's sitting outside, digging up the ground," he reassured my girl at her concerned glance.

"Well," she said carefully, "will you tell us why you brought us to Corant?" She still sounded tentative about the planet's name.

"Simple," I murmured absently. "The Commander ordered us here. Zar came to Earth to inform me, and we brought you through the tunnel. *Why* we're supposed to be here, we haven't discovered yet. I suspect it is for Robert's sake. He's rather discordant with the idea of belonging to the Commander. Perhaps something on Corant will change his mind."

Zar's eyes suddenly flickered with understanding. "Oh!" he exclaimed. "Suri, that's it!"

I glanced at him listlessly.

"The prisms!" He looked directly at me and Channeled his excitement to me.

I caught on, connecting his delight with his words. "Yes."

"What? What are the prisms?" my girl demanded.

Smiling, I turned to her. "They are the delight of Corantas. Crystal prisms, gathered in circles. They are places of worship scattered all over Corant." I stood. "Come, we'll show you."

Zar and I led the Earthlings from the seor. Sitting against the exterior wall, Robert glanced at us in derision. To his left sat a pile of the spongy ground; on his right, the trench he had dug it from.

"Will you come with us?" I asked him politely. "We're going to look at crystals."

While normally the prospect of seeing crystals would have roused his interest, now he was determined to be resentful. He narrowed his eyes and turned his head away. With another angry jab at the ground, he pulled up more of the purple terrain. There was a loud tearing noise as it came free and he added it to the growing pile.

I shrugged. "We'll return presently." Turning, I began to walk away.

"Wait!" my girl demanded. Her eyes flashed angrily. "We can't just leave Robert here alone!"

I glanced around. "Yes, we can. There are no Embers here, and the only Corantas who would find him will do him no harm. He's perfectly safe." Under my breath, I added, "Of anyone here, he is the most dangerous."

My girl continued to glare at me.

"Come on," Zar said softly. "Suri's right. There's nothing harmful on Corant that Robert can't handle. There are no creatures around, and the Corantas are friendly. At worst, they will invite him for a feast."

I turned my head away to hide my grin.

Finally satisfied, my girl followed as Zar led us away. We left Robert and the dwelling place behind swiftly. In moments, my girl's anger dissolved. She marveled over the texture and color of the ground and often stopped to bounce or rock back and forth. Her eyes lit up whenever she did this and she gave a most childlike smile. Eversen gazed outward over the landscape, eyes wide at the Coranta trees and the pink-tinged sky. My girl didn't notice the trees until she walked right under the bark of one. She stopped short.

"Oh," she murmured, reaching out a tentative hand to the bark, but pulling it away before she touched it and glancing at me.

Zar and Eversen also stopped beneath the broad, shady peelings to watch.

"It won't harm you," I reassured my girl. "You can touch it." To demonstrate, I took the smooth, fibrous bark between my fingers. I bent it back and forth, but it didn't break. "These are called yures," I said, gazing up at the underside of the huge trunk. "The bark is edible, and also provides shelter from the heat in the summer." I grinned at my girl. "Now it's wintertime. We're not likely to be too uncomfortable."

My girl reached out again and ran her palm along the stringy texture. She had a pensive expression, which quickly turned delighted. "They have a very soft surface," she noted, flipping over the bark to reveal the underside. "Almost furry."

"That part is scraped off to eat," I said and pulled out my knife to cut a foot-long piece off the end. "It adds a very unpleasant feeling when you eat the fibers. Almost like chewing hair," I muttered, bent over shaving the bark. "I tried it once. I won't ever do it again."

My girl laughed.

I glanced at her briefly in surprise, then looked back at my work. Gently, I made a slit in the middle of the broad peeling, wiped my knife on my pants, and sheathed it. Using my fingers, I peeled the slit wider to expose the meat underneath. Once the covering was discarded, I tore out the elastic beige paste.

"Here, try it." I offered my girl a small piece of the bark meat.

She took it gingerly. "You're sure it won't harm me?"

I nodded, grinning cheekily. "I wouldn't give it to you if it were harmful." I turned to Zar and Eversen. "Would you like to try it?"

Zar shook his head, but Eversen reached out for a piece.

I popped the remainder in my mouth. It tasted like almonds with a hint of pomegranate, slightly sweet but not overbearingly so. The texture was chewy, but dissolved rather swiftly, leaving a pleasant aftertaste.

My girl also ate hers. At first, her expression was concentrated, then it turned to happy surprise. She chewed slowly and swallowed. "It's delicious."

"Completely harmless," I said, tossing the rest to the side, "and plenty nourishing."

Eversen, too, looked pleased with the yure bark. He smiled.

Zar brushed the drooping bark aside and led the way onward. "We're nearly there," he told us.

As we walked on, I pointed out the blue sun. This, too, had a remarkable effect on them. My girl looked astounded. Eversen's jaw dropped. Zar laughed at their reactions.

Soon, we came out onto a bare patch of land, empty but for the crystal prisms. No yure trees grew around the circled gemstones, and no Coranta dared live near them.

We stopped to take in the sight.

Directly in front of us stood seven crystals, each nearly ten feet tall, slanting up sideways from the ground in a circle fifty feet across. They looked imposing, sparkling in the starlight and casting colored lights between them, each one giving off a different tint of the rainbow. In the center, the lights converged into a glowing orb. It was there we headed.

As we drew nearer, soft music wisped in the air around us, on the very edge of hearing. It grew louder with each step until it was distinguishable as a song. Chiming bells, dulcimers, and lyres blended together to form a beautiful harmony.

The Earthlings were awed. Zar led the way between two towering prisms into the center. Light bounced around us, no longer stationary in its paths, so bright it was nearly blinding. Only our shadows, cast darting among the light, kept the circle dim enough to see. There, in the middle, the faintest sound of rustling water, as soft as wind through leaves, tantalized us, merging with the music.

We stood together in a group, looking around at the glistening colors that bounded between us. Warmth accompanied them, peaceful and comforting. We remained silent as we stood, and gradually the song hummed louder.

Murmurings of voices mingled amid the melody, but the

words were unintelligible. Combined with the tranquility of merely being among the gemstones, the song stirred something deep inside each of us.

I dropped to my knees, overwhelmed, and bowed my head. Piercing guilt at my disobedience to the Commander welled in me. I whispered remorse aloud, and my words fell in with the song; rather than diminishing its beauty, they enhanced it.

Zar gripped my shoulder tightly. Beside us, my girl also knelt. The movement sent her shadow flickering among the dancing colored lights.

The song rose to a crescendo inside me, a mixture of warmth and light that was utterly glorious. The heat seared through every pore of my skin, down into my inner being, until it felt like I was burning. The lights moved inside me, brushing every part of my body and strengthening everything they touched. It was staggering.

Finally, the heat receded and the light dimmed. I rose from the ground, stronger, utterly peaceful. There were no words to describe the change that had been wrought in me. I only knew the Commander was wholly worthy, and I was wretched.

Reluctantly, we moved out from the prisms in tacit agreement. My girl and Eversen both trembled slightly, which made me smile. Zar was silent and serious, two things he rarely became. I turned to face my companions.

For a time we remained silent and reflective, still wondering, unwilling to end the moment. I met my girl's gaze and grinned. She returned a smile, somewhat hesitantly.

"The prisms are Corant's pride," I said, glancing back at the circle of stones. "As you can understand."

"How did they come to be here?" my girl asked, following my gaze.

As one, we began meandering away from them, back to the seor where Robert waited.

"The Commander placed them there," Zar explained on

the way. "He placed them in different places around the planet as dwellings of worship for the Corantas – and any who might travel here."

We passed the yures that had been so enchanting on the way to the crystal prisms. My girl glanced at them with a faraway look. "Amazing, isn't it?" she said in an aside, "that something so astonishing is no longer appealing?"

I nodded, also casting a glance at the yures. "They are nothing compared to the Commander's presence," I said softly, reaching out and rubbing the peeling bark in my fingers.

We came upon the seor only moments later. Robert was no longer outside, though his pile of turf remained where he had sat. I took a breath, a dart of anger blinding me at the thought that the boy could be so obstinate in embracing shadows.

Zar stopped. "He's not alone." Listening for a moment, he grinned and motioned us onward. "It's only Corantas, come to welcome us. They desire to see the Earthlings."

My girl looked nervous as she led the way down the stairs into the seor. Eversen went after her, followed by Zar. I went down last, to find everyone gathered in the main room. Robert stood by the newly-made table and chairs, with three visitors.

The Corantas were gangly and taller than the Earthlings or Zar and me. Grey, flaky skin stretched over their bodies, speckled with brown splotches. They had no hair, and their eyes were an eerie green, almost luminescent. Strips served for their clothing, fashioned expertly from the husks of yure bark. They turned to greet me, moving jerkily.

"Welcome," the first spoke. He wore a band around his head that was crafted from red and black feathers, marking him as the leader. His eyes were shaped like a cat's, now wide with curiosity. "My name is Yahn," he introduced himself. Motioning to his two companions with that same jolting motion, he continued, "My fellow warriors, Kein and Uli."

The two dipped their heads curtly as their names were

spoken. Smiles stretched across their features, revealing sharp, pointed white teeth.

"I was just speaking with Robert," Yahn said. "He claims to be an Earthling?" His voice carried a light accent that resounded like the whisper of wind. His tone ranged from deep to high as he spoke, making the words sound like a song.

"Yes," answered Zar. "He is an Earthling, as are the maiden and the young man." He motioned to my girl and Eversen.

"Most intriguing. I have not met their kind before." Yahn sounded enthralled. He craned his head to the side and stared at Robert, a faint smile playing on his lips. Then he jerked his head to me. "Are you the leader?"

I glanced at Zar. "No. My brother, Zar, has brought us here."

"Yes, we felt the disturbance in the atmosphere," Yahn mused, looking up at the ceiling and swaying slightly.

Uli grunted and settled into a crouch, his posture perfectly mimicking that of Yahn's. Kein ignored their movements and seemed content merely to stare, unblinking, from one Earthling to the next.

"What brings you here?" Kein inquired. His voice was deeper than Yahn's, subtler, hinting more at water than wind.

"The Commander," I told him. "I am guardian of the youngest Earthling. Zar came to find us and brought us here on the Commander's orders. I have been sent from Wynaeria to lead the boy to our master."

This seemed to both perplex and please the Corantas. They spoke quickly together, far too swiftly for me to make it out, though I knew it was in their own tongue, Ghui, and not the language of the universe.

Uli glanced at me with raised eyebrows. They were dark and broad, a stark contrast to his brilliant eyes and pale skin. "You are Suri?" he asked.

I looked back with equal incredulity. "Yes. How could you know?"

Three more of their strange smiles greeted my eyes. Kein came toward me and raised his hand, palm upward. On his wrist, in the identical place of my own mark, was a small, golden ringlet.

"We serve the same master," he said. His tone was reminiscent of the air itself. "Our Commander engraved it on each of us. Will you join marks?" He offered his arm to me.

I clasped his wrist, meeting his eyes. "I will." His skin was warm and felt as fragile as it looked.

Uli and Yahn both stretched their wrists out in greeting. After Zar and I had clasped arms with each of them, the atmosphere heightened to that of a celebration.

"We are delighted that you have come to us," Yahn spoke kindly, his eyes darting over each of us. "We were only just beginning to gather loni when we saw you arrive. We would be honored if you accompanied us."

Zar grinned. "Thank you for the offer. I, at least, would be delighted to come with you and gather."

"We will all come," I told the Corantas. "It has been many long years since I've gathered loni."

My girl gave me an incredulous look. Her thoughts were abundantly clear. She wanted nothing to do with the strange Corantas and whatever loni creatures were.

I grinned back at her.

"It will be great fun," Kein assured her. "The community gathers at the riverside to gather together. There will be food and good company. Tonight, we will have a feast with the loni we harvest. Don't hesitate. You must come with us!"

"Will we be safe?" my girl asked.

The most extraordinary sound filled the seor. The Corantas' laughter mingled together to form the perfect cadences of a crackling fire. I could almost see the flames and feel the heat.

Uli answered. "Yes. There is nothing to harm you, if you stay on the riverbank and allow the young men to gather. The rest of the community will ensure your safety." He bowed his head with a quick motion.

Robert's face brightened with the prospect of meeting more strange Corantas. He thought if it sounded dangerous to my girl then it must be a good idea. "Please!" he begged her.

She saw Eversen's eager glance and sighed grudgingly. "All right. We will come."

"Wonderful!" Yahn exclaimed. His luminous eyes sparkled. "Come, then, let us go!"

Chapter 8
A Foreign Feast

The journey to the riverside was far from leisurely. The Corantas walked quickly, almost gliding over the ground. Their twitching movements gave the impression of spiders as they took one leaping step after another. It was easy to see they preferred running and were adjusting their pace to accommodate us as best they could. Were I alone, I could have stayed level with them; since the Earthlings hindered their progress, however, I followed suit.

There was no occasion for speech, as we focused all of our energy on following the Corantas. We descended down into a dell filled with scattered yures. The sound of rushing water reached our ears, and soon a river came into view.

"Our community waits beneath the yures!" Yahn called back to us.

I saw the group of Corantas below staring curiously at us. They stood or sat, lounging, in the shade of the yures on our side of the river. As with Uli, Kein, and Yahn, the Corantas had flaky grey skin and glowing green eyes. Some children were playing together at the riverbank, splashing in the calm shallows.

The Coranta men began speaking quickly with Yahn in

Ghui as we approached. The children stopped their playing to come over and stare at us. One little girl stood at my girl's feet and looked up at her. She touched a finger to my girl's smooth tan skin and breathed a word of awe. My girl stood still, eyes wide, her breathing a little tremulous.

Several Coranta women stood grouped together beneath a yure. When they saw my girl, they hurried over and began running their fingers through her hair and exclaiming loudly with delight.

My girl looked at me nervously.

"They're admiring your hair," I assured her. "There's nothing harmful in their attention. None of them have ever seen an Earthling before."

The women beckoned my girl over to the shade beneath the yures, where they had her sit so they might play with her golden hair. They spoke in eager, chattering voices, apparently taken with her.

Robert scampered toward the Coranta children and began playing with them, running wildly on the riverbank and around the yures. Several older boys motioned for him to join them in the river. Robert glanced my way, then grinned and followed them to the water.

The Coranta men gathered around Eversen, Zar, and me, eagerly speaking in Ghui. Zar and I had learned the language from previous excursions to Corant. Throughout our conversations, we acted as translators for the Earthlings.

"How are you here?"

"Are you going to gather with us?"

"How long are you staying?"

"Will you eat with us?"

Yahn quieted them by waving his hand and clucking his tongue loudly. "They are here to gather with us," he announced. "We will prepare a feast for them with the loni we catch. We gather before our celebration to eat with them!"

Cheers broke out among the Corantas.

"Let us begin!" Yahn cried over the rabble.

As if the motion was rehearsed, the Coranta men lined up along the riverbank. One by one, they dove into the clear trickling water. They broke surface and swam out to the middle of the river. Even from the distance where I stood, it was easy to perceive that they were standing on the riverbed.

"Join us, Yahn!" one cried out in Ghui.

The Coranta leader turned to me. "Will you come into the water to gather with us?"

"Let us watch first," I spoke for us all.

"Will you and your companions be comfortable on the bank?"

"Join your friends, Yahn," Zar urged him, smiling. "We will manage well by ourselves."

With another of his eerie smiles, the Coranta departed, flinging his body into the river with his companions. Zar, Eversen, and I found shade beneath the yures and watched as the hunters began their gathering.

Standing with sure footing in the middle of the river, the Corantas tilted their heads down to peer through the water. Their eyes were sharp and unwavering, piercing through the clouded blue to the very bottom, where lay the loni. These are small, orange balls with a tough, rubbery skin and a juicy, pitted center, a type of Coranta vegetable that strengthens bones and aids in agility. The Corantas prize them above all others for the nourishment they provide.

Shouts of laughter broke from the men standing in the river. Yahn jumped away from the others, a look of surprise on his face. The others laughed at him and imitated his movements. I guessed some type of fish had startled Yahn.

A young, thin Coranta ducked swiftly under the water. He came up with a triumphant shout; between thumb and forefinger he held a slippery loni. The other men clapped him on the back in congratulations, and began gathering in earnest.

It is a difficult job to harvest loni, which is why the Corantas gathered as a community and spent an entire day doing it. First, one has to locate the loni, either by feel, or by opening one's eyes under the murky water. Once grasped, the loni have to be twisted, almost screwed, off the riverbed – a difficult feat as they have stubborn roots that cling to the rocks, and slippery slides that make it nearly impossible to hold onto them.

Loni are rare in most parts of Corant, and since they have such short seasons, it is a great success to gather them, and a tradition among the Coranta tribes.

More than once one of the men lost their footing in the water and swept away down the river until they could make it to the bank and walk back to join the group. Each time this happened, the gathering stopped, and everyone watched as the man fought against the current. Once he rejoined the group, he was awarded a chorus of laughter as each gatherer submerged him by turns.

Many times, one of the men would suddenly duck beneath the water and come up grinning, triumphantly displaying his prize. With each success, the women cheered and the children jumped up and down, clapping their hands and ululating.

While the men gathered loni, the women wove clothing out of the yure peelings. They showed my girl how to split the rough bark and tenderize it by pounding it with their feet. My girl took to it with a girlish smile on her face, glowing at the praise showered on her.

Zar and I wrestled and raced along the riverbank, while Eversen remained content to merely watch the proceedings and enjoy the beautiful day.

For several hours we stayed at the river. At intervals, the gatherers would come to shore and stand with us, dripping wet, to celebrate their catches. After receiving praise and entrusting the vegetables to the women, they returned to their task.

When the children complained of hunger, the women provided snacks of dried lizo, a type of deer-like meat. Robert tried it to my girl's dismay. Eversen also took a bite, and encouraged my girl to as well, which she eventually did, surprised that she liked it.

After snacking, the children ran back to the shallows to play. Eversen followed them and sat in the shade of a yure to watch their frolicking. My girl continued to sit with the Coranta women, and learned several Ghui words as they worked with the yure peelings. Robert left with the older boys, who showed him how to gather the loni. Though the current was too strong in the center of the river for them to join the men, they practiced searching and ducking under the water in the shallows.

After a while, Zar and I attempted loni gathering. It was difficult to keep our eyes open underwater as it was denser than that of Wynaeria's or Earth's, but with a little effort, we managed. Each of us retrieved several of the orange vegetables and brought them up amid thunderous applause.

"You're not nearly so agile in the water!" Yahn crowed.

This brought gales of laughter from the Corantas.

When the day began to ebb, we climbed from the river and stood dripping on the shore. Mothers called their children and fathers divided the cluster of loni between the families. Yahn selected some of the finest for us.

He spoke swiftly in Ghui to the community. The Corantas glanced at us with happy, kind faces, and answered Yahn with nods and affirmation. When he had finished his address, he dismissed the families to their seors.

"They go to their own homes for the evening meal," he told me. "They have agreed that this is the best way. We would not all fit comfortably in your seor."

"Will others come with us?" Robert asked eagerly.

"Yahn, Uli, and I will join you," Kein assured him. "The others decided they will wait. The proper preparations for a feast of celebration cannot be made tonight. Instead, we will postpone it until tomorrow and have a community feast in honor of your visit."

~ ~ ~

Back in the seor, Kein, Uli, and Yahn set about to prepare our meal.

"There is more lizo meat to be had," the leader informed us. "It is freshly killed, so we will have to clean it properly. We can summon it, if you would like."

Zar grinned. "Pray, do."

"It will not harm us?" my girl asked, though her tone was not as hesitant now. The afternoon among the Coranta women had greatly changed her perspective of the living ones.

Robert rolled his eyes in exasperation.

"Of course not!" Kein waved away her worry. "We would not harm our Earthling guests!"

"Surely you will join us for the meal?" Uli asked.

"Yes," smiled my girl.

"Good," Yahn said. "Shall we summon the food?"

I motioned for them to proceed. "Yes, by all means."

We watched as the Corantas gathered in a circle. Yahn began speaking swiftly in Ghui, his voice rising and falling in pitch and volume. Uli joined in and then Kein. They began jumping slightly back and forth, in a jerky sway, and bowed their heads to look deliberately at the floor. Abruptly, they stilled.

Yahn reached out his right hand – mark down – over the space between them. Uli and Kein did the same and quite suddenly, there was a long, loud ripping noise. A large bundle sprang from the ground under their hands.

My girl gasped, wide-eyed. Eversen looked awed. A wide grin stretched Robert's face.

Zar raised his eyebrows, a crooked smile twitching his lips. "I've heard of this before, but I've never seen it. It's quite amazing."

The Corantas turned to us, holding up the kill. It was an animal, much the same size and shape as a deer. The coloring, however, was closer to that of a zebra's – black and white stripes that zigzagged over the body. The animal had black, cloven hooves, and a single curlicued horn in the center of its forehead.

"A lizo," Uli informed us. "They are quite common in the northern regions of Corant, though harder to find here in the south." He grinned widely. "Lizo is our favorite and the largest prey on our planet." He gave a rigid bow. "We are delighted to share it with you."

Zar turned to Yahn. "Is there anything we can provide for our meal together?"

The Coranta looked shocked. He shook his head vigorously, his jagged movements making it appear to disconnect and reconnect with each motion. "We have other delicacies to provide," he assured us, looking pointedly at Kein. "You will sit out and clean the beast. Uli and I will summon the remainder of the meal."

Zar muttered to me, "I didn't think they would allow us to share anything, but I thought I'd offer. Stubborn beings."

I worked hard to keep my features neutral.

"I'm sure Kein would refuse any help with preparing the lizo, too," he went on. He sounded grumpy, but I knew better.

"Offer," I suggested. "He can only say no, and with Yahn preoccupied, he might allow you."

Zar sighed and rolled his eyes, but went over to Kein, who had picked up the lizo and was now shuffling awkwardly toward the stairs with it to clean it outdoors.

"Will you allow me to assist you in preparing the beast?" Zar asked politely.

Kein stole a glance at Yahn and then smiled widely at Zar. "Absolutely," he said. "We'll be done before the rest arrives." He allowed Zar to help him carry the lizo and they disappeared up the stairs.

I turned to my girl, Eversen, and Robert. "None of the provisions they bring will be harmful, but don't be afraid to refuse something if you're wary of it. They won't be offended." I searched their faces carefully for a moment, then turned to the table. "We should make a place for the meal. I'll create more chairs."

Leaving the Earthlings standing bewildered in the middle of the room, I turned to the table and five chairs. Not without some difficulty, I was able to make space for three more chairs around the table. The work left me slightly out of breath. I ran my fingers through my hair and then cleared the table of the Earthlings' sacks, which I put against the wall out of the way.

By the time I had finished my work, I heard Zar and Kein climbing back down the stairs. Uli and Yahn had summoned the rest of their food from their homes and were preparing it quickly. There appeared to be different varieties of fruit, breads, and vegetables, including the loni we had harvested.

I looked around with a satisfied smile. This was turning out to be quite a feast.

When all the preparations were made, Uli placed mats to eat from around the tabletop, which Yahn had thoughtfully summoned along with the side dishes. There were no cups or utensils, as Corantas don't drink at their meals, and use their fingers to eat.

Soon, we were all seated at the table together. I only recognized a couple of the foods Yahn and Uli had provided.

Everything was delicious.

There were three separate types of bread: one black, one brown, and one a startling white. The black bread was knotted, and seeded, and very heavy, giving off an aroma of caraway. The brown bread, shaped into braids and kneaded with hard nuts, smelled of cinnamon. It was a sweet bread, flavored with a Coranta fruit reminiscent of apples. The white bread was formed into rolls, easily the lightest bread I'd ever tasted, almost dissolving in my mouth. It reminded me of snow, with a scent of tarragon.

"Sua," Uli said. "It is our most delectable bread, and has the longest baking process of them all."

There were evies, elongated white tubers – a crunchy, slightly spicy vegetable. Bunches of green leaves had a strong, rich flavor, and were exceptionally chewy. Yahn called them vue. Also spread with the vegetables were the many loni we had harvested.

"It has been many long years since I've seen a Wynaerian gather loni," Kein commented, plucking one of the balls from the others and turning it over in his hands. "It was delightful to observe." He flicked his hand and threw back his head in one jerky movement. The loni landed in his mouth. He chewed, swallowed, and spat out a pit into his hand.

"Wynaerians' eyes were not made to withstand the pressure of water." Uli grinned. "I'm amazed yours survived."

Zar scoffed around a mouthful of sua. "We are known for our many talents!"

Small blue strips of leathery sweetness, called ulen, were one of the fruit dishes. Accompanying them were stringy, translucent noodles. These tasted far too sweet to be a fruit, but coupled with the ulen, they became bearable. Together, they tasted and smelled like blueberry pie. The final fruit was a large, sun-yellow melon. When Yahn cut it open, it revealed a vibrant red center. Called a kulso, it was juicy, and mostly sour with a vague sweetness. It was most similar to a grapefruit, though it lacked the bitter aftertaste.

The lizo meat had been cooked over a fire in single portions. It was tender and spicy, pleasantly moist with a wild tinge. Dipped in a white sauce that tasted suspiciously like cheese, it was superb.

The Earthlings sampled each dish, and my girl, for one, was surprised at how well she liked the foreign meal. When finally our appetites were sated, the Corantas refused our help in cleaning up and returned the leftover food to their homes in the reverse way of summoning it.

After everything had been cleared from the table, the Corantas once again gathered in a circle. This time, they summoned water to wash down our meal. Rather than sitting together, the Corantas showed us their tradition.

We gathered in a circle, each holding a goblet of water. Yahn spoke a blessing, thanking the Commander for the good meal and abundant water, then, as one, we tipped the goblets back and drank. Only when the water was gone did we lower the cups again. Yahn, as the leader, stepped to each of us to collect the chalices and said, "May we drink together again."

Once the chalices had also been returned to their homes, the Corantas lowered themselves to the ground and sat, cross-legged.

"Now tell us the long story of what brings you to Corant," Yahn requested.

Zar and I joined them on the floor with the Earthlings, where it was more comfortable. Once we were all seated, Zar began the narrative, from my exile from Wynaeria up until he was commissioned to find me.

"After the Light Dancing" (Kein interrupted to ask what Light Dancing was) "of three nights ago, the Commander asked that I speak with him apart from the others. I said my farewells and good nights and walked with him into the forest. He had changed from the Beam to a Wynaerian form.

"Once in the shelter of the trees, the Commander informed me of Suri's whereabouts. He told me I had to find him and bring him to Corant.

"'The Earthlings will travel with you,' he said. 'They will be safe on Corant. One day they will need to know about it.'

"I was confused by his statement. 'What on Corant will the Earthlings need to know about? Will they not be afraid?'

"The Commander merely smiled and told me he would show us what to do once we arrived. I suspect there will be trials ahead and Corant will be a safe haven for them." Zar gazed at Robert. "Perhaps the Embers will be involved."

For the second time since meeting Robert, my vision filled with blinding white. I gasped and leaned forward, head in my hands.

Before me rose a multitude of translucent balls, stretching out to the horizon of a planet. A deep sense of dread filled me, and pain shot along the bond I shared with Robert. Sharp screams pierced my ears, mixed with maniacal laughter and the clank of manacles. Flames rose before my eyes and heat seared me.

I opened my eyes. This vision was much more similar to those I'd had before meeting Robert: indistinct noises, shapes, and ideas, nothing concrete. It was unusual for the vision to end so quickly, but what I discovered from it was enough.

We're leaving the Earthlings on Corant, I confirmed to the Commander. *We're going to be attacked by the Embers, and someone will be captured.* I glanced at Robert, suspicious. The Commander didn't answer and I was silent for a moment. Then the memory of the fire's heat hit me with a sudden certainty.

Someone will die. The realization disturbed me. *Who?* I wondered, more to myself than to the Commander this time. Then another thought broke in. *If Corant is to be a safe haven for the Earthlings, where are Zar and I going?*

You, Eversen, and Robert will leave, the Commander replied. *The others will remain on Corant.*

I considered that for a moment. *Where are you sending us?*

Jaada.

That jolted me. *Jaada? Why the Embers' planet?* My musings were introspective, but the Commander answered anyway.

There is a purpose for each of you. You must meet someone. Robert must be challenged. Eversen will be encouraged.

"So interesting," Yahn murmured, and it took me a moment to realize he was talking about the Commander's commission to Zar.

I raised my head to look at him. It appeared that only a few seconds had passed. No one seemed to notice my brief thoughtfulness.

"Why should Corant be important to Earthlings?" Uli asked, eyes flicking to them. The Earthlings were each silent, watching the exchange.

Deciding now was no worse a time than some and better

than others, I spoke. "They are protected here," I answered. "The Commander has another commission for us. We're leaving."

Zar's eyes widened. "Where are we going?"

"Not you," I clarified. "Robert and Eversen will accompany me. We are going to Jaada."

Silence met my pronouncement.

The Corantas were flabbergasted. Uli's jaw dropped. Yahn blinked quickly, and Kein gave a shake of his head. Zar stared at me for a moment. The Earthlings looked bewildered.

I grinned at their reactions. "I've had another vision," I informed them. "We're going to be assailed, and someone will be captured by the Embers." Before anyone could speak, I answered their question. "No, I don't know which of us." I darted my eyes to Robert. "You, however, will be tested." To Eversen, "You will be encouraged; and I must meet someone."

"Is that all?" Yahn asked.

"I believe it's enough," I said. "The Commander didn't name any specifics, but I have no doubt we will be challenged."

"When will you go?" Zar prompted.

"Why not immediately? As there is no time limit, I can't imagine the Commander would want us to delay."

My girl's eyes narrowed. "You're taking Eversen and Robert to another planet? You're leaving me here with Zar?" Her voice rose.

"I must obey the Commander," I countered. "He told me to leave you with Zar, so yes, you will stay."

"What will happen to you?" my girl shot back.

I lifted my lips in a half-smile. She didn't care about me; she wanted to make sure Robert would be safe. "I don't know. Whatever happens, the Commander will protect us and we will be in his care. Is that enough for you?"

She looked away, which was answer enough for me.

Yahn rose. "We will sustain you for the journey. Our provisions will travel through tunnels without spoiling. We will summon the most nutritious food for you, to keep you strong. It will be hard to find sustenance on Jaada, I think."

"Provisions are no matter," I said, waving a hand impatiently. "We need to leave as soon as possible."

"You won't be departing before morning," Kein interjected. "You need strength to withstand foes you will encounter on Jaada. Come tonight to the celebration between the stones. We're gathering in worship. We will commission you, and you will be encouraged before you go."

I dipped my head in acknowledgement. "Very well, then."

My girl looked disgruntled, but remained silent.

Robert had watched the exchange without speaking. His eyes shone with the excitement of an adventure. A somewhat sly smile lifted the corner of his mouth. "What sort of people live on Jaada?"

I looked at him shrewdly. "They are called Embers."

His reaction was as I expected, though he quickly quelled it. His eyes flickered and brightened; and an expression of delight crossed his countenance. It was only there for a moment, but I knew he was not nearly so innocent to Embers as he proceeded to convey.

"What are Embers?" he asked, staring unwaveringly at me.

Inwardly, I recoiled in disgust. "They are a race of living ones, though most are so aligned with demons that they are incapable of a single act of goodness. They are shadowy, human-like creatures that bring darkness, cold, and fear to those they encounter."

Robert was not in the least disconcerted.

"Suri," admonished Zar.

Unable to stand Robert's egotism, I glanced at my girl. She looked fearful.

"Can they traverse to Earth?" she asked Zar.

"Yes. They journey to Earth quite frequently," he answered.

"Yes," I responded to her unspoken suspicion. "One was

outside Eversen's hut."

She looked aghast. "You can read my thoughts?"

I grinned. "When I wish to, yes. You were once my charge, as Robert is now. Because I am a guardian of the Commander, I have been granted the ... abilities necessary to draw my charges to him."

Yahn, Uli, and Kein all wore amused expressions as they turned away to summon provisions for traversing to Jaada.

"'You were once my charge,'" my girl repeated. She wore a strange expression that unnerved me.

I coughed, paying close attention to her confused thoughts. "Many years ago, I led you away from your father's hut and restored you to your family. In the process, you submitted to the Commander, thus enacting and fulfilling my purpose in your life."

Her eyes flickered to Robert and understanding dawned in her mind. "Is your purpose always fulfilled?"

I exchanged a wary glance with Zar. "No," I said gently. "At least, not in the way you mean." I drew a breath, thinking quickly. "All charges do not come to the Commander. Yet his will cannot be thwarted. While sometimes it seems to be a failure of guardianship, the lessons learned and wisdom gleaned is for the Commander's greatest honor."

My girl nodded in acceptance, despite her disappointment.

"In the end," Zar murmured, "it falls to the Commander's decision as to who becomes his."

Eversen stepped to my girl and squeezed her shoulder reassuringly. She smiled.

"You ran away from home?" Robert inquired, apparently oblivious to the depth of our conversation. He looked elated at the prospect of such a daring exploit.

My girl's voice reeked of bitterness. "Yes. I've told you. My father –" she winced "– was not a very good or kind man. He killed my mother when I was about ten, and I ran away." She cast a glance at me. "It seems I was not alone, but had a guide."

Smirking, Zar lifted his eyebrows at me. "Yes, and I'm sure he was the greatest guardian available."

I grinned back sheepishly. "At least I was sent on the assignment," I reminded him.

"What happened?" Robert's eyes bored into my girl's. "Where did you go?"

"My aunt in New York raised me until I came of age. I left her to find what became of my father. He had died a couple of years previously and his house near Bedwin stood empty. As I had nowhere else to go – I was tired of living in the city with my aunt – I stayed and took over his property. I've lived there since."

Robert gaped at her. "You mean that's the place where I met you?"

She nodded.

Kein approached us, and spoke to me. "We will depart and leave you in peace for the remainder of the day." Gesturing to his companions, he said, "Yahn and Uli will leave the provisions here with you. After the celebration tonight, and a good night's rest, we will farewell you in the morning." He twitched his head downward.

"Thank you." I extended my hand and we clasped marks.

Yahn, Uli, and Kein wished us farewell, and departed. Against the wall remained the products of their summoning. Three bulging sacks were bundled together, light and durable for traveling.

Chapter 9
The Prisms of Light

Once the Corantas were out of sight, Robert spun back to my girl. "Why would you go back to where your father lived?" he demanded. "Didn't you hate him?"

My girl gazed steadily at him and spoke slowly, softly. "I did, for many years. I was hurt and angry. I never wanted to see him again, or even think of him." Again, she glanced at me, and took a step closer to Robert. "Then the Commander came to me. The burden of hatred was too heavy for me to bear any longer. So the Commander took it, and I have been free ever since."

There was silence in the seor after this pronouncement. Looking for something to do, I strode over to the sacks left behind by the Corantas. Crouching, I flipped back the covering flaps and peered inside, but as I rummaged through them, my mind was far away, remembering the assignment I had failed.

I had unpacked and repacked the three bags and started again when Zar crouched beside me. He placed a hand on my shoulder.

"I assume based on your expression and attitude, that she did not explain the entirety of her journey."

I barked a bleak laugh. "Not hardly. Though I was contemplating more my exile from Wynaeria than her worst night."

"What happened, then? I don't recall this story." Zar was nearly amused.

"Screaming, nightmares, torture." I shrugged. "Every evil the Embers can employ were assailed against her. My shield was insufficient, and they reached her." I straightened and Zar stood with me. "It was the hardest night I'd ever had, and probably a close contender to the worst she's ever had."

I was not blind to the stares of the Earthlings, nor deaf to the very quiet breaths they took as they eavesdropped on our conversation. My eyes caught Eversen's; his countenance was etched with empathy. A pondering look came into his face and he broke away from my gaze, flicking his eyes toward my girl. He looked back to me and lifted his eyebrows in question.

His inference was clear.

I shook my head, disgusted with myself.

"Ah, don't be so cold," Zar advised, crossing his arms reflectively. "You're leaving in the morning. It's best to have good fellowship before the departure."

Half exasperated, half amused, I motioned to the stairwell. "Then, to expand our good fellowship, let's explore the planet we're on. There won't be any other time before we leave."

"Those in favor say, 'aye,'" muttered Zar.

Stifling a grin, I strode purposefully to the stairwell. "You will most likely find me among the yures," I informed my spectators. With an exaggerated bow, I bounded up the stairs and out into Corant's sunlight.

The air was fresh and sweet, with a hint of peaches distinct to Corant. A gentle breeze ruffled my hair and for a moment I stood still in the doorway, enjoying the subtle sensations.

"Any day you want to continue, that would be lovely."

I stepped aside onto the spongy ground.

"I mean," Zar continued, stepping out beside me, "I understand your fascination and infatuation with everything, but some of us would actually enjoy a walk in the pleasant weather. By all means, continue your idle thoughtfulness. Only allow us to pass first, so we can go on."

I chuckled and reached out a hand to help the Earthlings climb from the seor's entrance. "I didn't realize your excursion was so incumbent," I said lazily.

Zar walked forward, calling back over his shoulder, "Excursions are the way of guardians, Suri! Surely by now you have realized the importance of them!"

I left the Earthlings and jogged toward my brother. With a well-timed jumping kick, I sent him sprawling.

"Oho!" he cried, rolling onto his back before I tripped over him. "A fight, is it?" He kicked out his foot to trip me.

I stepped back, easily avoiding his retaliation. "Do you ever wonder," I began, looking down at him with a smirk, "why the Commander allows such immature guardians?"

"Well, I'm glad you've finally put yourself in that category," Zar approved with bravado, as he got to his feet. "As for myself, well, you know the Commander chooses only the best warriors –"

I tackled him before he finished his boast, knocking us both to the ground, where we wrestled.

"Tut, tut, Suri," Zar gasped, holding me pinned to the ground. "I would think after all your *excursions*, you would be more agile than this."

I couldn't prevent my laughter, which spilled over raucously.

"Still no match for your older brother," Zar sniffed pompously, releasing me to sit back on his heels. "*Wherever* did you learn to survive?"

I stayed on my back, laughing, unable to stop. "Not from you," I gasped. I tried lifting my head to stand, found that it required too much exertion, and dropped it again. "Otherwise, I would stand a chance against you."

Zar, now standing above me, reached down a hand to

help me up. "I trust you won't attempt another foolhardy match again." His tone would have been disparaging had it not been steeped in humor.

I gripped his hand and used his strength to pull myself up. The Earthlings were staring, agape, but I ignored them and turned to Zar. "It's not as easy on Corant," I asserted brashly. "The bouncing ground does not help. Were we on a solid surface, I could easily vanquish you."

"I should have left you on the ground," Zar exclaimed. "Such bold taunts when you were justly defeated!"

Robert grinned. "Zar's stronger," he stated. At my mock offended expression, he continued, "He's older. It makes sense that you can't beat your older brother."

I shook my head in disbelief.

Zar laughed. "That's the second time I've beaten you, on as many planets. Shall we try for a third on Wynaeria?"

He was only teasing, but I couldn't help the resentment that entered me. All merriment vanished into sullenness. If only I *could* return to Wynaeria.

Zar sighed. "I'm sorry, Suri." He reached up a fist to lightly punch my arm. "Come on, let's explore." He turned away to lead us.

I followed quietly, trying to regain the sense of lighthearted adventure I'd had in the seor.

"You must admit, though, that the Commander picks the best warriors to traverse Open Space." He threw me a sly look over his shoulder.

It roused me from my sudden melancholy. "I take that as a compliment!" I called to his back.

Robert sidled over to walk beside me. "Where are we going? Will we see the crystals?"

I peered down at him. "We already visited the crystals," I reminded him. "You will have to wait to see them until tonight at the celebration. Now, we are going to look around. The yures form a kind of forest, where animals live."

He didn't seem disgruntled in the least. "What sort of animals?" Once again, he reverted to being an innocent boy rather than the arrogant lad that was becoming more common.

"There are not many that populate Corant." I noticed Eversen and my girl drifting closer to overhear, and adjusted my volume for them. "Lizoes are the largest, and we're unlikely to find one. There are some bird-like creatures as well. They are ... unusual." I couldn't think of a better word to describe the vibrant beings. "They are called umplies, and are much more prevalent than lizoes."

"They live in the forest?" my girl inquired. She had begun walking beside me, and was closer than I had anticipated.

Taken aback, I stared at her for a moment, then recovered myself. "Yes. They make their nests in the uppermost branches of the yures, and feed on insects that live in the bark."

"What do they look like?" Robert pressed.

"It's difficult to describe," I began.

"Come, come, Suri. Surely you won't spoil all the surprises before we get there?" Zar had doubled back and joined us, apparently lonely.

I raised an eyebrow at him.

We neared the yure stand now, and fell silent. Robert looked keenly at the bark to try and find the insects I'd mentioned. As we walked further in, my girl and Eversen joined him in his search. Several paces on, the yures grew denser, and we often had to duck under the peeling bark as we continued. Strange chirruping resounded around us. A bright blue flashed against pale pink sky.

"Look."

I crouched at Robert's side and pointed up at the yure branch where the umply perched. My girl, Eversen, and Zar followed the direction of my finger.

"Oh," my girl breathed.

I chuckled. "Difficult to describe, aren't they?"

A large, snowy white head peeked down at us. The umply had a thin neck that broadened out into bare-skinned shoulders. The wings protruded from what looked like black sticks, no more than an inch in diameter, but several inches long. At the end of each stick a bush of brilliant sapphire feathers spread out to form the wings. From the tips of the wings protruded three small appendages. They couldn't be rightly called claws or fingers, but some strange mixture of both.

"The umply uses those to dig into yure bark," I explained. "They claw out insects to eat. The claws also help the umply climb."

The umply's body was sinewy and strong, only a slight shade lighter than the flamboyant wings. It was not covered in feathers, but thick, woolly fur, and ran down into two legs. For feet, two more of the black stick-like bones jutted out and ended in large, golden claws.

The umply cocked its head at us, its eyes a mosaic of color, like that of a supernova. Its beak was small and pointy, a deep mahogany color. It seemed to be smiling at us.

As we watched, the umply opened its beak. A high, burbling sound pierced our ears – the same chirruping we'd heard when we entered the yure forest. With another purring cry, the umply dove. Or rather, it plopped from the yure branch. Its movements were so uncoordinated and bulky, it seemed to be falling rather than flying as it swooped toward us.

"Duck," Zar warned. "It's going to attack."

We needn't have bothered. The umply landed on a yellow yure branch a few feet from us and gave us another piercing glare.

I got to my feet with the others.

"Ah." Zar understood. "There's a lady-bird."

Sure enough, another umply, this one a vibrant yellow, dropped to the ground only a yard from us. The only distinction between the male and the female was the pomp of plumage. Her feathers were much bushier, frilly compared with the male's. She began preening, completely ignoring the male when he squawked in indignation.

I turned to my companions with a smirk. "I think we can safely exit the scene now. While he's preoccupied, the umply won't charge us. It's a good thing the female arrived. Otherwise we would have discovered what it is to be nipped by an umply."

"A most unpleasant sensation," Zar agreed.

We turned away from the umplies and continued on through the forest.

"What other kinds of creatures are here?" my girl asked in delight. Her face was aglow from the encounter with the umplies. She looked at me for an answer.

"Um ..." I looked to Zar for help, but he snickered and pointedly turned his back on me. "In this region there aren't many others that I can recall. Those that do live here are either nocturnal or so rare it would be nearly impossible to stumble across them."

"What are they like? Are they like the umplies?" She said the word carefully.

I smiled. "No, not really. The closest to umplies are rugles, and they are much more like bats. In other regions of Corant, there are types of fish and reptiles. Here," I gestured to the yures surrounding us, brushing blue bark with the back of my hand, "is the most barren part of Corant. It grows the hottest in the summer and the coldest in the winter, due to the position of the sun. Most life in many other parts of Corant could not be sustained here."

"Will we see any nocturnal animals?" she asked next.

I bounced my eyebrows. "Well, Robert, Eversen, and I won't be able to, as we're leaving. You, however – as Zar will be here with you, I'm sure he'll take you to see some." I bored my eyes into my brother's back, sure that he heard my words.

"Yes, yes," responded he. "I can take you out after dark sometimes to see the night creatures."

Robert scuffed his feet against the ground, head bowed. He appeared disappointed.

"What's wrong?" my girl asked him, putting an arm across his shoulders.

He mumbled, "I want to see the night creatures, too."

"Oh," my girl blustered, "I'm sure you can see them after you return from Jaada. Won't he?" She rounded on me.

I stopped walking and held up my hands beseechingly. "I can't promise he will. The Commander may not have us return ..." her glare quelled the rest of my sentence. "Yet," I continued hastily, "if we do return, I will make certain that he sees night creatures."

"There." She squeezed Robert's shoulder. "Once you get back we can all go and look for them."

The only trouble was *whether* we would come back. Only the Commander could know, and he was indisposed to divulge his knowledge to us.

~ ~ ~

Corant's sun was drawing near to the horizon when our companionship stepped out of the seor again. The Earthlings, Zar, and I had already eaten our evening meal, preparing for bed as soon as we returned. Against my personal preference, Zar insisted I sleep before journeying again, though it had only been a few days since my last respite.

"There's no purpose in wasting the night away in unconsciousness," I argued as we walked across the plains toward the circle of crystal prisms. "If I need rejuvenation on Jaada, I am fully capable of finding a laie to sleep in."

Zar retorted adamantly. "Your body needs as much physical strength as it can possess before you travel there. You have no idea who you might meet or the challenges you will face, and you should sleep on Jaada as little as possible. Laies may not be safe or nearby for your repose. It's an unnecessary risk."

"You're a mother hen!" I exclaimed.

Zar continued, undeterred, a half-grin quirking his lips. "I'm a firstborn. I suggest you turn in early and sleep as long as you can." He ducked, laughing, out of reach of my swinging arm.

"Mothering firstborn," I grumbled. Though I was only jesting, a spark of real anger ignited in me at Zar's protectiveness.

The Earthlings laughed.

Just very slightly to our left the blue sun had nearly touched the horizon. Deep maroons, purples, and violets reached up into the sky from the sun's rays. Vibrant colors of orange, yellow, and red from the east and south splashed the sky. Finally, the north threw hues of green and blue. Merging together at the peak of the sky, the rays displayed the normally pink sky as an explosion of color. It was breathtaking.

We grew quieter and trod more softly as we continued, the beauty around us a silencer. Gradually, we became aware of that tantalizing music from the crystal prisms. It drifted through the air on the edges of our consciousness, comforting and peaceful. Just beyond a pink yure, the circle of stones came into sight.

It was then that we saw the Corantas. They were gathering together from all around, striding slowly up to the outer edges of the circle. There were nearly a hundred of them, young, old, and middle-aged. In contrast to their lighthearted spirits earlier in the day, they were now solemn out of respect for the Commander. They stopped at the crystals as one, hands joined together and every head bowed. The circle of Corantas grew larger as we watched.

A younger man coming from the east noticed us and strode forward to meet us. It was Kein.

"Welcome," said he softly. His eyes were wider than before, bright with excitement. He lifted a hand to clasp marks with Zar, Eversen, my girl, and me. "Come and join us," he beckoned.

We followed Kein silently to enter the congregation of Corantas. They made space for us between them. Robert stood back and did not join. He had no interest, as he did not belong to the Commander. Only those who possessed the mark joined the celebratory circle. All others remained in their homes. Kein took a place on my girl's left. Yahn and Uli were also among the circle, heads bowed, lips moving swiftly in Ghui.

For several moments we remained in the same posture, no one looking at another, as the tension eased in each. The music, once so elusive, now resounded clearly, so loud it seemed to enter our bodies. We no longer felt our hearts beating, but the music beating inside us. Again, the lyrics of the song rang out, lilting and indecipherable.

Around the circle the song's effects became apparent. One by one, the Corantas dropped to their knees, overcome. No one released their grip on their neighbor and as the song went on, warmth began spreading through our marks. From one to another, the heat intensified until it felt like burning, nearly unbearable. Yet it was not painful, merely strong.

I glanced down at my burning wrist and blinked, unable to believe what I saw. My skin, clasped by Eversen on one side and Zar on the other, was glowing pure white. The light began to move, traveling from my wrists up my arms and across my shoulders and chest, then down into my stomach and legs, until it reached my toes. With the light, the fire spread. I looked around the circle, and noticed I wasn't alone. Everyone clasping marks was now illuminated with bright light.

I cast a look at Robert, my curiosity thoroughly aroused. I wasn't surprised by what I saw, but greatly disturbed.

He stood on the edge of the circle, leaning haughtily against a yure with his arms crossed. Instead of light, a muddy brown color muted him. He looked around, apparently unimpressed, and his eyes blazed red. He couldn't see the lights shining from the rest of us. Rather, his features twisted into disgust and a sneer curled his lips. His heart, I noted, was no longer enshrouded with misty shadows, but completely encased in a dull black crust.

I turned away from the sickening sight to my girl. She glowed brightly, and her heart was too white to gaze upon. It shone out from her chest, illuminating her entire body. I wondered how hot the fire was in her. As I watched, she dropped to her knees, and tears fell into her lap. The Commander had overwhelmed her as his own.

I bowed my head once more and breathed in the light and the heat and the song.

It could have been minutes or hours later that the first voice joined the music. Not long after, another began, and then another, until the entire circle was singing. I added my voice to theirs and the music swelled to a crescendo that never seemed to end.

The sun had set completely and was in the throes of its most glorious exhibition when our celebration ended. It was only then, when I released the wrists of Eversen and Zar, that I realized Robert had gone.

The lights shining from us faded slowly, but Robert's darkness would have been hidden from the moment the circle broke. Anger cut through me at his disappearance, and in its wake the glory of the celebration faded.

"Where's Robert?" my girl murmured, eyes still luminous with a soft luster. She looked to me for explanation. As well she should have, as I was Robert's guardian.

I inwardly kicked myself. "He's gone," I answered, voice tight. "I don't know when he left or where he went."

"Let's find him," Zar said wearily. "You have a journey to make in the morning and his presence is necessary."

Now subdued and sullen, our fellowship spread out to look for the Earthling boy. We scoured the area, which now dimmed into darkness to hinder our search. I wandered away from the others, not bothering to call out to Robert, knowing he wouldn't answer.

I found him under a green yure, once more playing with fire. His fingertips were alight with it. Slowly, the flames grew and formed together into a ball. Robert sneered and tossed the ball of fire into the air, catching it lightly. Now, I was sure that if I could penetrate the swirling mist, I would find his heart black to its very center.

I walked silently up to him and leaned against the yure's trunk. For a moment, I couldn't speak, too angry to form coherent words. I seethed watching him; Robert threw the fireball several more times and caught it. His fingers and palms were completely unharmed.

When I was certain my voice would not shake with anger, I spoke. "What are you doing?"

Robert didn't bat an eyelash. His eyes, now reflecting the fire he held, remained focused on the ball resting in his fingertips. Flickers of red danced across his face. His sneer lessened, but remained.

"I came away to practice," he said in a cold voice. "I think I have more power here. It's easier to command the fire than it was on Earth." He looked at me and his eyes looked dead and grey away from the firelight. "It was uncomfortable at the celebration."

"Uncomfortable," I repeated in disbelief.

"Yes," continued he as though I were merely an errant thought whispering in his ear. "It felt like I was freezing, or burning." He cocked his head and extinguished the flame by closing it in his fist. Then he stood and looked at me. "We can go back to the others now. I was only waiting for you to finish."

Incensed, I didn't answer.

We walked back to the others, who had gathered together to wait for us. It was nearly dark now; the sun was lowered beneath the horizon.

"He was under a yure," I answered curtly before they could ask.

"What were you doing?" my girl demanded to Robert. "Why did you leave?"

Robert had an air of superiority as he answered. "I didn't like the celebration. I left to practice ..." he let his voice trail off.

"Practice what?" asked Zar. He glanced at me.

I didn't unclench my jaw.

"I learned some things on Earth," Robert said evasively.

"Fire," I told Zar. "He was lighting and extinguishing fire."

My girl and Eversen were stunned.

"I suggest we return to the seor and get some sleep before something else happens tonight," I said.

Zar nodded.

It was a quiet walk back, though once or twice I heard my girl berating Robert under her breath. Whether he heard or not, I couldn't tell. The atmosphere of the celebration had been completely decimated in the wake of Robert's disappearance. It seemed almost a thing of the long-gone past.

The Earthlings climbed into the seor first and Zar detained me.

"The Ember?" he inquired.

"I don't believe there was one nearby. I think the Commander's presence repulsed him because of the darkness he already possesses." I ran my hands through my hair wearily. "Whichever Ember implanted the darkness in him has done a thorough job. Robert is as far from the Commander as Malevolence himself."

Zar nodded, as though he expected as much. "Perhaps Jaada will help."

I snorted. "More likely, he'll join their ranks than turn to the Commander. Did you see him at the celebration?"

"Yes. It was unsurprising." He frowned. "The Commander knows what he's doing, though," he reminded me. "Jaada might awaken Robert to the reality of his damnation."

"In the meantime, we'll all suffer." I ducked to enter the seor and Zar followed.

At the bottom of the stairs, the Earthlings had already bid each other goodnight and settled into their various beds. Robert was lying on his back, staring at the ceiling. His fingers glowed and dimmed, but did not create fire again. He glanced at me and grinned.

I glared back and clenched my jaw.

Undaunted, he grinned more widely and returned his

eyes to the ceiling.

Stalking to the seor's wall, I bent down and began manipulating the material. The work was a very small and inadequate way to release my anger at Robert. Too soon, the bed was erected. I threw myself onto it and bored my eyes into the ceiling.

Zar grinned at me from where he sat on the stairs.

I gave him a withering glare and closed my eyes. For a long time sleep evaded me, and I drummed my fingers on my chest. To occupy my mind, I thought of the Earthlings, the celebration, Robert's insolence, the journey to Jaada on the morrow. Groaning, I turned over.

"Can't sleep?" Zar asked innocently, his voice low to keep from disturbing the others. "I thought that was an Earthling problem."

I opened my eyes, lips compressed, refusing to answer his taunt. He now stood at the foot of my bed, mouth twisted into a smirk. I threw my arm over my eyes and grunted.

Zar chuckled at my obstinance, but didn't speak.

I felt the change in the atmosphere and didn't care. A few minutes later, my mind went blank, my body relaxed, and I succumbed to unconsciousness.

Chapter 10
Unruly Claims

Some time had passed before I awoke. The seor gleamed faintly, reflecting the light in the sunrise. From the silence surrounding me, I knew none of the Earthlings had awakened yet. I sat up in bed and yawned.

"Welcome back," Zar greeted me. "As you did not perish during your respite, I imagine it was not terrible."

"You wouldn't know," I retorted. "Suspending consciousness is a useless way to survive. Never again will I sleep twice in a week. I assume you Channeled the exhaustion, did you?"

Zar spread his hands in what he clearly believed to be an innocent gesture. Eyebrows raised, he grinned affirmation.

"Of course." I stood and stretched my arms behind my back. Zar poked me and I grinned, dropping into a protective posture. "None of that," I protested.

The Earthlings woke before long and we prepared for departure. Our sacks we slung over our shoulders, and, after a hurried breakfast, left the seor for the tunnel.

The walk to the tunnel-site was quiet and short. It was unsurprising, though no less astonishing, that the tunnel had not disappeared, which would have been inherent to their nature. I wondered why my tunnels were different from the others, why they didn't disappear once their purpose was fulfilled.

"Where is the tunnel?" Robert's tone was sneering.

Reining in a harsh rejoinder, I just managed to keep my voice level. "Would you like to see it?"

For a brief instant, Robert's eyes lit with excitement. Then arrogance overtook him. He shrugged. "Why not?"

I reached out my hand.

Robert adopted a haughty air and for the scantest moment, he thought about spitting on it. Then curiosity overcame him and he took my hand. Immediately, his eyes widened and an involuntary gasp broke from his lips.

"Can I see?" my girl queried. A burst of excitement welled in her and she extended her hand without waiting for an answer.

I reached out my free hand to hold hers.

Her mouth opened in a perfect circle. "That?" she breathed, stretching out her other hand to pass it through the tunnel's walls. "That is what we traveled through?"

Zar and I chuckled. "Yes." I tried to look at the tunnel objectively, trying to imagine what it would be like to see it for the first time. It was impossible, but I had a vague idea of the tunnel's grandeur and singularity.

Eversen looked left out, unable to see what we stared at, though he didn't seem upset. Zar put a hand on his shoulder and then he, too, could see what stood before us.

"Now that we have gawked at our transportation –" I began.

Zar shook his head at me. "Ruin the moment, Suri. Go ahead. This will likely be one of a very few times any human sees a tunnel, and you want it to be finished with as quickly as possible."

"That's not what I said," I protested, but I didn't finish my previous sentence.

The Earthlings wanted to look all around it and touch the

blood-red line at the ground. The tunnel was the texture of glass, but easily passed through, which posed a quandary for them. It glimmered with every color, and hummed faintly. For several long moments they examined and exclaimed over the tunnel. Finally, my girl and Robert released my hands. My girl stepped back and looked up into the sky, trying to penetrate the tunnel's invisibility.

"Well, this is farewell, then," Zar said.

My girl brought her eyes back down to mine. Resigned sorrow played over her features. She turned from me to Robert, and knelt to encompass him in her arms.

He embraced her with a passive air. He seemed determine to be detached from everyone. Perhaps he considered himself valuable to the Ember in his dream and therefore superior to the rest of us. His aloofness did not discourage my girl, however.

"I will miss you, Robert," she murmured, voice soft. "Please be cautious, and do what you're told." She turned to Eversen. "Thank you for everything. I wish we didn't have to part ways so soon. I will eagerly await your return." She smiled.

Eversen stepped to her and gathered her in his arms. He set her back to look at her and grinned broadly.

"Well, let's go then," I said, eyeing the tunnel.

"Suri, wait."

I froze. Shock surged through me. She probably didn't know it, but it was the first time she had said my name.

Zar raised his eyebrows, smiling, and nudged my elbow with his arm.

I turned to look at her. "Yes?"

My girl was embarrassed. She scratched her arm absently and didn't fully meet my gaze. "I'm going to miss you, too," she said. "You've been a good companion, not only recently, but also when I was a young girl." Hazy thoughts of nightmares and being comforted flitted into her mind, but she didn't dwell on any of them.

I rearranged my features into a smile and spoke gently.

"You've been ..." I picked my words carefully, "a delightful charge. I'm glad we were finally able to meet in person." It wasn't all I wanted to say, but it would have to suffice.

My girl's eyes shone, and it may as well have just been the two of us, the way the others faded from my mind.

Then Zar chuckled and clapped me on the back. He engulfed me in an embrace and muttered, "*Someone* will be eagerly awaiting your return."

I felt my ears burn. "Thanks." I stepped back and looked up into my brother's face. "Don't neglect your duty here, or I may just come and relieve you of it."

He smirked. "I'll be careful."

"Should I get into any perilous situations, don't forget to come rescue me," I jested.

Zar's eyes were serious as he answered, "I will always come back to you, my brother."

I caught his serious tone and nodded soberly. I turned to Robert and Eversen. "Let's depart before something else delays us," I suggested, glancing over at my girl.

Zar laughed. "That could only be you, Suri,.."

I ignored him and stepped into the tunnel with Robert and Eversen. Immediately, we traveled through Open Space. Once more colors and lights and planets sped by. This time, Eversen's and Robert's eyes were opened to tunnel-traveling.

Unlike on Corant, as we drew near to Jaada the tunnel darkened considerably. The gloom grew heavier and more tangible the closer we came, until it was impossible to distinguish anything. When we landed, the darkness enshrouded us from each other and a deep coldness washed through us. A heavy stench of sulfur and smoke hung in the air.

Eversen shivered.

Robert turned around blandly, hiding the fear that assailed his shadow-encased heart. A vaguely curious expression entered his face before his eyes faded to grey as they had when he'd left the Coranta celebration.

"Welcome to Jaada," I said mordantly. I looked around, my eyes stronger than the Earthlings and able to penetrate the darkness further. Still, I could discern nothing more than my companions. The only pinpricks of light were gems embedded in the marble ground – diamonds, rubies, and emeralds. The rest of the landscape was bare and eerily silent.

"What are we doing here?" Robert asked. "What did the Commander have in mind?"

His words were icy and grated. I turned to glare at him. "It is not our prerogative to know what the Commander has in mind. We are to obey, and that is what we're doing. Now come on." I tramped off in no specific direction, forcing the Earthlings to follow.

"Suri?" A voice I'd never heard before called my name. It was low and hoarse, but not unkind, and it came from behind me.

I turned. Robert stared at Eversen, whose eyes were wide.

"Suri?" the voice spoke again, almost jubilantly. This time, I saw Eversen's mouth form the sounds of my name.

I stopped in my tracks and stared at him, as dumbfounded as Robert, and equally speechless.

Eversen grinned incredulously. "Robert," he said, turning to the boy. "I can speak." His words were little louder than a whisper, but whether from long muteness or awe, I couldn't tell.

I took a step toward him. "*How?*"

"I can speak," Eversen repeated. He reached a hand up to his throat to feel the vibrations of his speech. "I can speak!" He threw his head back and laughed.

I grinned, astonished, though a portion of my mind cautioned against his loud exuberance. Jaada was not a safe planet to parade our presence. Embers are ruthless in any form, but much more powerful in their own homeland.

"We need to exercise caution," I warned Eversen; a trifle of rue struck me at dampening his excitement.

He nodded in spite of my tone and grinned. "I'm sorry." His eyes shone with the knowledge of his new ability.

The Commander's words entered my mind. *Eversen will be encouraged.* Now I understood. My thoughts whirled on. If Eversen received speech, there would be a reason for it. He must talk with someone.

"We need to find shelter," I said. "There are crystal-like spheres on Jaada, called laies. We must find one to sleep in. They are Jaada's form of tree."

"What do they look like?" asked Eversen, reveling in his newfound ability.

I snorted. "That's the complication. They're invisible."

My words plunged us into silence, and I began walking again, straining my eyes in the gloom for the signs of a laie. It is very difficult to find them, besides the obvious reason of invisibility. Their exteriors are made of a diaphanous material that makes them nearly insubstantial. Other than Embers, only those accustomed to the infinitesimal difference in the atmosphere can detect the location of the laies; or so Juris had once told me.

I was neither. *Commander, help me.* Twice before I'd trekked to Jaada, and both times I'd stumbled upon a laie by shining light on their reflective surface. Each time I'd also narrowly escaped with my life.

As we walked, I tried to concentrate on detecting a difference in the air. It felt ludicrous, closing my eyes and paying close attention to the surface of my skin. I noticed only the cold chill of Jaada's atmosphere.

"How can we find one?" Eversen asked.

"For what are you looking?" a curious, tinny voice asked. Amusement laced its tone. "You look disoriented."

Surreptitiously, I darted my eyes toward the sound. I knew already we had been accosted by an Ember. How we were to fight it – or escape it – I didn't know.

"Where are you?" Eversen queried. His voice remained

steady, though he was visibly shaken.

"Show yourself!" I demanded. "By order of the Commander."

The voice chuckled, a rumbling, rustling sound that reminded me of dragons shifting their wings. "As you wish."

A spark of fire lit through the darkness and before us materialized an Ember, lounging in what appeared to be thin air. He faced us, hands folded together around his knees, violet eyes piercingly bright, flitting over us in study. His head cocked slightly to the side and his lips curled back into a leer. His weapons were currently retracted, which was good. Thick deception surrounded him, nearly visible in its intensity, yet it seemed rather to be something worked in his mind by another than his own design.

"Which are you?" I asked coldly, tensing to fight.

The Ember's leer grew larger, revealing his pointed teeth. He relaxed his nonchalant stance and dropped to the ground before us, appearing to hoist himself down from something.

A laie. He had been sitting in it, watching us. For how long? I gritted my teeth. How many had we walked through? Where there is one laie there are a hundred.

"My name is Unruly," he introduced himself, spreading his arms and bowing flamboyantly. "At your service." His voice carried a metallic ring to it, like the sound of a sword being unsheathed. Overlapping the tinny sound was a calm, almost adolescent, tone. He was certainly a strange Ember.

"We are Suri, Robert, and Eversen." I motioned to my companions without removing my eyes from the Ember's.

"Visitors," Unruly breathed, his leer widening. Excitement danced through his eyes. "Lost commodities. Jaada has become most fortunate to receive a Wynaerian and two Earthlings."

How he penetrated my guise, I didn't know. It is easy to distinguish the Earthlings – their skin-tones, eye color, and body movements are unique. In the guise of the universe, I appeared as merely a traveler, neither Coranta, Wynaerian, or Ember, but more of a muddied combination of them all.

For an Ember, he was uncommonly sedate. He didn't seem to be thirsting to kill, or aggressive, merely curious and excited.

"I've been waiting to meet a Wynaerian for many Jaadani years," he informed me. He reached his hands up and grabbed hold of what must have been the laie's door, swinging himself into the air. He remained suspended, looking down at us, perfectly at ease in his bizarre position. "What brings you here?" His grin returned.

"Are you an Ember?" Eversen inquired.

I had the same question, but for different reasons. The being before us acted more Coranta than Jaadani. There was something very odd about his complacent manner.

"Yes," answered Unruly. He laughed exuberantly, the rustling sound ricocheting through the air. "Can you not tell? How else shall I prove my nature? Perhaps fire?" Without waiting for an answer, the Ember landed lightly on the ground, blazing fire dancing in his palms. The flames reflected off the translucent bottom of the laie.

"What are you doing?" I asked, narrowing my eyes.

He extinguished his fire and ejected two sinister, jagged scythes from the ends of his arms. "Would you like to play this way?"

"I don't want to play," I told him forcefully. "We are seeking shelter."

Unruly gave a maniacal chuckle and rolled his eyes eerily, looking all around us, no doubt at the invisible forest we were in. "Looking for a laie?" He was greatly amused. His weapons retracted. "Dear friends, surely you are not so blind and unfeeling as all that! Insensitive to the gossamer material surrounding you? It seems incredulous." He shook his head in bewilderment.

Something was definitely different about this Ember. Impossible though it may be to change one's identity, I strongly suspected him of subterfuge.

"Welcome to the forest," he announced grandly, with another bow. "If you so wish, I can leave you to enjoy the laie alone. There are many more to serve my purpose."

Robert stepped toward Unruly. He had been quiet since meeting the Ember and did not seem nearly as afraid as he should have been. "Your name is Unruly?" he confirmed.

"Yes." A lopsided leer twisted his features. Mist pulsed around him, darkening and then lightening. It encroached on Robert, but stopped before it touched him.

I snarled, stepping between Robert and Unruly. Though the Earthling was hardly in my good graces at the moment, he was still my charge and I was commanded to protect him. The Ember, under no circumstances, would flout my authority.

Immediately, the mist recoiled and reentered Unruly. "Does that concern you?" he questioned playfully. At my look, his tone softened. "Forgive me," he requested, though the mischief did not entirely depart from his demeanor. A flicker crossed his face, and then inquisitiveness pierced his eyes as they bored into Robert's, wide and luminous. "I do not understand this Earthling. He has been touched by one of my kind – claimed. Yet he is not overcome."

I tensed, knowing what he would say, and determined to keep Robert safe. "He is also claimed by the Commander, who has a far greater authority than one of your kind."

Unruly turned his gaze on me. "The Commander," he said. He staggered backward a step, chest heaving, as though he'd been punched. His features twisted into pain and for a moment he breathed sharply.

All this from the name of my master?

"Allow me," Unruly gasped, clutching his chest and glancing up at me. "Allow me to join you in the laie. There are many things about which I wish to question you."

"The Commander's name harms you?" Eversen looked horrified. "How can that be?"

Whatever my prejudices and doubts regarding Unruly, I knew so long as the Commander remained in me, I was far more powerful than the Ember. Never before had I seen my master's name command so much power. It was illuminating.

"You may join us, and explain your mystifying character."

Unruly jumped and swung into the laie in one swift, limber movement. "Come, come!" he cried, reaching down a shadowy hand to Robert. "Come, join me!"

Robert cast one uncertain glance at me. His eyes hardened and he purposefully grasped Unruly's hand. Instantly, he gasped and flinched, but Unruly did not let go, though he gave a little whimper. Robert's hand turned white from cold for only a moment before he disappeared into the laie.

I motioned for Eversen to follow. Again, Unruly reached down and lifted the Earthling up with a single, forceful motion. A shriek pierced the air, a chilling sound of pain.

Warily, I stood alone outside the laie. Unruly poked his head out to look at me. A strange gleam came into his deep, dark eyes, and a mischievous sneer curled his mouth.

"Perhaps," he whispered. "You trust too willingly, great guardian." His words were saturated with rancor. His eyes lit maliciously; a hint of deception curled his lip.

"Perhaps," he said again, composing his features and reaching down his hand to me, "perhaps I am only a fool."

I grasped the freezing, darkened hand. Something like fire burned in me and shot down my arm into the tips of my fingers.

Unruly flinched away from me and screamed in agony, but refused to release his grip on my hand. His eyes bored into mine, wide with terror and, I suspected, for the first time empty of subterfuge. For several long seconds he seemed frozen. Then his arm twitched and he raised me into the laie. As soon as I was inside, Unruly dropped my hand and scampered to the farthest side.

The sphere swayed crazily from the sudden movement. Unruly slouched, his back to the solid black interior, cradling his hand against his chest. He no longer looked at any of us, but examined his fingers. They had turned grey from contacting light, a color I had beheld often on Embers.

I took advantage of his listless position to examine the laie. It was large enough to hold several more beings. Much like the ground of Jaada, its substance was black marble, but it did not contain any gemstones. Smooth and hard, the laie was most uncomfortable. I could now see the opening of the sphere, through which only the tangible Jaadani murk was visible. Unruly's voice made me look at him.

"Do not touch me again," he muttered. His voice trembled, and he raised his eyes to mine. They carried the same blatant terror as when he'd reached to hoist me up.

"What happened?" Robert and Eversen asked in unison.

I stared mutely at Unruly, awed and perplexed.

The Ember got to his feet unsteadily. His hand slowly dimmed into black again. Drawing a shaky breath, he lowered the hand to his side and looked at us.

"You belong to the Master," he said in explanation, voice now controlled and rustling. "I am a charlatan. When light meets darkness, what is impacted must die." He turned over his hand, flexing his fingers and bouncing his eyebrows. "In this case, my hand."

"Why the difference in reactions between my touch and Eversen's?" I asked shrewdly.

"You are a Wynaerian. The Earthlings have never been in the presence of the Master's son, as you have. They have light in them, but your light comes also from outside of you, when you have wandered on the planet of light."

"There's light in us?" Eversen wondered.

"From the Master," affirmed Unruly, folding himself into a sitting position once more – a fluid, graceful movement. "His presence is pure. It lights up a living one's being from the inside out to the skin. When this light comes in contact with something as dark as an Ember, it is so utterly repulsed, it strikes as electricity. That is what happened between Suri and me."

I settled down into a seated position. Robert and Eversen followed my example. Unruly ignored us, still curling and uncurling his fingers in examination.

"I'm glad you've come," he said brightly, eyes shifting up to our faces. "I have so many things to question you on."

"Of what nature are these questions?" asked I warily.

Unruly's grin was delighted. "I must ask about the Master and – his son." A confused look touched his eyes for a moment.

"His name harms you?" Robert was disgusted at the weakness. "The Commander? Why can't you speak it?"

Unruly flinched and shuddered, but his gaze did not waver. "I am an Ember," he said lightly. "I cannot be accosted by light without experiencing excruciating pain, as was just demonstrated. Even the mention of the Master's son – it is like boiling acid over my mind. Physical touch," he gestured idly to me, "is the same. One is physical, the other mental. The two pains are equally devastating. Why would I weaken and torture myself by saying the name?"

"What curiosity can you have toward him?" I countered. "You are an Ember, as you have so rightfully pointed out. How can one such as you be interested in someone of light?"

"Ah," Unruly sighed, rolling his head back on his shoulders and sinking into a curled position against the laie's interior. His movements were fluid and graceful, almost unnaturally so. "Now we come to the purpose of my life." He closed his eyes, reveling in the words he spoke. "I want to be freed."

"Freed from what?" Empathy laced Eversen's tone.

"Darkness. I don't want to be inherently evil any longer. I want to know about the Master and his son. I want to come in contact with the light and not be burned. I want to live, instead of dying in the guise of life. I want to meet the Master's son." His eyes, however crazed, shone ecstatically.

"You want to come to the Commander?" I asked in disbelief. As the Ember had spoken, he was a charlatan, and steeped in deception. This could all be an extensive trick to weaken and destroy us. In spite of my cautionary thoughts, though, I suspected he was being sincere. Something checked me from disbelieving him.

"Yes." Unruly's expression transformed into a hopeful look. "I want to meet him. Do you think he would accept one such as I?"

What could I respond to his query? How could I know? Would the Commander accept someone who had been seeped with evil and night since his inception? I didn't know.

"Why do you want the Commander?" Robert scoffed. "He's got nothing on the Burning Ember."

Unruly twitched, clenching his jaw. A dark shadow crossed over his eyes, one that was not a part of his wispy being. "You speak his name?" His voice was low, warning.

"What is there to be feared by speaking the Burning Ember's name?" I countered.

Unruly's eyes darted to me and slowly the fiery warning faded from his mien. He shook his head, a sad smile stretching his mouth. "I had no idea," he murmured. "I didn't know there is a freedom I can possess. *Is* there? I don't know. Teach me, please. I want to know if I can be accepted. I want to know if my darkness can be changed into light. You have life in you and a way to believe in something greater. Can I?"

"Why? What will you gain?" I challenged.

"If I gain anything, it will only be understanding, I'm sure," he mumbled to himself. "There must be some reason why I have not been attacked in all this time. Can everything be backwards? Can it be a lie?" He caught his breath, his eyes awash with calculation. Finally, they cleared once more and he spoke forcefully to me. "What I want to gain is the opportunity to become something more. Will the Master's son accept me?"

I gazed at him unblinkingly. He was certainly sincere. Even the best charlatan could not uphold this charade so scrupulously.

"Surely," Eversen exclaimed. "He would never turn away someone who desires him!"

I looked at the Earthling, but did not speak.

"Why?" Robert asked Unruly. "Why do you want to come to the Commander? I don't understand."

"Please," Unruly gasped between his teeth, "stop saying his name. Call him the Master's son. I cannot speak with you much longer if you continue to weaken me." His eyes flashed over us. It was clear that his body had begun to grey with the constant use of the Commander's name.

To Robert, Unruly responded, "I want redemption."

My mind lurched in pain at his admission. I stared at him. Could it be that we both longed for the same thing? Could it be that the Commander had sent me here for Unruly?

"Then listen," I said. "Listen and receive. Be changed from darkness to light." I nodded to Eversen. "As you were granted speech, I have no doubt –" I glanced at Unruly, "– the Master's son wishes you to speak. Offer him the truth and let's pray he takes it."

Silence abounded. Unruly waited expectantly.

"Redemption," Eversen mused. "Do you know," he hesitated infinitesimally, "the Master's son's history?"

Unruly nodded.

"He became a human, discarding his supremacy, and traveled to Earth. He spoke truth and life for three years, healing humans."

"Then one day," Unruly murmured, blank eyes staring at his hands, "the Embers rallied with the Adversary and his cohorts to bring the Master's son to his knees."

"We stood by and watched," I inserted quietly, studying Unruly. "Embers and Wynaerians alike were there that day."

"There were Corantas, also," remembered Unruly. "All living ones of the universe had gathered to watch, some in anxiety, some in triumph. I also rejoiced that day."

"Yet now you sit here proclaiming you want to know the Master's son and turn from your darkness," I accused. "You know his story. Perhaps we should hear yours."

Unruly jerked his head up, eyebrows raised. "I have been waiting for a Wynaerian to come to me for a hundred years," he announced softly. "Will it make a difference what I say before I hear the truth?"

"You know the story," Robert commented. "So then why are you so confused? What is this redemption you're talking about?"

Abruptly, the Ember stretched his fingers toward Robert. A shift occurred in the atmosphere; the laie grew darker. The mist around Robert's heart swirled angrily.

"What are you doing?" I demanded, rising into a defensive position, knife in hand.

"I'm siphoning away the shadows," Unruly responded calmly, flicking his eyes up to me momentarily. "He cannot listen to the truth while his heart is black with whispering lies."

I watched closely. The dimness inside Robert lessened. Drifting grey mist and shadows seeped out of his chest and floated toward Unruly. When the mist touched the Ember's fingers, it disappeared instantly.

A smug leer overtook Unruly's lips. "An Ember planted the darkness and doubt. An Ember can take it away," he explained, lowering his arm.

Robert's heart was no longer shadowed. A very faint golden shield surrounded it, worn and fragile. If the blackness had continued in him for much longer, it would have overcome the shield and changed him into an Ember.

I shuddered, slowly lowering myself to the ground again. The laie rocked gently.

"Of what is the shield made?" asked Unruly, settling back against the wall, hands folded behind his head. With his chin, he motioned studiously to the golden case around Robert's heart. "It's not merely light, for the depths of gloom can overcome it after time. It cannot be only love, either, for love requires trust and trust can be broken."

"It's both," I answered, "but they are from the Commander, not a mere living one. His strength cannot be thwarted."

Unruly hissed at my use of the name. "I know," he

answered, looking troubled. "I learned so on the day he died. Then what happened? He rose, didn't he?"

"Yes," said Eversen. "He defeated death and darkness, by life and light. He defeated despair with love. All of his followers were encouraged and strengthened by his power."

I added, "The Embers left Earth to cause mayhem in the universe. Yet you returned, attempting to break the might of life and light and love." I glared at Unruly.

"As a race of living ones, we are taught to hate the Master and his son. We are raised in the way of darkness and evil. We go to other planets in order to make chaos and turn those of the light toward the Adversary."

"If he is your leader," I challenged, "why do you call him the Adversary? That is a Wynaerian name. It is not from Jaada."

Unruly grinned sheepishly. "I've turned from him. He is no longer my master, but my enemy. I want nothing further to do with him. I want to come to the Master's son."

"You continue to express that desire," Eversen noted. "Why don't you, if you are so eager? What holds you back?"

"I don't know how." Unruly jumped to his feet, causing the laie to sway, and paced. "Yet he must have heard me, for I asked him to send me someone and here you are." He whirled to face me. "We are getting nowhere. You have not told me how I can approach the Master's son. How do I tell him I don't want to be dark anymore? How can I embrace light?"

"It may kill you," I warned. "If the touch of light harms you so severely, coming before *the* Light may destroy you."

Unruly waved that away. "I want to meet him," he reasserted, as though convincing himself. "If doing so ends my life, it will be an end justly deserved. At least I will have tried."

I shook my head, disbelieving still. How could an Ember have changed his nature to the point that he wanted to meet the Commander? How could wickedness so deep be overcome?

Unruly snorted. "You still don't believe me. Am I right? Of course I am. What other way can I prove I am an Ember and

I want to change? Perhaps commanding the nature of my planet to show this is where I belong?" He snapped his fingers.

The landscape changed instantly. Our laie grew translucent. It hung suspended in air, attached to nothing, like a stationary bubble. Through the walls, hundreds more came into view, overlapping each other, as far as we could see. We were in the midst of a laie forest, just as Unruly had professed.

"I can bestow seeing on your eyes," he crowed. "I can siphon away shadows or make them stronger at my will. I can create and extinguish fire. I can see laies. In what other way can I prove my nature?"

"I believe you're an Ember," I told him bluntly. "There's no other explanation. I don't believe your desire for repentance."

Unruly chuckled, an unnerving sound that slivered under the skin. "You think I've brought you here under deception?"

"You are utterly evil. Naturally you are deceiving. You cannot speak truth, so how can I believe you?"

"I could call on the Master's son," Unruly offered. "Would it convince you if I asked him here?"

His dauntless sincerity gave me pause.

I gazed at him. "If he doesn't answer?"

Unruly swallowed, but shrugged. "He's answered me once before," he mumbled to himself, looking stoically at me. "Perhaps he'll answer again."

Suri, the Commander rebuked me. *Listen to him. It is for you as much as him that I sent you here.*

I dared not disobey the Commander again. "What did he answer you before?" I asked, though I already knew.

"I asked him to send me a Wynaerian who knew the truth," Unruly answered blandly, lounging back against the wall once more, hands folded in his lap. "For two hundred years I've resided in this forest, far from any living one. I have been in exile, you see." He lifted his face to the ceiling, gazing out upon Open Space. "Did you know you can see Wynaeria from here?"

181

I glanced up quickly, following his stare. Shining down at me was indeed, my home planet. It shone brightly and warmly in the low sky.

"I've been watching her for many, many years, waiting for one of her inhabitants to come to me." He sighed.

"Why were you exiled?" Eversen asked after a pause.

Unruly's cheek twitched. "I rejected the Adversary. The Embers banished me from their community. They branded me a traitor. I would have been killed had it not been for the strength I possessed at the time. I was the strongest – a leader of Jaada's inhabitants. If they had attacked me, the ensuing battle would have destroyed the entire planet. In time, I would have been overpowered, but the toll was too great a price to pay. They dared not assault me."

"Then what happened?" Robert's eyes were rapt.

"I was stripped of my authority and influence. The Embers erected this forest for my prison. Their combined forces proved strong enough to force me in here. I could not leave, even then, at the peak of my power. I have remained among these laies ever since.

"None ever travel here, nor could they break the barrier if they tried. The might used to create this place has long since diminished among the Embers. There are very few now who possess that power, and even they would find it difficult to discover a weakness in the barrier. After many failed attempts to escape, I accepted my fate. I cannot travel to other planets, nor can anyone trek into my forest. Until today."

Only our faint breathing disturbed the atmosphere.

"After the first century," Unruly finally continued, apparently unable to bear the silence any longer, "I began to despise my nature. I longed to receive light and love and life – anything to escape this dungeon. After many weeks of trying to starve myself, I sought the Master's son. He didn't answer, but I never stopped trying. I knew he could hear me if he wished. I thought if only I continued long enough, he would grow weary and listen. I asked him to send me someone from Wynaeria –

someone who could teach me about him. I begged him to answer me and believe my sincerity."

Unruly closed his eyes languidly, no longer trying to convince us of his sincerity. "I accept if you disbelieve me," he said softly. "I ask only that you teach me a way to converse with the Master's son before you leave."

Eversen gave me a loaded glance, full of compassion.

I rebelled against speaking the truth to an Ember. Deep-rooted prejudices cautioned me against his woeful story, yet the Commander had implied it was for Unruly that I had come.

"I will answer your questions," Eversen pledged. "Only the Master's son could take me away before our conversation is exhausted."

I sighed in resignation. "I will answer as well as I can."

Robert suddenly cried out. He wrenched sideways and fell, shuddering. I cast a glare at Unruly, but he seemed as confused as me.

"What's happening?" asked Eversen.

I darted to my charge's side and knelt beside him. Placing my hands on his shoulders, I murmured to the Commander under my breath. Some wicked thing was swirling in Robert's mind, but it was indistinct and shrouded with mist.

"They have discovered you," Unruly breathed, eyes focused far away through the laie's transparent wall. "Your light is easy to distinguish and target, and they have done so. They are standing on the edge of the barrier." Understanding dawned on his features. "They're attacking Robert as best they can. He has a propensity to evil, which they're using; the shield around him is growing insufficient. They'll kill him or convert him to an Ember."

"How do I know it's not you attacking him?" I hissed, leaning over Robert and muttering the Commander's love around his heart.

"I have been stripped of my influence," he reminded me. "The most darkness I can command is just enough to encase him. I cannot penetrate the shield. I am far too weak."

Robert gasped, his face beaded with sweat and his hands clammy as they grasped my tunic. His eyes gleamed. "Please," he murmured, once more a little boy, filled with the terror of a nightmare. "Help me." His voice broke and tears filled his eyes.

"Commander, I invoke you. Grant me the power to overcome these shadows." The circlet of thorns on my wrist burned, as it hadn't since the Coranta celebration. I looked down at it in surprise. It glowed and pulsed with my heartbeat. Without hesitation, I pressed the mark to Robert's chest, over his heart.

Immediately, I plunged into his mind.

"Come to us," a hundred voices hissed, crawling over each other, pervading the atmosphere. They came from dancing shadows that shot sparks just ahead of him beneath the cover of trees. "Join us."

"How?" the boy breathed. He took a step toward the silhouette-like beings. Embers, he remembered they were called. They were fascinating, and strangely endearing in their darkness. "How do I join you?" he repeated.

Harsh laughter rose around him from every side.

"Take another step," several voices chanted. They rasped like a multitude of weapons clashing together. "Come to us."

The boy obeyed, stepping toward the edge of the forest, but stopped abruptly. A barrier blocked him from going further. "I can't reach you." The desire to reach them welled fiercely in him; he thought he might cry if he didn't. "Please. Help me."

A single Ember detached himself from the others and stepped toward the boy. One of his eyes glowed violet, the other red. The Burning Ember. "I can break the barrier," he said softly. His voice was warm and soft, soothing. It washed over the boy from head to toes, like an embrace. "Do you want me to break the barrier?"

The boy gazed up at him, letting the words seep into his mind. As silence settled between them, he began to feel comforted and at home with the Burning Ember, whom he knew to be

Malevolence. A sudden memory of his father entered him, and he wondered if this being would abandon him too.

"No, of course not," the Burning Ember murmured, reading his thoughts. "I will set you free from all fear. You will love me, and I will be good to you. Will you join me?"

The boy knew that these promises were not idle words – that he would be free, and he would love the Burning Ember. And he knew that he wanted this freedom and affection more than anything. A desire to worship this being entered the boy.

"Do you want me to break the barrier?" Malevolence repeated.

The boy blinked, an adoring expression overtaking his demeanor. "Yes," he breathed. "Yes. Let me come to you."

Malevolence smiled, a flash of white teeth in the darkness. His eyes sparked flames. "You will become one of us," he promised silkily. "We will grant you power over your enemies and over those who claim to be your friends. You will have the authority to destroy all who stand in your way. Do you remember playing with fire?"

"Yes," the boy answered, lifting his hand to the Ember. It came up short, held vertical against the invisible barrier. "I remember." A burst of excitement blossomed in his chest.

"You can have more," the Burning Ember whispered, leaning forward. "Much, much more. You need only join us."

"I will," the boy said. "I will join you."

"Swear it," Malevolence demanded. "Swear it with your blood."

Taken a little aback by the ferocity of his voice, the boy lowered his hand. "I swear it," he said solemnly, meeting Malevolence's gaze. "I swear it with my life, my heart, and my blood."

A twisted sneer enveloped the Burning Ember's features. "Come forward," he ordered. "The barrier is lifted by your vow."

The boy took a step forward, unhindered. A wide grin spread across his face. "I am yours," he breathed in awe, "and you *will give me power."*

"Much, much more than power," Malevolence promised. His leer did not diminish as he held out his hand to the boy.

This time, when the boy touched the silhouette-like being, no blast of cold or fear entered him. Rather, a pleasant warmth tingled up his arm. He felt it creep its way into his heart.

The Burning Ember placed his fingers lightly on the boy's chest. "I extinguish the work of our Enemy," he said. "I squelch the light in you and take you as my own. Obey me, and you will be rewarded. Do not forget who is your master."

"Never," the boy answered, reveling in Malevolence's touch.

"You are mine," the Burning Ember whispered. "All mine."

A searing pain shot through my arm, centered on the circlet of thorns that branded my wrist. It writhed along the bond between me and Robert, bristling like a branding iron. Screaming accompanied the fiery pain. I opened my eyes, jerking my hand away from Robert.

Immediately, the pain in my arm ceased, and the screaming turned to ragged breaths.

Robert gasped, looking up at me. He wore a smugly triumphant expression and his eyes flickered. They were no longer green, I noted. Now, a deep grey, almost black claimed them. Robert smiled, a crooked leer identical to Malevolence's. He looked older, and not only from tunnel-traveling. In the past few moments, he had grown.

I lurched away from him, causing the laie to tremble. Horror, disgust, and hatred barraged my mind. I could not speak through my anger at the boy.

"Hello, Suri," he said, a low, vile tinge to his voice, to match his altered features. He had not turned into the wispy shadow of an Ember yet, but his skin was visibly darkened. He was transforming from an Earthling to a Jaadani.

When I didn't respond for rage, Robert grinned, turning to face Eversen and Unruly. "The atmosphere is not so oppressive anymore," he remarked.

"Robert?" Eversen asked, a horrified expression on his face. "What happened to you?"

"He has joined Malevolence," I spat, finding my voice. "He has weakened my bond with him and vowed his allegiance to the Embers."

Eversen's eyes widened. Unruly shook his head, slowly, as though in disbelief.

"Commander," I vituperated aloud, "why have you allowed this?"

This time, both Unruly and Robert grimaced and groaned at the name.

I couldn't prevent vindictive glee at their reactions. "Commander," I repeated harshly, no longer speaking to my master.

"Suri," Eversen said quietly, sternly. "Do not speak of him in that fashion."

"It is a punishment justly deserved," I returned, glowering. "If the Commander's name harms them, then they should be flogged with it for refusing his love."

"Will upbraiding them reveal his love?" Eversen challenged, his tone icy.

"Will allowing their contempt?" I retaliated, irate. "The Commander would not tolerate their impudence in his presence. He would scold them."

"Do you think so?" Eversen's voice rose in volume. "You think the Commander is a harsh master, bent on exacting vengeance on all who refuse his love? Why are you so quick to mete out judgment on them?"

Neither Unruly nor Robert spoke, but both appeared to be enjoying our argument. Robert grinned despite his pain at the Commander's name. Unruly had a curious expression, neither gleeful nor troubled, but more nearly thoughtful. Both allowed us to continue, their winces at the Commander's name the only sign of something more than indifference.

"Commander," I spoke again, this time invoking him,

though I allowed a cruel smile at the pain it caused in Robert and Unruly. "Show them the truth! Reveal your love to them!"

Suri, the Commander rebuked me, severe.

His tone was the first thing that broke through my furious thoughts. I paused in my outburst and allowed myself to cool slightly. The Commander continued.

Who are you to condemn them? Shall I not show them the same grace I have extended for you? What have you done to merit my love? I decide who will receive my mercy. Is that not enough for you?

I cringed before him, a terror rising in me unlike any I'd had since coming to the light. "Commander," I whispered aloud.

I have endured their contempt as I have endured your arrogance. Would it be fair for me to destroy them and let you live?

I couldn't answer.

Do you wish me to destroy you all? Are you ready to stand before me?

When I still didn't respond, the Commander's voice softened into his usual tone.

I love them, Suri. I love them as I love you. I do not wish any of you to go astray from me.

Then why do you allow us? I finally asked.

Do you not know? he countered gently.

Pressing my eyes closed with my fingers, I bowed my head. *Yes,* I answered slowly. *I do know.*

Tell me, he prompted. *Remind yourself.*

It's your love, I said. *It's your love that allows us our arrogance and will. Without your love I would be as they. I would never come to you.*

Remember your own journey, Suri. Do not judge harshly those who have not yet received me. Become a leader worthy of them and bring them to me.

Yes, sire. I lifted my head and gazed at Unruly and Robert. Eversen still stared at me with a tight expression.

Swallowing, I pushed aside my pride and said in a low voice, "Forgive me. I have no cause to hurt you."

Unruly and Robert looked at me with surprise, though my charge did not relinquish his sneer. Eversen merely nodded.

"The Master's son will deal with you as he sees fit," I continued in the same contrite tone. "It is not my position to pronounce his judgment."

"You are forgiven, Suri," said Eversen. His anger melted from his features and he smiled. "It is a difficult thing to stand up to the Master's son and withstand his returning tirade."

"Reprimand," I corrected quietly, casting him a smile. "The Commander does not rage against his own. He only disciplines them to teach them the depth of his love."

Robert scoffed. "You cannot truly believe that *taskmaster* loves you. What kind of love rampages against one who merely questions it?"

I clenched my jaw before answering, boring a steely glare into him. "Questioning the Commander's love is questioning himself. He *is* love. When one is ridiculed, so is the other."

I received no reply to that, and shortly thereafter we turned our minds to other things. Eversen broke out food from our sacks and we ate a cold, silent meal, after which the Earthlings settled down to sleep. Once they slumbered, I wandered outside, where I looked up at Wynaeria. It had been a long time since I'd set foot on my homeland and a stab of longing entered my chest, followed by discouragement and anger about Robert.

How do I lead him to you? I asked the Commander. *He wants no part in the light or in your love.*

The night quietened into silence. The Commander's presence was nearly tangible.

I closed my eyes, resting in the pregnant air. Slowly, my mind turned from my charge. *What of Unruly, Commander? Can he become your own?*

He has guilt he must overcome, the Commander answered

sadly. *He is drowning in fear. He does not yet know what living in the light entails. He must only go forward and discover whether I am worth the sacrifice.*

You will not reject him?

If he comes to me, I will accept him.

Will he?

I could almost see the Commander's smile in his response. *Watch, and discover.*

"You miss her, don't you?"

I opened my eyes and glanced at Unruly, who had joined me silently. He didn't look at me, but into Open Space toward Wynaeria, features indecipherable.

"No one can be truly happy anywhere but in their own home," I responded quietly. "Naturally, I miss her."

Unruly chuckled. "I don't think I'd miss Jaada if I left. It hasn't felt like a home since my imprisonment." He was silent for a moment. "Is that how his love truly works?"

"Yes. He loves the unlovable and brings them into the light so that he will not have to live without them. He did the same with me, and I have forgotten it."

"How could you forget?" A faint note of mocking laced his query.

I shook my head, suddenly weary. "I don't know."

I didn't say anything further. After a few minutes of silence, Unruly left. I watched him stride away, black swirls in his wake drifting up to Open Space. I sighed and averted my gaze.

No more than ten minutes passed before Eversen jumped out of the laie. "Suri," he panted. "Robert's gone."

Chapter 11
Commission to Zeker

We searched all through the laie forest that night. Robert was nowhere to be found. Neither Eversen nor Unruly had seen, heard, or felt Robert's departure. We did not know when he'd left, or where he would have gone, though I had my suspicions.

"He's gone to the Embers," I muttered to Eversen once we returned to the laie. Unruly sat on the opposite side of the sphere from us with a sober countenance. He had been mostly silent since I questioned him to be sure he had not aided Robert's disappearance.

For several long moments, we were quiet.

"Where do you think Robert is?" Eversen ventured.

"If he's gone to the Embers, he will be on Jaada or Zeker," Unruly iterated.

"Can you find him through your bond?"

I laughed bleakly. "No. A bond is not like that. It's an acute relationship that travels between space and time. I can only discern that he is alive. I don't know where he is or what is happening to him. For all my knowledge, he could be an inch from death."

Troubled, Unruly murmured, "That may be true."

I glanced at him.

"Once Robert serves his purpose, Malevolence will destroy him," he answered my unspoken question. "To my kind, Earthlings are mere toys, to be discarded when their use has been exhausted."

"What are we going to do?" Eversen asked.

I bowed my head, rage once more welling in me at the brash young Earthling who served as my charge. "I don't know. We need direction."

He held out his hand to me, wrist downward. I took it and we crossed marks. "Commander," he spoke quietly. "Lead us."

Return to Corant, the Commander whispered in our minds.

"Robert –" I began.

Not now, the Commander interrupted gently. *Return to Corant with Unruly.*

I dropped my wrist from Eversen's, frowning.

"Corant," the Earthling murmured, confused. "We have to go to Corant."

Unruly raised his head to look at us. "Why?"

"You're coming with us," I informed him.

He scoffed and chuckled. "I cannot leave prison." He waved an arm to indicate the laies. "I am bound to the forest and Jaada's ground."

"Then the Commander will break your bonds."

He flinched, but otherwise concealed his pain. "I am not–"

"You are coming!" I snarled, whirling on him. "I refuse to disobey my master."

"How?" Unruly challenged. He spread his arms in a show of being chained. "How are you going to release me from this prison?"

I shrugged. "It doesn't matter. We need to leave."

"What about Robert?"

"'Not now,'" I quoted. "I assume we'll find him later."

~ ~ ~

Several moments later, we were heading toward the tunnel. It occurred to me as we walked that if my tunnel had broken through the forest, and it didn't disappear, there would be nothing preventing Unruly's departure. I said as much to him.

"We'll see," he grunted dispassionately, repositioning the sack over his shoulder.

I harbored a doubt that, as an Ember, he would be unable to travel through my Wynaerian tunnel, but I kept it to myself. There was plentiful dissension among us already.

My tunnel shone like a beacon in the midst of the laie forest. Colored lights traveled up and down the length of it, making the circle where it stood glow. As on Earth and Corant, when we reached the tunnel-site, warmth and peace permeated through us.

I stepped forward confidently, closely followed by Eversen. We stopped just shy of the tunnel and turned to Unruly. He remained in the shadows beyond the circle of light. His jaw dropped and his eyes gleamed with something akin to fear. He didn't step into the light.

I couldn't resist a grin at his aporetic expression.

"It's not going to harm you," I said snidely.

Unruly shook his head slowly. "It might," he murmured. He took a hesitant step forward and stopped, his eyes never moving from the dancing lights. "The Master's son's name harms me. Your light and touch harms me. How do I know one of your Wynaerian tunnels won't?"

"It would be a cruel thing for the Commander to do – order you to come with us and punish you for doing so," Eversen said practically.

Unruly shuddered. "It would fit with my knowledge of his character," he murmured.

"It wouldn't fit with mine," I opposed.

Unruly clenched his fists and strode forward. He reached

out a hand and passed it through the dancing colors of the tunnel. A faint hissing noise sounded, but he didn't withdraw his fingers. He sighed and dropped his hand.

"Well?" Eversen demanded.

He looked askance at him. "It won't kill me," he admitted. "It won't be pleasant either."

"Well, then, let's go." I stepped into the middle of the tunnel. Unruly and Eversen joined me and the tunnel served its purpose. We successfully left the atmosphere of Jaada, Unruly in tow.

"Look," I said, pointing to the looming image of Corant.

Unruly shifted apprehensively.

I laughed. "There's nothing to fear. Landing will be no more uncomfortable than tunnel-traveling."

Zar and my girl awaited us when we arrived. It was mid-afternoon on Corant.

"Where is Robert?" my girl asked, her gaze sweeping over each of us and landing on me.

"Robert has disappeared," I said bitterly. "He joined the Embers."

My girl's eyes widened with shock, and Zar looked taken aback. "What happened?" she breathed.

"Did he assist Robert's disappearance?" Zar asked, looking at Unruly. "Who is this? Why do you travel with an Ember?" His voice seeped bitterness.

"His name is Unruly. He wants to come to the Commander, but he is not ready yet," Eversen explained.

"You can talk," my girl exclaimed, momentarily sidetracked. Zar, too, looked surprised.

Eversen smiled thinly. "The Commander enabled me when we landed on Jaada."

For a moment, Zar and my girl merely looked at him, speechless. Then Zar turned to Unruly.

"How can we trust you?" he demanded.

Unruly dipped his head and dropped his sack to the ground. "I have proven my sincerity to Eversen and Suri. When they first arrived with Robert, I could have annihilated them, yet I didn't. I remain unopposed to them and they have yet to find fault in me."

Zar eyed him doubtfully. "An Ember seeks the Commander?"

Despite all the times we'd mentioned his name, Unruly still flinched at hearing it. Obviously its power didn't diminish with time.

"Yes," he answered unwaveringly. He proceeded to relate his story of imprisonment. "What more can I say to convince you?" he asked when he had done.

Zar raised his eyebrows. "Nothing, at the moment." He turned to me. "Come back to the seor, and explain all your doings." He shot a skeptical glance at Unruly as we began walking and murmured, "Tell me why you travel with an Ember."

"Only by the Commander's orders," I muttered. "I distrust him as much as you. As far as I can discern, he did not assist Robert's defection. The boy went to the Embers on his own. Unruly has not done anything suspicious since our acquaintance, but trusting him would be ill-advised."

"I won't. Not until he's proven true."

"He seeks the Commander," Eversen inserted.

"Did you know Embers could deviate?" I asked Zar.

He shrugged, casting another dubious glance at Unruly, who walked a little apart from us. "They are living ones, and so have a choice, though I've never encountered one who chose light over darkness."

"He seems sincere," I informed him. "Despite the pain that both light and speaking the Commander's name cause in him, he has not shied from it. He was eager to accept the Commander, but he hasn't let go of the darkness." I yawned.

"Yes, I know you're tired," Zar conceded. "Food first, though. Friends with an Ember ... who would ever have imagined it?"

I shook my head. "Only the Commander." I paused.

"There was no death on Jaada. Unless Robert's birth as an Ember qualifies."

"Did he actually transform?"

"Not completely. His eyes had begun changing to violet and his skin became a shade darker."

Zar grunted.

I didn't have a chance to continue, for Unruly said, "Is that a fabled seor? I have never seen one."

The seor gleamed in the distance, just visible beyond a few yures.

"Have you ever left Jaada?" Zar asked.

A hint of Unruly's leer curled his mouth. "Yes. I've never traveled to Corant. Earth was the greatest planet to destroy. So easy … so simple." His voice lowered to a whisper. "It has always been the largest target. Fear runs rampant in Earthlings."

His low, rustling voice crawled along my skin. I shuddered to shake off the sensation.

"They are easy prey," Unruly continued, apparently oblivious to the audience he now commanded. His eyes looked at the ground he traipsed over, wide with incredulity at his own words. "They doubt so quickly and completely. It's no secret why Embers enjoy terrorizing Earthlings. The power is intoxicating."

Zar shot me a dubious glance. I nodded and shrugged.

Unruly saw the exchange and chuckled nervously. "I don't miss the terror," he admitted. "Only the power of influence over others." He went on quickly, "I won't harm an Earthling again. For many long years I've been forced into practicing restraint. Now, I'd rather embrace light than feed on fear."

"How could you enjoy that?" my girl demanded tremulously. A horrified expression stretched across her face as she thought of Robert.

"It is in my nature," the Ember muttered. "Even after so many years it would be far easier than walking through this torture." He motioned to the ground.

It was then that I noticed how lightly and quickly he

stepped, almost in a shuffling manner, rather than in the fluid way that he used on Jaada.

"Does it hurt?" Again, my girl expressed horror.

Unruly barked with his metallic laughter. "Any light hurts the darkness. Only very strong, tangible darkness, like that of Jaada, can swallow light completely. I was stripped of that magnitude of power long ago. Even the light of Corant's sun is uncomfortable."

Pity flooded my girl. "Isn't it warmth to you?"

"More like fire," Unruly corrected. "Cold creatures like us cannot be warmed. Heat burns us." He cast a glance at my girl and saw her empathy. "Don't feel sorry for me," he said adamantly. "I am an *Ember*."

"You are a living one," my girl said emphatically. "If you can feel remorse, you can come to the light."

"I want to come to the light," he murmured wistfully.

"Why don't you?"

For a brief instant, Unruly curled his fists into curved, jagged blades. He retracted them before they fully formed. "I don't know."

My girl opened her mouth to question him more, but then we came upon the seor and Unruly stopped short.

He blinked rapidly several times before staring at the gleaming fluid marble. It was a brilliant golden color in the sunlight. Unruly reached out a hesitant finger and lightly brushed the seor's exterior. Trembling, he pulled it away.

"I have to go inside?"

"If you wish to fellowship with us," Zar confirmed. "Otherwise, you can remain out here, where there is little shelter from the light."

"There is far more light *in* the seor than out of it. It doesn't merely reflect the sun. Light is woven into the marble." Unruly looked at the opening of the seor. "I think I can endure the pain."

"Join the Commander," my girl suggested. "Then there

won't be pain."

He laughed bleakly and shook his head. Again, he reached out a finger and touched the seor, self-consciously this time. He pressed his palm against the surface and held it there for several long seconds. When he withdrew it, his hand didn't seem as dark. He examined it for another long moment.

"Let's go," Eversen urged.

Zar acquiesced, ducking into the seor. My girl and Eversen followed. Unruly gave one last, uneasy look at the fluid marble, and ducked inside. I skipped down the stairs after him.

~ ~ ~

Unruly patiently endured the scorching heat of the seor as we related our adventures to Zar and my girl and shared a meal. He kept as still as possible, grimacing whenever he shifted his position. Every hour or so his feet became grey, at which point he left for the shade of the yures where they could heal.

When the sun set, we left Unruly beneath the yures, and walked to the crystal prisms. There, we celebrated with the Corantas and greeted Yahn, Uli, and Kein, who were delighted to see us again. Zar invited them to return to the seor with us, but they declined after hearing of Unruly. They, also, were suspicious of his professed sincerity.

Wishing the Corantas farewell and goodnight, Zar and I led the Earthlings back to the seor. I dragged my feet, tired.

"Is this my little brother, exhausted from his worldly travels?" Zar teased. "What happened to the great warrior of only three days ago?"

"Be quiet," I muttered listlessly, and yawned.

Zar chuckled, but reacted instinctively when I stumbled. "You can't be that weary, surely?" he asked, shocked, as he helped me back to my feet.

"The last couple of days have been long," I responded.

"You really are exhausted," my brother marveled. "Not objecting to sleep; falling as you walk. What did they do to you on Jaada?"

"I survived. Though my vision could have been referring to tonight, when you kill me with jests."

Zar scoffed. "I would never dare such a feat."

I didn't bother to retort, focusing on using the remainder of my energy to reach the seor and the bed I hoped was still formed. I swept past Unruly, and fell onto the marble bed. Immediately, I fell asleep.

~ ~ ~

I blinked and opened my eyes. It took a few seconds to focus on the swirling gold above me. I groaned and rolled over, trying to clear my foggy head. Then I remembered the words that had been spoken in my mind while I slept.

Go to Zeker. The voice had been adamant, and sounded vaguely familiar.

I frowned. Zeker was an Ember planet – the only other one besides Jaada. What would I do there?

Find Robert. Take him to Tarjik.

I recognized the voice then. *Commander?*

He is being held captive by the Embers. There is not much time. The Commander's voice turned urgent.

Will we confront the Embers? I dreaded the thought. Fighting Embers on their own planet would be suicidal.

Instead of an answer arriving, the world lurched.

Everything turned a blinding white, but I could not shield my vision from it. I stared, wide-eyed. Slowly, figures formed in the whiteness. Cold swept through me, reminiscent of Jaada, but much worse; stronger. The figures before me began dancing and singing, but I could not understand what they said. Then flames rose up and swallowed them before they grew distinct. Screams filled my ears, prolonged until my head buzzed.

Gasping, I bolted upright. I turned my head to the side and retched. My stomach felt heavy with lead and my heart pounded.

"Suri?"

I looked up into Zar's anxious face and shook my head warningly. A headache stabbed my temples. Zar waited as I closed my eyes for several moments, and then turned to look at him.

"We're going to Zeker," I said thickly. I swallowed hard and spoke again. "Robert is there and we have to take him to Tarjik. The Commander didn't say why."

Zar looked surprised, but nodded. "And what happened with you?"

I groaned and swung my legs down onto the floor, carefully avoiding the mess on the floor. "I saw another vision. Or, rather, the Commander showed me something; I'm not sure what."

"Enough to make you sick," Zar said pointedly.

I grinned halfheartedly. "It was the same as before. Someone's going to die. I don't know who." Idly, I wondered if it would be me. As the flames had been so scorching both times, it seemed reasonable that I might be the one who would burn.

I shook away the disconcerting thoughts and stood, poking Zar in the stomach. He bent double protectively and grinned at me. I looked around and noticed the seor was vacant.

"Where are the others?"

"Unruly's beneath a yure, healing. The Earthlings went to join him shortly before you woke and made a mess." He strode to the sacks, removed a long strip of cloth, and stooped to clean the floor.

I crouched to help him. "What do you think of Unruly? Do you think he's sincere?"

"It's not his sincerity I doubt. I doubt his ability to come to the Commander. If light hurts him so fiercely, how can he stand before the purity of our master?"

"I don't know." I stood. "As a living one, he must have the capacity to be redeemed."

Zar looked up at the word. His stare penetrated.

I stared back steadily, knowing what he thought. "The Commander redeems all who come to him," I continued. "If he created the living ones, he can restore their darkness to light."

Zar stood slowly, finished cleaning. "If redemption comes for him, do you think it will come for you?"

I shrugged. "I see no reason why one can be redeemed while another cannot."

Zar averted his gaze. "Come, the others will want to hear of our new mission from the Commander." He started toward the stairwell. "Zeker and Tarjik?"

"Yes," I answered, sprinting after him. We ascended the stairs before he responded.

"An Ember planet and the empty planet," he mused. "Interesting, don't you think?"

"I don't claim to know the Commander's plans in sending us around the universe," I responded coolly. I gazed out over the landscape, looking for the yure where the others were gathered. It was perhaps fifty yards distant.

"For all your pride, you hide it well."

Instead of responding, I clapped his back and started running toward the yure. Zar scoffed in exasperation. I heard his footsteps behind me, and pushed harder. We arrived at the yure together and came to a stop, breathing heavily.

"Unfair," Zar gasped, doubling over to catch his breath, hands on his knees. "You gave me no warning."

I chuckled breathlessly.

"What was the urgency?" Unruly asked, looking at us curiously. He stood beneath the yure, arms crossed over his chest, keeping a careful distance from the trunk and peelings.

My girl and Eversen stood beneath two peels of the yure's bark, also staring.

"We have a mission from the Commander," I announced. "First we travel to Zeker to find Robert, and then we go to Tarjik."

"Who?" my girl asked, eyes narrowing.

"All of us," Zar responded.

"Myself included?" Unruly asked in disbelief.

I nodded. "Everyone standing under this yure." I motioned to the plant. "As the Commander didn't single anyone out, I assume he means you as well."

Utterly astounded, Unruly couldn't retort.

"We just returned and now we leave again," Eversen said cheerfully. "What are Zeker and Tarjik like?"

Unruly turned to him and answered in a low voice. "Zeker is similar to Jaada only in its nature. The darkness and cold on Zeker is not merely in the air. It rises from the depths of the planet to pervade everything. The Embers there are crueler than those of Jaada. On Zeker, there is not even a lightening of the day. It is always swallowed in impenetrable gloom."

My girl shivered.

"Tarjik," Unruly continued, "is a neutral planet. It is smooth and empty. There are no inhabitants, and very little life. The only creatures I have discovered there are sembils, small fish who live in pools of water. Tarjik is usually used only as a shelter when one cannot return to one's homeland."

"Is it safe?" my girl queried.

Unruly smirked. "Completely. The Master engineered the atmosphere so that weapons are useless. It is a safe haven and place of regeneration, nothing more."

"Even your fire could not be sparked there?" she checked.

Unruly laughed this time. "My fire is useless on Tarjik. At the peak of my power, it was only a feeble flame in my palms, incapable of any damage."

"Why were you on Tarjik?" Eversen asked.

Unruly shifted his gaze away and stared out over the Coranta landscape. "I had my reasons," he said heavily.

I studied the Ember. My suspicions grew as I thought of taking him with us. He would be doused again in cold and shadows, his natural element. Would the evil of Zeker destroy the interest he had in the Commander?

"We need to leave," said Zar, after a moment of silence. "We don't know what position Robert is in and if it is bad, it would be better cut short."

"It would be his own doing," I said.

Unruly lowered his arms. "Are you ready to depart?"

"We need supplies," I said.

"We have enough for the journey to Zeker," said Eversen.

"That's enough, then. The sembils will sustain us on Tarjik." I motioned back toward the seor. "We should depart quickly. If I'm not mistaken, Yahn, Kein, and Uli will wish to pay us another visit. We should be gone before they arrive."

Zar laughed. "They visited during your previous excursion as well. If they knew our venture was expedient, they would only stay in order to provide us with sufficient provisions."

"Well, come then. Robert will not wait forever."

As we walked back toward the seor, my girl sidled up next to me. "Do you think he is all right?" she asked in a low voice.

Zar quickened his step and left me to walk with her alone. "No," I told her honestly. "He is alive. Aside from that, I have no knowledge of his condition. If Unruly spoke truthfully, Malevolence will destroy him."

My girl was troubled. In a lighter tone, she asked, "How much older is he?"

I smiled half-heartedly. "He is a young man now." I told her of Robert's transformation when he had awakened in the laie, and how different his features were.

She nodded. Motioning to Eversen, who walked in front of her, she commented, "He looks older as well; but you don't. You haven't changed at all."

"My body is accustomed to tunnel-traveling. Other climates and planets besides my own will do nothing to change my form. Only my homeland can increase my age. Also, I am a Wynaerian, and we age much more slowly than Earthlings."

She didn't say anything to that, and we proceeded to the seor with the others in silence.

Yahn, Kein, and Uli awaited us. The trio seemed to have

an uncanny knack for knowing when we were on Corant.

"Welcome back," Yahn said joyously. "It is good to see you again so soon." He cast a quick, appraising glance to Unruly and returned his gaze to me. "Zar tells me you plan to leave for Zeker now."

"Yes," I answered. "First Zeker, and then Tarjik. The Commander's orders."

Yahn dipped his head in one swift, jerky movement. "My friends and I will send you with provisions." He motioned to Kein and Uli, who were already summoning bread, dried fruit, and meat. They also provided us with several precious loni.

"Thank you," I said.

The Corantas were careful not to look at Unruly very long, as though he might contaminate them. They were eager and quick in their preparations for our journey. Mere moments after we had arrived back at the seor, we stood outside it once more, ready to depart.

"Come back again," Kein invited. "We will miss our companions in the abandoned seor."

"We'll return when the Commander allows us," Zar promised.

The Corantas dipped their heads in acknowledgement. "Farewell to you all," Yahn said, looking us over. A frown pulled at his lips for a moment as he gazed at Unruly. Then he turned on his heel and the three Corantas left.

"Once again to the tunnel," Zar muttered. "After all this traveling is ended, I will lie down and sleep for a week."

"I'll wake you before a week passes," I promised. "What would I do without your constant jesting?"

"Yes," Zar consented, "you would be useless without me."

Chapter 12
Death

We traveled through the tunnel in silence. As Unruly had warned, the shadows of Zeker grew deeper and stronger as we neared the planet. Even through the warmth of my tunnel, icy blasts barraged us.

When we landed, Zar and I crossed marks with the Earthlings to create a sphere of light and warmth around us. Unruly stayed a safe distance from us.

"We will be attacked," the Ember warned in a low voice. "The others know we are here."

"How long?" asked my girl, her teeth chattering despite the heat we radiated.

"Minutes. We need to hide. Or move."

I shook my head. "If they can sense your presence, moving won't help. Perhaps if we meet them, they will lead us to Robert."

"When we are all captives, what then?" Unruly's tone was biting. His rustling voice cut into my ears like knives.

"Commander," Eversen spoke aloud.

An almost visible shift occurred in the air. Unruly flinched back a step, the most severe reaction he'd had since our first meeting. The oppressive darkness lightened marginally, and the warmth we emanated spread deeper inside us to penetrate the cold.

Unruly cried out and stumbled forward a step. "You have weapons," he conceded, panting. "The Master's son's name is powerful here – far more potent than on Jaada or Corant. If you ask in his name, perhaps the Embers will lead you to Robert."

Resounding laughter danced on the air around us.

"You think you can escape with a mere name?" hissed a harsh, wispy voice.

"They don't know the nature of Zeker," a second voice quipped.

"What's this? Unruly with those of the light?" The first voice came back angrily this time.

Darkness was all I could see, no matter how I strained my eyes. For one moment, a flicker of violet appeared in the murk, then vanished.

"Commander," my girl whispered.

"Silence!" This voice I recognized. With it came a pervading cold that swept through us. It took several moments before our warmth extinguished it again.

The final voice had its desired effect. All around us grew eerily silent. There were not even sounds of animals or breathing. Everything hushed at the voice's command.

"Welcome to Zeker," it continued.

My girl tightened her grip over my mark. Her face blanched.

"Who are you?" Zar demanded. "By the power of the Commander, show yourself!"

A snarl hissed through the air, together with howls of pain. Sudden brightness lit up the dark, enough to illuminate hundreds of Embers in ranks, bristling with drawn weapons. The brightness was fire from Malevolence, who stood before us. His swords were wreathed in flames and a sneer curled his mouth.

"A traitor in your midst," he crowed. "Traitors receive the greatest penalties." His words were directed at Unruly, as harsh as his glare of hatred.

"I have betrayed no one," Unruly asserted. "I merely seek a greater existence than yours."

The Burning Ember laughed raucously, accompanied by his minions. The noise brought torrents of fear washing over my mind. I suddenly found it difficult to grasp Eversen's and my girl's hands, yet I did not relinquish my hold.

My girl whimpered.

"You are outnumbered," Malevolence bellowed. "You will all be murdered."

"What of the boy, Robert?" my girl asked shakily. She lifted her head stubbornly and glared at Malevolence.

The Burning Ember leered. "The boy is no more use to me than one of you. I merely brought him here in order to bring you. Now that his task has been completed, I thank you for allowing his vow to me." He gave a mock bow, much to the enjoyment of his followers, who snickered.

He continued, raising his voice in mimicry. "Now I behold in person the Ember who would betray his kind. I see the Earthlings of bravery, and the Wynaerian brothers. Here I awaited the contenders, and they are mere frightened children, grasping at names to save them from evil." He laughed.

Unruly trembled.

"Stay where you are," Malevolence ordered with a snarl. "You, I will treat like a traitor, once the others have been dispatched. You deserve the torture due the Enemy." He raised a sword-arm toward Unruly and ropes of fire shot from it.

The ropes bound Unruly and seared into his shadowy form, turning him grey. A lone rope of white-hot fire wrapped around his mouth as a gag. He stood immobile, eyes wide in fear.

"Do not fear," Malevolence soothed at my girl's gasp. "He will not burn. It will be a great discomfort, true, and it will end far too swiftly, but he will only turn grey. Nothing more will happen to the traitor until you have been killed."

I snarled wordlessly.

Malevolence began pacing, his swords illuminating the front lines of his horde as he passed before them. Shadows danced over their eager faces before they were lost in darkness once more. Malevolence didn't seem to notice his troops, his concentration wholly absorbed in us.

"You," he said, stopping and pivoting suddenly to face me. "You are Suri. You were there on Wynaeria, the day I destroyed your village. Do you remember?"

I gritted my teeth. "How could I forget?"

The corner of his lip pulled up into a lopsided leer. "You weren't so brave then, were you? Now look at you!" He waved a sword toward me, which shot out sparks.

I jumped back reflexively, though I needn't have bothered. The flames stopped short of the little circle of light surrounding us.

Malevolence showed no irritation at his foiled attack. "You have come before me with a group of desperate friends. Tell me, do you wish to die?" He stepped toward me menacingly and lowered his voice. "I can annihilate you all."

"Can you?" I shot back, suddenly bold. His failed attempt at burning me gave me courage. I had the suspicion that he couldn't penetrate the barrier of light surrounding me and my friends.

Malevolence's eyes narrowed into slits, one violet, the other red. He raised both swords and pointed them at the center of my chest. "You think I cannot slay?" His words Reverberated around us, from above, below, and every side, piercing.

Where the hilts of his swords ought to have been there glowed a deep maroon light. It licked down the sword blades, dancing and hissing loudly, until the silver gleam of metal became enshrouded. For a moment, the light paused at the point of the blades. Then it shot forward in a beam of fire, directed at my heart.

"No!" cried my companions simultaneously.

At their word, the shield of light glowed brightly and hardened to form a golden barrier, exactly like the

Commander's from so long ago. I took a wavering step back as the beam of fire hit the shield at the point of my heart.

The barrier held and the fire extinguished.

You will not harm my children.

A wide grin stretched my face, unbidden, at the cold voice.

Malevolence stepped back unsteadily and dropped to his knees, roaring in agony. His swords turned into black hands of shadowy mist, and his fire dissipated.

Allow them passage, the Commander's voice ordered. *You will not harm them.*

Malevolence cowered, covering his ears with his hands. "Yes!" he shrieked in a terrified voice. "They will go!" He raised his head to meet my gaze. Hatred filled his face, but he turned to his horde and shouted orders for them to leave.

The Embers dissolved into the night.

Eversen dropped to his knees. "Thank you, Commander."

My girl looked up at me and smiled tentatively. Her eyes drifted to something over my shoulder and she nodded toward it. "We have to go to him."

Without releasing the Earthlings' hands, I turned to gaze at Unruly. He remained bound with fire ropes, staring at us. Together, we stepped toward him. Zar dropped my girl's hand and reached for the bonds around him.

"Suri, your knife." My brother held out his palm to me.

I fumbled in my tunic for the blade and passed it to him.

With swift strokes he severed the fire ropes, and they fell away from Unruly. The Ember trembled, an awed look on his face. Zar cut his gag before returning the knife to me.

"Thank you," Unruly stammered. His face was ashen-colored, whether from fear or the contact with fire, I didn't know.

Zar grinned. "Don't you know better than to irk Malevolence?"

Unruly shuddered. "He's not the one I fear," he

murmured, glancing at me.

"You need only fear my master," I said, averting my eyes from his stare. "Come, let's find Robert. Where is he?"

"Do not expect to find him unharmed," he warned. "Malevolence's idea of reward is the beginning of his destruction. He will never allow an Earthling to be freed once the vow has been made."

"Regardless, we will free him and take him to Tarjik," I said firmly. "Where is he?"

"He'll be in a laie forest, like I was." Unruly motioned in a westerly direction. "There is one over there. I cannot perceive Robert, but that is expected. If he's bound in a forest, only those who guard him will be able to see him."

"Lead the way," Zar offered.

We walked in silence, still gripping hands, except for Unruly. In unspoken mutual agreement, we had decided it was safer to be connected than separate. Zar and I Channeled what comfort and peace we could to the Earthlings, thanking and beseeching the Commander as we did so.

"Here." Unruly came to a stop.

"Where are the guards?" Eversen asked.

Unruly chuckled. "There are other creatures than Embers on Zeker. The guards are invisible creatures of the deep, transformed to live on land."

"Invisible?" My girl looked around in trepidation.

"Not to me," Unruly assured her. "I see nothing here, except the laies. Wait." He stared hard at something for a long moment, then gave a swift jerk of the head. "Yes. He's here."

"How do you break into a laie prison?" Zar inquired, eyeing the seemingly empty expanse before us.

Unruly grinned. "With that blade of yours, I would assume you can cut through the barrier."

I stepped forward and unsheathed the knife. "Where?"

"Cut through here, a hole large enough for us to walk through." Unruly made the rough shape of a doorway in the air with his finger.

"Just cut through it?" I checked.

"Yes."

I lifted my knife to the right upper hand corner of the invisible doorway. It stopped short, as though there were a solid wall before it. Interesting. I added a little pressure to the knife and it sank into the barrier.

"Is it working?" I asked.

"Yes. Bury the knife up to its hilt. It should crack the barrier."

I shoved the knife in until something clearly stopped it. I assumed the blade had gone in as far as it could. A brief thought of leaving the knife hanging in midair occurred to me. I smiled and pushed it aside.

Slowly and carefully, I began slicing along the edge of the invisible doorway Unruly had drawn in the air. It was difficult work, not only because I couldn't see what I was doing, but also due to the strength of the barrier. After several long minutes of hard work, the doorway was cut.

"Now push inward," Unruly directed.

I sheathed my knife and outstretched my arms. My palms rested flatly against a cold, vertical wall that I couldn't see. I pushed. Deep groans and a high-pitched squeal sounded; then a thud.

"Well done," Unruly approved. "Now we step through and retrieve Robert."

"Will we be caught?" my girl inquired.

Unruly barked a laugh. "The Embers are incapable of attacking you after the Master's son's warning. They will not come."

He led the way through the invisible doorway. When I stepped through, hundreds of laies suddenly came into view all around us.

"You see Robert?" I asked Unruly.

He pointed directly ahead. "Yes, though I can't see what condition he is in."

"He's alive," I said. "That's enough for now."

Zar spoke quietly. "How will we heal his wounds?"

"Let's see them first," Eversen said practically. "He may not be close to death."

"He may be very close," Unruly countered. "He hasn't moved since I first spotted him."

We continued among the laies in silence. After passing several dozen, we came upon the one which held Robert. This one's membrane was diaphanous. An obstruction of shadowy mist encased the outside of the laie, outlining it, and covered the opening so that we could not see inside it. Only Unruly's vision could penetrate the wall.

"He is sickly," the Ember reported quietly. "He's very close to death."

"How do we get inside it?" Zar demanded.

Unruly lifted a hand and brushed his fingertips over the laie's opening. He gave a low hiss and dropped his hand. "There's a binding over the opening," he announced. "It burns Embers. Perhaps your knife can penetrate it."

"Can Robert hear us?" my girl asked.

"No. He is unconscious, and there are shields over the laie to prevent sight and hearing. It helps discourage the prisoner from speaking with his captors and influencing an escape." Unruly motioned to me and stepped aside. "Use your knife."

I pressed the knife into the thickest part of the dark binding over the opening. For a moment, nothing happened. Then the mist converged powerfully on the knife and it took tremendous effort for me to keep hold of it. With a loud, guttural whine, the darkness dispersed and a gaping hole appeared before us. Fire swirled away and dissipated in the air.

Unruly staggered backward, mouth slightly agape. "You – you destroyed all of the bindings!"

"Isn't that why you suggested I use my knife?" I asked.

Unruly gave me a look, still wide-eyed. "I didn't expect it to work so effusively."

"Can we go in?" my girl asked.

Unruly nodded mutely.

My girl rushed into the laie. I followed more slowly, anger toward my charge and fear for his condition mingled in my mind.

Robert lay on his side, tightly bound by chains of glowing red. He looked no longer like an Earthling, but an Ember. His skin had darkened into the shadowy substance of the Jaadanis. Still, it was easy to distinguish his mottled features. An arm stuck out at an odd angle, one eye was swollen shut, and he breathed shallowly. His features had aged to that of a young man, rather than a boy.

My anger abated at his appearance, despite his new Jaadani form, and gave way for compassion.

"Oh, Robert," my girl breathed, dropping to her knees beside him. She touched the manacles around his wrists and began to cry.

"Shh," I murmured, crouching beside her. My head whirled at Robert's condition. He looked minutes from death. "He'll be healed," I told my girl soothingly. I reached a hesitant hand out to the manacles.

As expected, the fire glowed brighter and singed my fingertips. I yanked my hand away and stared at the chains.

Commander, lead me.

How could I remove the chains without burning myself or harming Robert more? I thought of my knife, but the chains were too tight. There was no room for the blade to fit underneath. Even if it did, I doubted the chains would break as easily as the fire ropes.

"Unruly!" I called.

The Ember was beside me almost instantly. He sucked in a sharp breath at the sight of Robert that sounded genuine.

"How can I remove the chains?"

"I will." He curled his fingers around the manacles and broke them apart. Closing his eyes and muttering something I couldn't hear, he ran his palm over the chain links. As he touched them, the fire dissolved into his darkness. Within moments, Robert was free.

My girl reached a finger to the grey burns around Robert's wrists, but yanked it away before touching them and hissed with anger.

"Vengeance will come," I assured her, also staring at the wounds. "For now, let's get him to Tarjik."

"Be careful carrying him," Unruly warned. "They will have broken a couple ribs, besides his arm."

Warily, I reached out a hand to the young man. When my light contacted his darkness, torment shot between us, in spite of our bond. Robert grunted and I jerked away.

"Carry him," I ordered Unruly. "You are the only one who will not be harmed by the contact."

Gently, Unruly gathered Robert into his arms and carried him from the laie. I followed with my girl. Eversen and Zar were aghast when they saw Robert. As a group, we all headed for my tunnel.

Hampered by Unruly's burden, we had a slower walk going than coming. He was careful not to rock Robert more than necessary because of his wounds. The boy did not make a sound, though at one point his breathing grew shallower. I Channeled to him, thinking about what I would say when he had healed. I couldn't deny the slight smugness I had that his injuries were a just consequence of his choice. Nor could I ignore the deep anger that lodged in me at his transformation into an Ember.

When we reached the tunnel, Unruly took a deep breath. Together with Zar and Eversen, he was quiet, staring at Robert's dark and burned body. My girl spoke only once, asking how long the trip was, to which I replied, "Several minutes."

It was in the middle of Tarjik's night when we arrived. The smooth curvature of the planet was barely distinguishable in the gloom, and any shelter to be found was impossible to see.

"Where are the mushrooms?" Zar asked lightly.

I scoffed, in no mood for japes. "They aren't mushrooms."

"We're here," Unruly said, chuckling. "Allow me to bestow sight on your eyes."

"It works on planets other than Embers'?" Zar muttered.

We all ignored him, and before us, the planet came into view.

A small dip in the landscape quickly leveled out into a full-fledged dell. Nearly a dozen large, white balls dotted the white grassy space: what Zar affectionately called 'mushrooms.' They stood on short, squat stalks, providing ample shade. In the middle of the dell a circular stream of water reflected the stars. This, I knew, was where the only Tarjikian animals dwelt: sembils. These are small, fish-like creatures with spiky spines and sharp fins. Thin and lithe, sembils have large teeth, with two fangs that hang from either side of their mouths. In the sunlight, their scales glitter silver and blue.

"There," Unruly jerked his head toward the largest of the mushroom-like balls, called pophins. "We can sleep underneath the overhanging top."

I led the way to the pophin and walked around to the far side. "Which way does the sun rise from?" asked I, glancing into Open Space.

"Directly behind us," Unruly said, setting Robert on the ground. He pointed briefly at the stalk of the pophin. "We should sleep here."

"Robert needs immediate attention. His wounds can't wait until morning," my girl interjected. "Set him down and let me tend to him."

I touched her shoulder. "It's all right," I told her. "We can heal him."

"Then why haven't you?" she demanded, eyes flashing.

"Zeker was full of angry Embers," Unruly reminded her. "It was necessary to come here. No Ember will come here unless they have no other choice. We'll be safe."

The Ember set Robert down gently and leaned over him, grasping Robert's left wrist. "Channel, Suri. I cannot heal all of his wounds alone."

Standing over the two Embers, I Channeled into Robert, praying to the Commander for healing. I closed my eyes as much to concentrate as to block the sight before me and control the anger that could so easily surface. My girl hovered worryingly over the boy.

When she gasped, I knew Robert had begun to mend. I concentrated harder and continued to speak to the Commander and Channel. A soft *pop* told me his ribs were setting. Three more from his ribcage and then another, louder *pop* from his broken arm. This last was audible to my girl, who seethed with anger, and Robert was healed almost completely.

Slowly, the grey faded from the boy's body and his burns disappeared. The Embers' darkness consumed him and his eyes fluttered open.

"Suri," he murmured, a hint of a grin playing over his lips. His eyes were playful. "I hoped it was you."

At his tone of voice, all compassion for him fled. "Sleep," I told him harshly. "There will be plenty to speak of when you awake."

He sneered, scrabbling to sit up. "The Embers would have healed me," he spat. "You needn't have come after me. Though it is a shame more of you weren't beaten." His gaze flickered to Unruly and he lifted an eyebrow mischievously.

I glanced at the Ember, who shook his head infinitesimally. At that moment, all my suspicions toward him were reborn.

"Go to sleep," Zar muttered to Robert, looking at me. He, too, had seen the subtle exchange between Embers. "Time for contention in the morning," he murmured so only I could hear, brushing past me. He dropped to the ground and leaned his head back against the stalk of the pophin. "Sleep well," he wished us, and closed his eyes.

The others followed his example, taking up places on the ground where they could sleep comfortably.

I scowled. Against my better judgment, I lay on the

ground with them. It had been several days since I'd last slept, and I knew it was time to do so again. Tonight, though, I was even more loath to than usual. I did not trust Robert or Unruly.

When no one had stirred for several hours, I released my tension and closed my eyes. Allowing weariness to overtake me, I slept.

Chapter 13
An Ember's Mark

A thrill snaked down his spine. He shivered with delight and rolled over onto his back. Above, the night sky shone with stars. Silence wrapped him in its embrace.

He thought of his rescue from the Enemy, and reveled in the remembrance of his master's touch. Again, he heard the words that had bought his freedom.

Come forward. The barrier is broken by your vow.

"I swear it," the young man repeated his vow aloud. "I swear it with my life, my heart, and my blood." Lifting his eyes to Open Space, he grinned, a crooked, leering grin. "Master, I will be yours forever."

Silence one more descended in the darkness, and wrapped around the young man. Then, raising the hair along the nape of his neck, a voice gently slivered the air.

"Come to me."

A smile flitted over his lips. "Always, my master."

The voice chuckled. "Yes. I broke the barrier and claimed you as mine. Now you must obey, and you will love me for it."

"I do love you."

"Then find me."

"Where are you?"

The silky voice did not answer the young man's question. "You are mine. You know where to find me. Where do you want to be with me? I will meet you there."

An image of darkness filled the young man's mind, lit only by stars in the sky. Deep contentment settled over him, and the surface of his skin warmed with delight. He rested in the feeling for a long moment, before it grew stronger and he could hardly bear it. Longing welled in him, so intense it forced a groan from his lips.

He stood to his feet in one swift, limber movement. He glanced around in the night, another grin stretching his features. The young man chuckled low in his throat and extended his blades.

"I am coming, master."

I woke with the lingering frigidity of the Embers' darkness tingling along my skin. Groaning, I rolled over and sat up. After blinking several times, I ascertained that Eversen was gone. Surprised, I looked around more carefully. Zar and my girl still slumbered peacefully. Robert sat with his back to the pophin, a wide grin plastered on his face. Unruly sat beside him, features impenetrable.

"Where's Eversen?" I asked.

Unruly flicked his eyes to me. "We don't know," he said quietly. "He disappeared during the night."

"You didn't stop him?"

"I didn't see him," Unruly corrected.

"Where were you?"

A half-smirk tugged his lips. "Sleeping."

I stood up angrily. "What happened to him?" I nearly shouted. "Why didn't you hear when he left?"

"Why didn't you?" Robert countered coldly. His gaze rested on me for the first time. "You are the guardian here, after all. You should be the one keeping count of your flock." He sneered.

"Don't, Suri."

I heeded Zar's words and said nothing, spinning to face my brother. He sat up as well, eyeing me with a bland look of exasperation.

"He's an Ember," Zar continued, keeping his eyes fixed on me. "Don't listen to his taunts."

I shot my brother a glare and grudgingly lowered myself to the ground once more, staring at Unruly. "Where did Eversen go?"

He looked silently at me for a long moment, then slowly said, "Last night he seemed different to me; more reserved and secretive. He reminded me of those Malice influences."

"Malice is dead," I said.

A smirk curled Unruly's lips. "Not all who are dispatched are destroyed," he said in a low voice. "Malice was not killed; he was merely returned to Zeker, where he belongs."

"Zar killed him," I said flatly. "He plunged a temberle blade into Malice's chest. How could an Ember survive that?"

Unruly's countenance turned calculating, but it was Robert who responded.

"Embers are resilient," he said sneeringly.

"A temberle blade, without the Master's son's blessing, is merely a blade," said Unruly. "You did not invoke the Master's son to destroy Malice. He was brutally harmed, but he returned to Zeker in time for Malevolence to heal his wounds." He jerked his head to Zar. "Wynaerians heal the same way, only with light rather than darkness."

"If you want to find Eversen," Robert said slyly, "I might suggest looking on Zeker. I suspect he was transported there sometime this past evening and is now imprisoned."

I clenched my jaw and spoke through my teeth. "Would you happen to know why he is on Zeker? Or who transported him?"

Robert lifted his head to meet my gaze directly. His cold, violet eyes stared at me with unbridled mischief and delight. "Naturally," he said calmly. "I took him there." He leered tauntingly.

"Don't, Suri," Zar repeated, harsher this time.

"It's the Embers' holding place," Unruly said softly. "All prisoners they take will end up on Zeker."

I narrowed my eyes. "He's a prisoner on Zeker," I repeated. My knife was in my hand before I realized I'd drawn it.

"Suri."

This time it was my girl who spoke.

I jerked my head to look at her. "What?" I demanded.

She stood watching me carefully, her features drawn with sorrow. She took a step closer to me. "Remember the Commander's love," she said softly. "Remember his patience with those who are against him."

"I'm not the Commander," I spat.

"No," she agreed, taking another step closer. "No, you are not. Suri, you are one of his own, and you are becoming like him. Follow him. Do what he would."

"You heard Robert," I retorted, disbelieving. "You expect me to act like the Commander when my own charge has betrayed one of my companions?"

"Yes." This time Zar spoke. "You should not have been surprised by the betrayal, Suri. You knew Robert would turn to the Embers and vow his blood to Malevolence."

"You should have known I could never follow the Master's son," Robert inserted belligerently. "Why did you try? I long for the darkness and fire the Embers have given me. I like the way I am."

I turned away from the dolt and headed toward my tunnel.

"Where are you going?" Zar called to me.

"You can come if you wish," I returned. "I'm traveling to Zeker."

"Suri," my girl began.

I whirled on her. "Do you think I am going to let Eversen

be destroyed by *him*?" I gestured to Robert without looking at him. "If he is on Zeker, his torture will be horrendous. I'm not going to let him sacrifice himself because of a traitor."

"You can't leave your charge," Zar said.

Shock doused me. "Are you serious?"

"Quite. The Commander has forbidden a guardian to leave his charge before the termination of the guardianship," he reminded me.

I stared past Zar and my girl to Robert, who still sat beneath the pophin, a grin smearing his face. He turned to face me and cocked an eyebrow. "Come," I snapped to him. "You must travel with me."

He allowed his grin to grow wider. "If I don't want to come?" he questioned softly. "Will you force me?"

Unruly glanced from him to me and stood. "Come, Robert," he said. "We will travel with them to Zeker. We are a companionship still, whether you partake of it or not."

Robert scoffed lightly and rose in one nimble movement. "Then let us go." He sauntered with Unruly to join us.

"What if this is a trick?" Zar muttered under his breath.

"Eversen is gone. If it's a trick, the Commander will protect us," I answered. No one was going to dissuade me from finding Eversen. "Neither Unruly nor Robert can be trusted. I will not hesitate to incapacitate either."

"Very well." Zar sounded resigned. "Do you have your knife?"

"Always."

I turned on my heel before the Embers reached us, and stepped toward my tunnel. Before stepping into the center to travel, I turned to Zar and my girl.

"Cross marks with me," I ordered, in a quieter tone than I had yet used that morning. "We will need the Channels on Zeker."

Neither argued, and we crossed marks before stepping into the tunnel. Robert scoffed, but Unruly merely looked curious.

Cold swept through us as we entered Zeker's atmosphere. The darkness once more blinded us completely, nearly tangible.

I shivered. I had hoped the last time I'd come would be the last, and here I was, only a day later, stepping foot again on the Ember planet.

"Don't break communion," Zar murmured as the tunnel deposited us on the black marble ground.

"If we're attacked?" Unruly asked.

"We do what we did last time," I muttered. "Hold wrists and speak the Commander's name." Even at the mention, Zeker visibly lightened a shade.

"What if Eversen's not here?" my girl whispered. Fear clutched her in its grasp, so that she was trembling not merely from the cold.

"Channel," I muttered to Zar, as I did. To my girl, I answered, "He is. Unruly, how long before the Embers arrive?"

"They're not coming," he answered.

"What?" Zar, my girl, and I spoke in unison.

"They're in the center of their city, gathered together," Robert related smugly. "Eversen is not with them. He's held near my old prison. I don't think the Embers will follow us."

A troubled look shrouded Unruly's features. "They aren't bothered by our presence."

"If they're not coming after us, what was the purpose of capturing Eversen?" Zar demanded softly. None of us wanted to speak too loudly.

Robert laughed, but said nothing.

"There's something different with him," Unruly murmured, his eyes glazed with a faraway look. "His light has smudged into grey – neither light nor dark." He took a step forward and motioned for us to follow. "Come. We will find and rescue him. Then we must depart. The Embers are planning something, and I don't want to wait to see what it is."

We followed Unruly, unnerved by the silence around us. Only Robert seemed comfortable in the still night.

"How can you tell where the Embers are?" my girl ventured.

"The darkness," Unruly answered. "Embers feel the differences in light and shadows. I cannot distinguish which Embers are where unless I know them well, but I can tell the difference in normal darkness and an Ember's tilling."

Robert sighed theatrically.

"How far away can you feel the differences?" my girl asked.

Unruly snorted. "Distance doesn't matter." He paused. "It's the same way we can distinguish when Wynaerians are nearby or not. Their bodies are woven with light that is impossible not to detect."

We walked several more paces before Unruly stopped us.

"Here," the Ember said. His eyes narrowed. "They did not rebuild the wall, or brutalize Eversen." He crept forward. "I don't understand," he muttered under his breath. Pulling to an abrupt halt, he straightened and stared. "Oh."

"What?" Zar, my girl, and I asked.

Robert snickered. "Tell them, Unruly," he said.

"Depart from us," Unruly muttered to the young man.

"Oh, will you lead them on?" Robert asked mockingly. "I'd prefer to partake in the entertainment. However," his tone turned breathy and eager, "my master is awaiting me. I don't know how you ignore him, Unruly. The pull is irresistible."

"Leave," Unruly answered.

With a short chuckle, Robert turned from us and headed away. "Fulfill the agreement, Unruly. Malevolence will be most displeased if you do not."

"What?" Zar demanded. We all turned to face the Ember.

Unruly shot a hateful look at Robert's back. Then he turned to us with an expression of sadness. "There is an agreement on Zeker," he said slowly, then closed his mouth again.

"What is the agreement?" I asked.

Unruly shook his head slowly, a spark of fire igniting in

his palms. He ignored my question and spoke of Eversen, "They haven't harmed him. Not physically. Come on." He stepped forward, leading us into the invisible laie forest. Under his breath, he muttered a few words, and the laies became visible.

"What is the agreement?" my girl pressed.

"Later," Unruly murmured. "I will tell you once he is free."

"Where is Eversen?" I asked. Even with the sight bestowed on me, I could not distinguish the movement or sound of an Earthling.

"Follow me." Unruly led us deep into the laie forest, in a nearly direct route. Finally, we drew up to the largest laie I'd ever seen. It spanned nearly three times the space as any other, with a gaping entrance much taller than Zar.

I opened my mouth to ask, but then I saw, and closed it again.

Eversen hung from fiery chains on the back wall of the laie. His hands were manacled to each other above his head, and a chain wrapped around his waist, securing his back to the wall. His head was up, staring at us, but his eyes were blank. Rather than the lively blue they had been, they now glowed grey. His heart also was shrouded in a grey mist, neither light nor dark.

"What have they done to him?" my girl gasped.

Unruly scoffed and turned to us. "Don't you see? They know your knife can penetrate any defense, so they've given us something else. We cannot win against this enchantment with weapons."

"Enchantment?" Zar echoed.

"What kind of enchantment is it?" I inquired, stepping forward to stand before Eversen.

Unruly wasn't listening. "I knew it was a trap," he muttered to himself, pacing behind me. "They wouldn't let us come and go that easily. If it were so simple, anyone could do it. No, they've made an agreement and the arrangement must be kept. There's nothing else to be done."

"Unruly?" I asked.

"The agreement," the Ember said in a low voice, his back to me, "is that someone must die. From as far back as creation, the Embers have been granted their own laws for their planets. Jaada is not nearly so dark, as you have experienced. Zeker, however, is the embodiment of evil." He groaned.

"What do you mean?"

He spun to me. "They're going to kill Eversen, regardless of what we do. His life is tied to the chains." He motioned to the manacles. "If we cut him loose, he dies. His eyes and heart have been mixed. The Embers, unable to extinguish a light, smothered him with shadows. The strength of their combined force turned him grey. He is now indifferent, in a state of suspension."

"That's the agreement?" Zar demanded.

Unruly nodded. "When someone visits Zeker, the Embers have the right to kill them for trespassing. Only those chosen to be transformed into Embers are allowed their lives. However," his tone brightened marginally, from black to bleak, "only one death is permitted, regardless of the number of companions."

Stunned, we were silent.

Unruly paced, muttering to himself.

"What do we do?" my girl finally inquired. Pity filled her eyes as she stared at Eversen's limp body. "We can't leave Eversen here."

"No; nor can we release him," Unruly spat. "He is currently unable to hear, see, or feel us. His death would be instantaneous and painless. I don't know of a way to escape with him alive."

He spun to me. "Do you see what they've done? They haven't come after us, because they know there is no way for us to release Eversen without killing him. That will pay their debt. We would be free to leave."

Dread filled me as a thought occurred. "No," I said in a low voice. "We left Zeker before and no one died."

Another silence descended.

Unruly nodded, understanding. His eyes flickered over us. "They will kill two of us."

"Eversen," Zar said.

"And me," I supplied.

My girl shook her head. "No. They can't kill you both."

"They can," asserted Unruly.

I brooded, studying Eversen. "That's why Robert left so easily," I muttered. "He placed Eversen in the state of suspension. If we release Eversen, he will die; and I will be the one chosen to be killed for our previous visit."

"Why did they let us go before?" Zar said. "Why didn't they kill you then?"

"Because Robert was close to death," Unruly answered. "If he had died, their debt would have been paid. When he lived, they invited him to capture Eversen. He agreed and they planned our return to rescue Eversen. The Embers would rather kill a guardian than a charge, so they agreed."

I studied the Ember, skeptical. I remembered the look that had passed between him and Robert and doubt crept into my mind. I didn't trust Unruly to tell me the truth. If he and Robert had made an agreement, he would lie about it.

"What other options do we have?" Zar asked, studying Eversen.

Unruly was silent, thinking. Slowly a grin spread across his face. He started pacing again. With a loud shout, he turned on us, features victorious.

"We cut him loose," he said. "The temberle in your knife, Suri, broke the enchantments of Robert's prison. It should also break the enchantments here. Your tunnels, also, can enter and leave any planet at any point. They reached through the bindings on Jaada when you came to rescue me. Once you cut Eversen's bonds, the Embers will come. We have to be quick."

"You suggest I create a tunnel from here?" I asked in disbelief.

"Can't you?" Unruly challenged, eyes flashing.

"Yes, of course," I retorted angrily.

"I suggest you cut Eversen loose first," Unruly said, boring his eyes into mine. "The Embers will know when your tunnel penetrates the atmosphere. You'll have to create it immediately after Eversen's release, or they will capture us. I can guarantee none of us will leave alive should that happen." He thought for a moment more. "There is one other condition. We can't return to Tarjik."

I stared blankly at him. "Why not?"

"Your tunnel has to travel from here to Earth – it's the only neutral planet besides Tarjik. They will expect us to go to Tarjik and will be waiting. Earth, however, will buy us a little more time to hide."

"You mean they'll come after us regardless?" Zar looked hard at Unruly.

He turned to my brother. "We will be violating an agreement as far back as creation," he said fiercely. "Once the bonds are cut and we travel through Suri's tunnel, every Ember will be alerted to Eversen's survival. They will know he hasn't died, as he should have. They will follow us. Fortunately for us, they can't tell where a tunnel goes, only where it begins."

"Once in Suri's tunnel, we're out of their sight for a time," Zar said softly. "They will travel to Tarjik, expecting us to go there for Eversen's health. When we aren't found, they will know we're on Earth and come after us."

"They can't go to Wynaeria," I said. "Why can't we?"

"No," Unruly rejected vehemently. "I cannot go to Wynaeria either. Nor can the Earthlings. They will die. Earth is the safest place to go."

I turned to face Eversen's limp form. "What did they do to him to smear him in grey?"

Unruly followed my gaze. "It's an old trick of the Embers," he shrugged. "We used to use it on enemies during the Great Wars. Hostages were held in states of suspension like Eversen. When the enemies came to rescue them, they discovered the deception, but there was nothing to be done. The debt was already paid. Our foes had to leave without their hostages. We often claimed victory for that reason. Over time, however, others discovered the deception and countered it. We haven't been able to use it for many years."

"I remember," I muttered.

"Go on, Suri," my girl urged. "Cut him loose. Let's leave."

I unsheathed my knife and stepped toward Eversen. "I have to create a tunnel instantly?" I reiterated, looking up into the Earthling's cold, blank eyes.

"Yes."

Hesitating only a moment to summon the energy required for making a tunnel, I reached up my knife and cut Eversen free. His bonds dissolved into ash and he crumpled to the ground, breathing heavily.

Unruly sighed in relief. "I'm glad that worked. I wasn't sure."

My girl gasped with horror and rounded on him.

I didn't hear what she said, already focused on forming the tunnel around us. I envisioned light gathering together, and a circle of red on the ground, surrounding us. Muttering to the Commander, I asked for a strong tunnel. As I concentrated, one began to form; at first a faint flickering in the air, the lights grew bright and hardened, and then the tunnel was made.

I grasped Eversen in my arms, sheathing my knife, and pulled him inside the circle with the others. Immediately, my world careened.

The planet was still and silent when he arrived, as always. Only stars glittering in Open Space lit the landscape before him, glinting off a multitude of laies. Warmth and welcoming encased him, and he breathed deeply in contentment. The young man stepped forward into the forest, anticipation making his feet eager. Quickly and lightly, he scampered among the laies. It was the far side of the forest to which he'd been summoned.

As he exited the laie forest, a tingle ran down his spine. Peculiarly, he broke out in a sweat. He was not afraid, however; a meeting with his master brought him only joy.

Before him, the landscape changed dramatically. A large dell sank into the surface of the planet, encased by jagged marble cliffs. In the center, a black, crude throne had been erected, upon which the Burning Ember sat. Blades extended, he lounged on the throne; a crown of fire encircled his head.

As the young man approached, he noticed the throne was crafted from bones. The stray, appealing thought that the bones were those of Embers crossed his mind. He strode forward, and knelt with bowed head before Malevolence.

"Master," the young man murmured. His throat tightened at his master's presence.

The Burning Ember merely looked at him.

"The human was released from his bonds by a temberle blade. Both humans and their guardians are tunnel-traveling. None have been harmed."

A moment of silence passed between master and slave.

"So then, you have failed," the Burning Ember mused. A smile curled his mouth, and he leaned toward the young man cowering at his feet. His hot breath curled around the young man's cheek. "How shall I reward your disobedience?"

He did not answer.

"Perhaps a branding?" A hint of a snarl laced Malevolence's voice. "Will that cure your insubordination?"

The young man flinched. "Master, please," he began.

The Ember leader sneered. "Now you plead with me for your failure?" His blades sparked with flames.

"I will rectify it," the young man muttered, eyeing the dancing lights. "They have only eluded us for a time. Not all is lost." When Malevolence did not respond, he continued, "I have a plan, master. There is a way that we can destroy the Earthlings and their guardians. Will you allow me to speak?"

"You have always been my favorite," the Burning Ember mused, sitting back in his chair once more, "yet now, when I send you on an assignment, you come cowering back in defeat. What

plan can you possibly have to restore my love for you?"

The young man was cut deeply at the admission of his master's rescinded love. He swallowed and spoke in a low whisper, begging, as though for the air he required to breathe. "Master, I can deliver the Earthlings and their guardians to you."

A flicker of interest ignited Malevolence's eyes. His blade retracted, shaping into a hand. He leaned over his slave and placed a shadowy hand on his head.

The young man trembled.

"Where are they?" the Burning Ember breathed, gently Reverberating his voice around his slave's ears. "Release them into my hands, and perhaps I will see fit to forgive you."

The young man felt tears rise in his chest at the mercy. "Thank you, my master," he murmured. He took Malevolence's hand and caressed it, lightly brushing his lips over the back of it.

"Do not think your fawning will revoke your punishment. Tell me where the Earthlings and their guardians have gone." A hard edge entered his tone.

"They reside on Earth."

A cruel smile twisted Malevolence's mouth upward. "Well done."

The words wrapped around the young man as warmth. He relished his master's approval. "I will do anything for you," he said softly.

"You will burn for me," the Burning Ember promised. "And when the light has finished flaying you, you will be imprisoned as I demolish the Wynaerians. Perhaps the time in seclusion will change your stance about failing me."

"You are just, my lord."

Malevolence chuckled. "Always." His blades wreathed with firelight and lit the clearing around them. All pretense of gentleness fled his demeanor as he rose. "Stand and accept your punishment," he ordered in a harsh voice.

The young man obeyed readily.

"Malice, Chaos, flay this jackanapes."

Two Embers materialized from the darkness surrounding master and slave. Malice sauntered forward, sneering. Chaos followed, features amused. "Master," the two said in unison, kneeling before Malevolence.

The Burning Ember gave no recognition of them. He turned his back on the young man and stood before his throne. Folding his hands behind his back, he tilted his head back to look at Open Space. He smirked. "If you can, protect your beloved," he taunted the Master. "See how he has turned from you? I give him love, where you have only demanded from him. He is mine, and you will never take him."

Silence fell among the Embers for several moments.

Malevolence flicked his blades out, keeping his back to those with him. "Brand him."

With a hiss of delight, Malice scampered toward the young man. He held in both hands whips created not of fire, but of golden light, like that of a star. Wrapped around his palms were the handles, black leather. Though he grimaced in pain at the sight of the light, a deep satisfaction rose in him as he raised the whips to strike.

Crack!

Crack!

Crack!

The young man stumbled under the blows, crying out in agony. Across his back, lines of red spread where the whips contacted his darkness. The red sliced all the way through his body to his chest, and faded into grey, scarring him front and back.

Crack!

Chaos joined his companion Malice and they whipped the young man rhythmically, relishing his torture.

Malevolence stood erect, proud and glad at each lashing. He did not watch the proceedings behind him, unwilling to be harmed by the contact of the light.

Crack!

A thump *sounded on the ground behind him: the young*

man falling forward, unable to stand. Malevolence's features broke into an uncontrollable, crooked grin. Fire curled around his jagged blades, shooting sparks to either side of him. He trembled, elated.

Finally, the young man could no longer cry out in pain.

"Enough," Malevolence whispered. He waited until the whips had been extinguished, and turned to face the young man.

He was unrecognizable. Malice and Chaos, rather than merely beating the young man's back, had extended their punishment to his head, arms, and legs as well. Rather than black and wispy as usual, the young man had turned a light grey. The lines where each lash fell were clearly visible, now a muddy brown color.

The young man breathed shallowly, the only indicator that he lived.

"Awaken," Malevolence snapped. A spark shot from his blade-tip to strike the young man's eye.

He groaned, but didn't stir.

"Awaken!" Another spark shot from the Burning Ember to wound his slave.

Malice snickered, and a leer curled Chaos' lips.

The young man's eyes fluttered open. Their vibrant violet hue had brightened from the lashings of light almost into a blue. A flash of uncertainty crossed his face. He licked his lips and croaked, "Master."

"No mercy is given to those who fail me," Malevolence responded coldly. "Your punishment is not complete." To Malice and Chaos, he snapped, "Place him in a laie with fire chains. Let him rot until we return."

"Where are we going, master?" Malice asked.

The Burning Ember met his follower's gaze and a slow smile curved his mouth. "Earth. Those who have escaped will be recovered. Assemble every Ember, save this one." He kicked the young man's ribs, earning a gasp that widened his smile. He turned to his throne, waving away the other Embers. "I will lead you to victory against the Wynaerians and their master. Now *depart from me."*

Hastening to do his will, Malice and Chaos roughly grasped the young man between them and left.

Malevolence leaned his head back on the crown of his throne and gazed at Open Space. "You will never defeat me," he said quietly. "None of mine shall be taken away, and yours will be destroyed."

His words drifted away on the air, unanswered.

Chapter 14
The Agreement

Gasping, I opened my eyes, disoriented. Deep pain sliced through my limbs and back and chest. I no longer grasped Eversen, for which I was glad. My mind reeled at what I had just witnessed, and my body throbbed with Robert's wounds.

"Suri?" my girl asked. She stood before me, a look of concern touching her features. An Earth-meadow stretched out behind her. "Are you all right?"

I lifted my head to look around. We stood in the middle of a wide open valley in Australia, in the light of morning. For a moment, I could only stand there blinking. As my eyes adjusted, I discerned a perimeter of trees surrounding the grassy meadow. It stretched a fair way into the distance, so that the furthest trees were mere blurs on the horizon.

Even disoriented, I knew I'd never seen this meadow. My tunnel had lead us to a place I had never visited before, which was odd. Only by the Commander's interference would my tunnel deviate from its nature and deposit us in a place I'd never been. I glanced up at Open Space.

The sun was just drawing up over the eastern horizon of trees. It was still early in the morning. Wynaeria blinked in the west. There were no other indicators of our position.

It was then, looking around, that I realized I was slouching back against someone. Straightening, I discovered it was Zar. Everyone looked at me, various degrees of concern etched on their faces. Sighing in relief and despair, I closed my eyes. "How long ago did we exit the tunnel?"

"Only a few minutes," Zar answered. "What happened?"

I winced. "Robert's betrayed us," I said quietly. "Malevolence knows we're traveling to Earth."

"How?" demanded Unruly. "No Ember can trace tunnel-traveling until the inhabitants have departed from it."

"Robert shares a bond with me as my charge. I don't know how he knows where I am when I can't locate him, but he does. He told Malevolence where we're going, and all of the Embers are being gathered to dispatch us."

"All of them?" Eversen asked solemnly.

"Not Robert," I amended. "He was beaten and imprisoned until Malevolence returns."

"You witnessed it?" my girl breathed.

I scoffed lightly, rolling my sore shoulders. Zar Channeled to me, looking stern as he healed my wounds. "I experienced some of it," I told her. "They used whips made of light."

Unruly grimaced. "Branding, we call it. They whipped him until he was completely grey, didn't they?"

I nodded wearily.

"He'll retain those scars the rest of his life," Unruly muttered.

"What of the others? They're coming here?" asked Zar.

Unruly answered with surety. "Yes."

"We should leave," Eversen said. "They'll find us here."

"We have to conceal the Earthlings," I said, glancing at my girl. "If they are found, they'll be killed."

"We'll all be killed," Zar muttered, already Channeling.

Quickly and silently, Zar and I forged a protective shell around the Earthlings. To us, it was golden and fluid and stalwart, much like the shields of the Commander's love around the Earthlings' hearts. The Embers, however, would be unable to hear or see anything from within it. Unruly watched in disbelief as the humans disappeared from his view.

"Go to the forest with Unruly," I commanded the Earthlings.

Unruly jerked his eyes to me. "How will I care for them if I cannot see or hear them?"

Zar chuckled. "They'll stay with you. Follow their footprints, if you must; surely as an Ember that shouldn't be difficult."

Unruly snarled but said nothing.

"What are you going to do?" my girl asked me.

"We are staying," I answered. Even as I said it, I wondered if I was strong enough to withstand the onslaught. "Embers have fought Wynaerians nearly since creation. Go with Unruly and Eversen. We can fight forcefully for a time."

"And when you can't fight any longer?" She glared at me.

"The Commander will fight for us," I murmured, staring back at her steadily. "If we die, it's his will. Go now, before they arrive."

With a terrified glance, my girl went with Unruly and Eversen. Zar and I watched as they hurried toward the forest. Moments after they'd disappeared at the edge of the meadow, loud shrieks rent the air.

The Embers had arrived.

I held out my wrist to Zar. "We'll fight to the end."

"I'll get there first." Zar's eyes sparkled.

Together, we turned to face the onslaught of Embers. They streamed into the meadow with loud cries and laughter. The sun dimmed with the magnitude of their darkness. Flashes of fire from eyes shot out toward us. Perhaps fifty yards from us, the Embers gathered and stilled, watching us with sneering faces.

"There are more than I anticipated," Zar murmured. "Do you think they'll come one at a time?"

"Do you have a weapon ready?" I countered, eyeing the

crowd of Embers. The longer they stood still, the darker the meadow grew. Soon it would be dark. Cold seeped along the surface of my skin, prickling.

"I always have a weapon ready, brother." Zar brandished his temberle dagger. "You think I taught you for nothing?"

A tall Ember stepped from the crowd toward us, arm swords already formed. I recognized him.

"Malice," I greeted, stepping forward. "Still faring well since the last time we met?"

"Only your brother saved you, Suri," he responded lazily. "Even with him at the beginning of this fight, I suspect our numbers will overpower you." He flicked his sword toward us.

A blast of icy wind scraped my cheeks.

"Fighting us with wind, are you?" Zar taunted. "Remember my light?" A golden beam shot from his fingertips and danced across the space toward Malice. It barreled into the Ember's chest.

Malice merely sneered. "You think I don't have the power to withstand a mere trickle of light? Surely you are not so naïve." He waved a sword-arm behind him to the rest of the Embers, now bristling in anger and anticipation. "My followers will gladly tear you apart," he hissed. "Take a few if you can, but do not expect to survive. When we have finished with you, we'll find your precious Earthlings, and the traitor."

"The Commander will protect those he wishes to live," I responded coldly. "If he wishes them to join him in the light, there will be nothing you can do to prevent it. If he wants them to live, who are you to defy his commands?"

Malice snarled.

I saw his motion a split second before the paralyzing coldness of Zeker seeped into my bones. Leaping, scampering, running across the field, weapons bared, flames flickering, the Embers charged as Malice's sword fell. His blade pointed at us.

"To the end!" Zar shouted over the fray. He caught my eyes and grinned. Then he was running forward to meet the Embers.

I followed my brother, any trepidation about dying vanquished, and together we raced toward our foes. For only a moment, the sound of our ragged breathing and pounding feet was all that could be heard. We met with the first Embers in the center of the field, blade to blade.

Thrusting, parrying, leaping, and lunging, we fought. Bodies fell before our blades, only to be replaced as soon as we drew breath. The Embers surrounded us as a wave, closing off any escape. Zar and I fought valiantly for a very short few minutes, holding our own. We came back to back, facing innumerable foes, and circling, weapons brandished.

The battle was over mere minutes after it began.

The Embers laughed and parted before me. Malice strode forward, flames snaking around his jagged swords. A sneer curled his lips as he stopped a pace from me.

"The two greatest warriors of the Master's army," he jeered. "Here you stand, encircled by his enemies, unprotected, outnumbered. Is this how he treats his most faithful servants?"

Zar snarled, "Better to be killed than serve the Adversary."

Malice grinned. "Your slaughter will be memorable," he promised, voice grating. He cocked his head and relaxed his swords, started pacing before us. "I don't want to forget your pain," he said softly. His eyes glinted. "We'll make it slow and torturous. We'll make your Master squirm."

"Try."

Before Malice could respond or act, a roar split the meadow around us. The Ember took a step back and looked up. His eyes narrowed and a hiss escaped his lips.

I followed his gaze to the sky, though it was unnecessary. Light flooded through the darkness over the valley. Exiting tunnels, inhabitants of Wynaeria flooded the meadow. There were perhaps two thousand – enough to level the disparity in numbers. All those able-bodied and willing had gathered to fight.

The Wynaerians landed among the army of Embers as a

single body, weapons wielded. Without preamble, they began striking down those nearest them. The fight resumed around us, and once more our enemies began to fall.

Zar joined the multitude that filled the valley, disappearing into the Embers' darkness and leaving a wake of dead behind him.

Malice turned to me, laughing above the sounds of destruction. "You think your family can save you? I welcome your feeble attempt. We will vanquish you, and my master will reward me." He raised his swords once more and threw his head back.

A silent, undulating scream pierced the air, dragged from Malice's throat. Rather than sound, the disturbance was a vibration that rattled into our bones and ravaged our spirits. The silent cry went on and on, paralyzing Embers and Wynaerians alike, for a time causing the strife on the battlefield to cease.

All eyes turned to Malice, who alone seem unaffected as his cry persisted.

When the sensation abated, silence swept through the valley. I could hear the ringing in my ears and nothing else, still wholly concentrated on the ululation. No one fought now.

The Embers riveted their gaze on Open Space, waiting eagerly. The Wynaerians Channeled to each other, restoring their disquieted spirits.

I felt the cry echoing in my chest, a faint tremor through my bones, and knew instinctively what was coming. I glanced up at the sky and saw the flaming tail of an Ember's tunnel. Dread consumed me.

Malevolence had answered the call.

~ ~ ~

With shaken spirits and absorbing dread, we resumed the fight. Wynaerians fought recklessly, knowing there was no chance of success as Malevolence landed among us. Still, we battled on.

The Embers would not be handed victory.

I fought with mounting fury as Wynaerians fell around me, slashing at every shadow within reach, and dodging forceful blows.

An Ember's blade caught my shoulder. Snarling with rage, I struck him down with a blow across his chest. The impact released a spark of shadow and light before the Ember disappeared. I turned, and found myself face to face with Malice.

He grinned roguishly. "I hoped to destroy you. Shall we play?" Without waiting for an answer, he swung a wide arc with his left sword.

I dodged and dropped into a crouch to kick his legs out from under him.

He fell heavily and grunted.

I jumped to my feet in a protective stance, knife raised.

He rolled and rose, wielding his swords. "You're learning," he approved, slightly out of breath. "I could still spare you, if you wish. Surely the Master's two greatest warriors needn't both be killed at once. Come with us and become an Ember."

I spat at him. "I will never turn from the Commander."

Malice didn't even blink at the name. "You don't doubt him?" He motioned to those fighting around us, no longer pressing me to fight, as he enjoyed taunting me.

"Look at all the carnage. Your Master can't want you all to be killed. If you continue with this battle, every one of you will die." He waved a sword-arm to indicate the warriors.

I took advantage of the lull to glance at the others. I kept Malice in vision, ready to defend myself; but he wasn't looking at me.

A laugh suddenly broke from his lips. "Look, Suri. It's your precious brother." He pointed out over the battlefield, toward the incline of the valley's walls. "He thinks he can defeat Malevolence?"

I flicked my eyes to where he pointed.

No more than a hundred yards from us, Zar dueled with the Embers' leader. He fought dauntlessly, but he was weakening, and Malevolence did not relent.

Zar left an opening and Malevolence nicked his arm. Zar recovered swiftly, but I knew it would only be a matter of time before Malevolence dispatched him.

Rage blinded me. I whirled on Malice with greater vigor than I knew I possessed.

For just a second, surprise ignited his face, before he swung easily back into the rhythm of fighting. He raised his swords, one to block, and one to thrust.

I twisted away from the attack and rallied. Every tactic I knew I used against him. Unable to draw near him to strike, I pranced around him carelessly, toying. When opportunities arose due to his rashness, I stepped in close to injure him.

The Ember hissed in anger at my wiles, unable to defend them.

During one such feat, I managed to trip him. He sprawled on the ground before me, scrambling. Unable to resist a little chuckle, I murmured, "We played."

Malice snarled.

"Commander, defeat him!" I invoked, eyes locked on the Ember before me. With a final downward swing, I stabbed my knife through Malice's chest.

A hiss erupted from the Ember. Sparks shot from his eyes and mouth, and then he shuddered, fell to the ground, and lay still. His body greyed nearly to white and his eyes stared toward Open Space, gaping holes. He was destroyed.

Turning in disgust from my defeated enemy, I scampered away, once more entering the crowd of warring bodies. I fought my way to the edge of the fray until I reached the incline where Malevolence and Zar still fought.

Zar back-stepped and fell to one knee, raising his dagger high to block a blow from one of Malevolence's swords. The other buried to its hilt in his chest.

Without waiting to see if he had finished his work,

Malevolence turned from my brother. A grin tugged the corner of his mouth and he entered the battlefield once more, slaying those in reach of his blade.

I stared for one horror-stricken moment at Zar, fallen on the ground. Outside the throng of bloodshed, my mind became strangely lucid. I pushed myself into a run toward him, skirting the fringe of the battle. Around me, the stench of death and clamor of war touched my senses, unabated. I ignored the impulse to rejoin the fight and continued to my brother. When I reached him, I dropped to my knees at his side.

Blood spread from the wound in his chest, soaking his clothes and the ground beneath him. He remained in the same position as Malevolence had left him, lying on his back, legs sprawled. His features were pale, eyes closed. One hand still clutched his temberle dagger. He did not breathe.

I grasped his shoulder, Channeling to heal him.

He was unresponsive.

"Commander," I invoked. "Heal him."

The Commander quietly resolved, *He is yours for a time, Suri.* Then, softer, *Only ever for a time.*

Zar gasped awake. His golden eyes looked at me and he grinned weakly. Impishness glanced across his face. "I thought you'd come."

"Always." I returned his smile.

"I can't stay," my brother said, closing his eyes again. His smile changed, became joyous. "The Commander's called me home."

"No," I protested. "He allowed you to come back."

"He allowed me to say goodbye."

I stared at him, disbelieving.

"I told you I'd get there first," jested he, slitting his eyes open to see my expression. "Come off it, Suri. It's better that I die before you. I'm older, after all."

"You seem to be getting stronger, not perishing," I retorted. "If you're dying, shouldn't you be saying what a wonderful younger brother I've been and how you'll miss me?"

Zar gave a snort, which turned into a cough. "I can't miss you in the Commander's presence," he murmured, winking.

Blood still streamed gently from his chest. His breathing slowed, became a rasp of agony.

I gripped his shoulder. "Then stay where you *can* miss me."

He rolled his eyes. "So vain, Suri." He added, "Stop Channeling. You make it difficult."

I ceased.

"The Commander has called me home," he repeated softly, closing his eyes. "I only asked that I could say goodbye."

I bowed my head, reeling with confusion that he could be so lighthearted about his death. But, it was his way to find the joke in everything.

"So you're going to leave me to finish the battle we've begun?" I challenged.

"Precisely." His grip on my hand failed. "I'll be waiting with the Commander for you."

"Of course," I muttered, studying his features. They relaxed under my scrutiny and Zar began breathing slowly, not so harshly as before.

"To the end." His body relaxed.

I swallowed. "Goodbye, brother." My eyes welled with tears, but I clenched my jaw and kept them from spilling over. Zar would not want me to weep over him. Abysmal emptiness congested my chest and I raised my face to Open Space, the last of my family. I felt alone.

After a moment, a black rage rose in me, directed toward Malevolence. I stood and turned.

The battle had continued, oblivious to Zar's death. The Wynaerians were falling, overwhelmed by the multitude of Embers.

I wrested Zar's dagger from his grip. Brandishing it in one hand and my knife in the other, I rejoined the fight, searching for Malevolence. Ferociously, I fought my way to him.

"Malevolence!" I shouted through the clash of blades and shrieks of the dying.

He heard me from several paces away. His laughing face turned to me. The living ones nearest us stopped their dueling to watch and listen.

"Your brother died, did he?" Malevolence jeered, sauntering through the armies to me. "It took longer than I'd expected. Now you plan to challenge me, avenge his death?"

I gritted my teeth. "I challenge you," I said tightly.

Malevolence gave a knowing look.

"Not to avenge my brother," I clarified, fixing my eyes on his. "I challenge you for the destruction you have wrought throughout the universe. It is time your darkness was destroyed."

"Zar, the strongest of the Master's army, could not defeat me. Now his younger sibling, full of courage and strength, thinks he can dispatch me. What makes you certain you can succeed where your brother failed?" he mocked.

"Commander, defeat him!" I roared.

Malevolence chortled, raising a sword-arm. "You think beseeching the Master's son will help you fight? You've challenged me brazenly. Now fight and prove your worth!" He swung the first sword toward me.

I flicked my knife up, ducking to avoid him. He chuckled and followed me. Using one sword as a shield, he raised the other above his head and brought it down where I stood. I skipped lightly out of the way, turning in a tight circle. In the same movement, I threw Zar's dagger, aiming for Malevolence's back.

The Ember shifted quickly and the blade thudded into the ground. He stepped back toward me, swords brandished.

For several more minutes, he hailed relentless blows down on me. I held my own, neither gaining nor losing ground. However, as had happened with Zar, Malevolence's attack was unwavering and inexorable. I fell back as blow after blow rained down and I managed to narrowly block them.

I stepped back and tripped over a fallen Wynaerian. Raising my blade to cover my face, I glared piercingly at the Ember.

Malevolence twisted his lips into a sneer, his sword-tip lowered to nearly touch my neck. He breathed heavily, but an expression of triumph twisted his demeanor. "The mighty Suri," he spat maliciously, "lying before me." He leaned close. "Practically kneeling, I would say."

"Only to the Commander," I returned coldly.

"After being soundly beaten, you still remain spirited." His eyes flashed. "Perhaps we can find a way to break that spirit of yours." Throwing his head back, he made the same silent, undulating cry that Malice had.

Immediately, the battlefield grew still. Embers and Wynaerians alike turned to face Malevolence.

When all stared at him, the Burning Ember stopped his ravaging call. "Take as captives those you fight," he commanded his followers. "Slay those who resist. We will make an offering to the Master – we will spill blood for him."

The Embers made a raucous noise that could only be their expression of jubilee. They grappled with the Wynaerians nearest them, and quickly all were subdued.

"Start with this one, and bind them to stakes. Use whatever force necessary. I want a fragrant aroma for the Master." Malevolence looked down at me, his eyes gleaming. "He shed his blood for you, Suri," he whispered. "Now do as he commands and follow him. Shed your blood for him."

A shudder went through me. I thought of the future I had seen, and knew I had been wrong. It was not only one death, but many. My brother, myself, and only the Commander knew how many more. Sickened at the thought, I closed my eyes, wondering why so many had to perish today.

"Yes, it is tragic," Malevolence said at my reaction. "So many lives lost because you fought against us, instead of joining us. Now, you are too late."

Do not lose heart, my son.

The Commander's words opened my eyes.

You will rise with me in life.

I smirked at the Burning Ember standing over me. "You may kill us," I conceded, "but don't mistake a triumph for victory. In the end, the Commander will destroy you."

Malevolence gave an angry shriek and blackness consumed my sight.

~ ~ ~

My hands and feet burned. Scorching heat swept up my spine and wrapped around my middle, digging into my skin. My insides were freezing, numb to the heat. I shook violently. Harsh noises resounded around me, metallic, acidic, cracklings and rustlings.

It was then that I realized my hands were wrenched behind my back, and I sat in an uncomfortable crouching posture, with my feet beneath me. I opened my eyes.

The burning came from the fiery bonds securing my hands, feet, and waist to a stake at my back. Darkness shrouded the scene around me – the Embers' darkness, which explained the numbness in my bones. On either side of me stood many more stakes, a Wynaerian bound to each. We all faced the same way – toward Malevolence.

The Burning Ember had ignited his shadowy body as no other Ember could – an ability which earned his distinctive name. He paced before us, a silhouette on fire, eyes shooting sparks. With each step, flames licked the ground at his feet. Already the once-beautiful meadow had turned black, exuding sulfuric odors.

"He awakens finally," Malevolence leered, coming to a stop before me. "I was awaiting your consciousness for my display. As you can see, our offering has not yet started."

"Offering?" I scoffed, pushing hard against the ground to

stand. My shoulders pulled in agony. "The Commander –"

Fiery cords sprang from Malevolence's fingertips to wrap around my mouth. "Always so voluble," he crooned softly. "Did no one ever tell you silence is a virtue?"

I stared at him in hatred, the fire in my spirit matching the fire burning into my skin.

Malevolence grinned back. "This is all for you, Suri." He spread his arms to indicate the pinioned Wynaerians and burning meadow. Fumes of smoke billowed around him, sometimes clouding his burning form. The rest of the Embers stood behind him, only their eyes visible in the night.

"For you and your brother, who, regrettably, was unable to attend our gathering. The Master has long revered the two of you," Malevolence spat with disgust. "As you are his favorites, I thought it fitting to offer you first. Zar has already been dispatched, as you know. Now it's time you began the burning ceremony."

The Embers behind him cackled with glee. He raised a hand to silence them, and the quiet grew far more intimidating than the noise. Even the fires' crackling seemed to diminish.

"Rest assured, we will find the lost ones," the Burning Ember murmured softly. His eyes pierced into me. The sparks flinging from them became fiercer and propelled further, nearly striking me. "The traitor will be dealt with as I see fit, and the others will join you in death through burning."

You forgot the freezing, I wanted to spit at him. My body trembled against the stake from the chill in my bones, a strange contrast to the heat searing from my bonds.

"Farewell, great warrior," Malevolence mocked, bowing meretriciously. He raised his blazing hands, which morphed into swords. The two tips pointed at my heart; they drew together and with a soft *cling* of metal, a beam of fire blasted from them.

In the split second before the heat reached me, I shifted my eyes from the blades to Malevolence's demonic features. Then an inferno combusted my chest.

My back arched in agony, my head thrown back against the stake. I could not tell if the fire came from without or within me. Perhaps it was both. The heat licked along my skin, joined by the flames of my bonds. Unbearable torture swept through me as my nerves lit.

Black encroached on my vision and I slumped.

Chapter 15
Hymn

Burn them," Malevolence ordered, eyes on the dying Wynaerian before him. At long last, his adversary was defeated. Burned by the Burning Ember. How fitting.

His followers obeyed his orders, skipping to the bound Wynaerians – weeping and screaming at Suri's death – and set them alight. Though none of the Embers had the capacity of Malevolence, their power was sufficient to rid the universe of these Wynaerians.

Malevolence stepped toward Suri's charred body as flames still licked along the stake, turning his enemy into ash and bones. Overwhelming triumph swept through him, strong and intoxicating. The firelight swirled with the blackness around him. He came to a stop just short of the Wynaerian's unrecognizable corpse.

In the night air, laughter and screams of pain mingled together, rising up to Open Space. Let the Master listen to his followers shriek, powerless to prevent their deaths.

As Malevolence stared at Suri, an idea sparked in his mind and a sneer twisted his mouth. "You are not finished yet, great warrior," he whispered, then turned to face the rest of the carnage.

"Scatter their bones. Let them dry in the heat of the air, a testimony to the universe of the Master's power."

The Embers howled with laughter at the mockery.

Malevolence grinned. Casting another glance at Suri, he pivoted to leave the massacre-ground. Behind him, celebratory exclamations mingled with the failing cries of the remaining Wynaerians. Smoke and sparks rose up into the air, a fragrant aroma for the Master.

~ ~ ~

A thrill of excitement ran through him. He stood alone at the top of the valley, looking down upon the scorched plain. Trees shaded him, keeping the sun's heat from beating on the back of his head. As he had commanded, the valley was full of bones, all now dry as dust. Many crackled in the heat of the sunlight. A gentle wind blew among them, creating a low moan.

Malevolence smiled joyously. Lightly, he skipped down into the valley and walked among the bones, ignoring the scorching sunlight. Today, it was worth the pain. Euphoria rose in him at the success of the previous night. He scanned the massacre-ground with evident pleasure, turning slowly among the carnage, to take in all.

His enemies: how far they had fallen!

Gleefully, he began to dance, a slow, fluid movement, casting shadows and sparks on the dried bones. Then, raising his jagged swords, he looked up into Open Space with a grin. Head tilted back, he began to shriek, high and lilting, a call that penetrated the atmosphere.

A responding shriek sounded in the forest behind him, followed by others. Soon he was surrounded by the noise, his Embers answering his call.

They materialized in the shade beneath the trees and watched him. Eagerly, they switched from foot to foot in restlessness, waiting for his command.

Malevolence ceased his dance to look around at them all,

unable to control his glee. "Glad you could join us." He spread his arms wide to include the bones.

The Embers laughed.

Malevolence reached down, his swords becoming hands, and plucked a long, slender bone from among the others. He weighed it in his hands for a moment, holding it like treasure. Delicately, he ran his thin fingers along the surface.

In one fluid motion, he lowered himself to the ground and bent over the bone. Legs crossed, he began scraping at it with his fingernails, eyes lowered to his hands. He ignored the Embers watching him, concentrated wholly on his work.

Shrak. Shrak. Shrak.

It was the only sound in the valley as he carved the bone. Within moments, Malevolence had finished. He now held a crookedly crafted flute in his fingers. Raising it to his lips, he began to play, a triumphant tune at the defeat of his enemies.

After a few notes, words entered his mind, which he Reverberated around the valley.

Among the decimated
laughter will reside:
bounding along the wind
until they're cold inside.

Come to me, my family;
shriek with lifted voice.
Raise your ears to hear me:
you have no other choice.

Dance over our defeated!
They go down to Death:
their fearsome, angry foe
who steals their final breath.

Sing with me, bonded friends:

cry with joyous shout.
Play upon their bones:
scrape and hollow them out.

Revenge on those who hate us!
Spite our Enemy!
Kill his chosen ones
and come celebrate with me.

Among the decimated
laughter will reside:
bounding along the wind
until they're cold inside.

With one hand, Malevolence continued playing; with the other he motioned his followers to join him. As one, they flooded the valley of bones. Darkness came with them until the massacre-ground was as black as the night before.

The Embers followed Malevolence's example, plucking bones from the ground and carving them into instruments. One by one, they joined Malevolence's song, until the dell was rife with it.

Listen, my Master, he thought. *Listen, Lucifer. We have defeated your enemies. Reward us well.*

~ ~ ~

The stench of the dead entered his nostrils, putrid and sickening. Down in the valley, the Embers danced with glee, unwilling and unable, to see the redemption before their eyes. He turned from the disgusting scene and tunneled away through Open Space.

On Wynaeria once more, the Commander strode through the village toward Juris and Lili's cottage. He stepped along the path and stopped outside the house, where two small children played together with rocks and sticks, laughing.

"Mena!" the Commander called in a low voice. "Poil!"

The two jerked their heads up. Smiles wreathed their faces and they began to run. Their little legs pumped ferociously and brought them barreling toward him.

The Commander dropped to a crouch, arms wide open to receive them. A smile stretched across his features as he caught the two children in his arms, red-faced and breathless.

"Commanner!" exclaimed Poil, burrowing his face into the Commander's chest. He rested his cheek there for a moment, trying to regain his breath.

"Oh, you've come, you've come!" cried Mena, hugging the Commander fiercely. "You've finally come!" She tilted her head back to look in his eyes disapprovingly. "It's been ever so long!"

The Commander chuckled. "I know, sweetheart." He smoothed back her hair and touched a finger to her pouting lips. "I've come again. This time I won't go away so soon."

"Where you go?" Poil asked, also pulling back to look at him.

"Ah, Poil, but that is why I have come. I must speak with your parents." He winked.

"Come, come!" Mena cried, tugging on his hand to pull him up. "We have another visitor!"

"You do?"

Both children stared at him in disbelief. "Don't you know?" Mena breathed, eyes wide.

"Know what?" The Commander stared back into her face steadily.

Then Mena laughed. "Of course you know! You always know! Hurry, hurry, Commander. He'll want to see you, too!" Again, she dragged on his hands to pull him to his feet.

This time, the Commander stood. Mena and Poil wrapped themselves around his legs, giggling as he took a stumbling step forward. In this awkward manner they made their way to the house. The door stood open to let in the spring breeze, and voices wafted from inside.

Mena jumped from the Commander's leg and rushed inside. "Momma! Papa! Guess who's come?"

Poil hung onto the Commander's leg, satisfied just to be with him. The Commander looked at him and whispered, "How are you, Poil?"

The boy's adoring eyes turned up to him. "Happy."

The Commander reached down and swung the boy into his arms. Poil leaned against his chest, closing his eyes, perfectly content. The Commander carried him into the house.

Lili, Juris, and Firen, a Wynaerian neither young nor old who had once sacrificed himself for his homeland, sat at the kitchen table. They spoke together in drifting tones, happy and lighthearted. Mena fluttered around, dancing in exultation and chattering away to no one in particular.

The Commander flipped Poil over, holding him by his ankles. The boy dangled in the air, laughing and giggling as the Commander swung him back and forth like a pendulum. "Thank you for the warm greeting," said the Commander, turning the boy upright again and setting him on his feet.

Lili rose and hobbled to the Commander, eyes shining. She curtsied before him and then gave him a hug as well as she could with her pregnant belly. Juris and Firen stood and bowed low; together they strode forward to cross marks with the Commander.

"I'm glad to see you again," he said to them. "My dear and faithful servants." A gleam of pride littered his eyes.

"Come, sit," Lili offered, motioning with one hand; the other rested lightly on her bulging stomach. "Drink with us."

The Commander took a seat at the table and accepted a cup of water. Mena and Poil clambered into his lap. He held one on each leg and watched as the others sat around him.

"Master," Firen said, dipping his head in respect. "Thank you for my life."

The Commander smiled. "Do you now see that when one sacrifices himself for all, he is raised in life?"

"Yes, my Lord," the ageless man said, returning the smile.

"Are you going to send us on another mission, Lord?" Juris asked.

The Commander flicked his eyes to him. "Yes. This one you'll find easier in some ways, harder in others." He lifted a hand to stroke Mena's hair and his features grew serious. "You know of the Embers' deeds," he began in a low, tight voice. "Suri, Zar, and all the others have been slain on the battlefield."

He continued uninterrupted, telling them of the Embers' attack and the Wynaerians' defeat. He told of the Burning Ember's slayings, and of the song he sang the next morning. Finally, he told of his plan to return to the valley of dry bones.

Silence pervaded the room. Even Mena and Poil understood the seriousness of the conversation, and remained quiet. Poil snuggled closer into the Commander's chest.

"Zar, Suri, and the others will also discover the truth of death. Until then, I want you to spread this story on Wynaeria. Teach it to your children, and remember the deeds of their bravery. It was an act of obedience to me that they went to their deaths. That truth should not be besmirched or forgotten, but told to all who will hear. Tonight at the Light Dancing, we will celebrate their obedience. When the time comes, it will be of great importance that all remember their sacrifice."

"Commander," Lili ventured quietly, "will you bring them back to life?"

"They *are* living, Lili," answered the Commander. "Their souls cannot die. They remain with me, alive in death."

Lili nodded in acceptance, though his answer did not completely satisfy her.

"Trust me," the Commander beseeched gently. "Watch, and discover." He set the children on the ground and rose. "I will see you tonight, my children. Do not lose heart. My message will be spread to the ends of the universe." He headed toward the door.

"Commanner!" Poil cried, rushing after him and grabbing him around the leg. "Don' leave!"

"Please!" Mena begged, eyes full of sorrow.

The Commander knelt. "I will never leave you," he told them. He leaned close to whisper in their ears, "Reach into my pockets."

The children obeyed and pulled their hands out. Each held a necklace: a silver circlet of thorns dangling on a chain. Mena gasped in delight and surprise. Poil gazed at his with wide eyes, a very serious expression on his childish face.

"Than' you, Commanner," he whispered.

"Thank you," Mena echoed.

"They are symbols of my presence," the Commander told them, as though it were a cherished secret. "Wear them and remember me. I am always with you." He pulled the children close and kissed them both. "I will see you tonight, my children."

Mena whirled to her parents, proudly brandishing the necklace. "Look what the Commander gave me!"

Poil stood where he was, still staring at his necklace.

"Come to me, Poil," the Commander whispered. "One day you will be a great warrior, and I will lead you. Don't forget me." He rose, cupped the boy's cheek in his hand, turned, and strode from the house.

Juris turned to face the others, determination etched in his features. "The Commander requires an easy task of us," he murmured. "There is no reason to fail him."

Mena and Poil came to him, holding up their necklaces. He fastened them around the children's necks, and sent them outside to play. Mena and Poil obeyed happily, skipping from the house.

"We should write the story," Lili suggested, turning to a small shelf, on which were set several rolled parchments and writing utensils. "If there are copies of it, the story will spread further."

Firen grinned. "Call it *The Adversary's Defeat*. Death, Embers, darkness – they will die in the end. The Commander prevails against all."

Lili strode to the table, pen and parchment in hand. The others gathered around and looked over her shoulder. Lili dipped the quill in the ink and looked up.

"What shall it say?"

~ ~ ~

The Adversary's Defeat
as written by Lili, Juris, and Firen

Once upon a time, in a land where heroes die,
the Commander called upon us
to battle those of darkness.

Tunneling from home first two brothers left, alone
obeying our Master's orders:
leaders against the darkness.

They arrived on Earth: landed lightly in the dirt
surrounded by grassy valleys:
the place of utter darkness.

Their enemies came, Embers who shadowed the plain.
Our warriors rushed forth to fight
without fear in the darkness.

Two opposing many, they battled the enemies,
pleasing their Lord: the Commander,
brave and strong in the darkness.

The Master sent more to join the brothers, in hordes;
and for a time we held our own:
diminishing the darkness.

Hymn

The greater numbers performed sufficient wonders.
Yet still outnumbered by Embers,
we fell back in the darkness.

Malice gave a roar: ravaging, to call his lord.
The Adversary came swiftly,
joining the fight in darkness.

Malevolence fought. The elder brother he sought;
he cornered the warrior Zar
and struck his shield with darkness.

Zar died in defense. Suri sought Malevolence.
The Adversary struck him down
but he lived in the darkness.

At their leader's words, the enemies stilled their swords.
A lull took place in the conflict:
in the field soaked with darkness.

The battle ended, our deaths only suspended.
Wynaerians were ordered bound:
roped with fire in darkness.

Malevolence jeered, mocking the Master he feared.
Vengefully, he sacrificed us
frigid, flaming, in darkness.

We died in honor, upholding the Commander.
Our foes ravaged our sacrifice:
scattered our bones in darkness.

In the morning sun, the Adversary returned,
euphoric at his victory,
when he slayed us with darkness.

The Commander knew: he watched, incensed; subdued.
He returned to Wynaeria –
> *left the curs to their darkness.*

Keep them in your thoughts: the Wynaerians who fought
in remembrance of the Master,
> *against the ones of darkness.*

Heed our Master's word – when the Embers flaunt their swords,
the Commander will vanquish them,
> *and bring the death of darkness!*

Epilogue

A large laie loomed before him in the darkness, illuminated by his Ember eyes. The opening gaped wide, sealed by his own bindings. His eyes pierced the diaphanous exterior to stare at the prisoner within.

The young man hung suspended in the air, arms widespread. Body greyed by his branding, head bowed to his chest, his only movement was that of breathing. Deep scars slashed across his body, identical throughout. His eyes, though currently downcast, were a livid blue from all the light that had penetrated him.

"This is how I love." Malevolence smiled. Unable to quickly end the gruesome sight before him, the Burning Ember began to pace. He walked back and forth in front of the prisoner, each footfall causing sparks to shoot out and burn the young man's feet.

"You thought to be rewarded," he taunted his unconscious slave. "You thought I would grant mercy to one who disobeyed me? Awaken!" He slashed a blade down, releasing the bindings on the laie and breaking the fiery ropes that secured the prisoner.

Groaning, the young man stirred on the ground and looked up. A look of utter disgust crossed his face, quickly squelched by adoration. "You returned," he murmured.

The Burning Ember crouched, grinning, and touched his blade-tip under the young man's chin, tilting his head up. "I always return for what is mine," he whispered. "And you: you are mine."

"Of course I am," the young man breathed, gazing into Malevolence's eyes.

"Your punishment was just."

"Yes."

"My love for you has returned."

Tears pricked the young man's eyes. "Master," he said past a lump in his throat, "you are kind and good."

"Yes." The Burning Ember caressed the young man's cheek in one hand, tilting his head back. "I have another task for you," he said softly. "I have forgiven you your failure and grant you another opportunity to prove your loyalty to me."

This time, the young man's tears spilled over. "Your love for me is too much," said he. "What can I do to repay it?"

"Obey me."

"I will, master. Whatever you wish, I will do."

Malevolence smiled, standing. "I thought you would answer thus. My task for you is this: destroy Wynaeria."

The young man's eyes widened. "Destroy Wynaeria?" he repeated breathlessly.

"Don't you relish such an opportunity?" countered his master. "What better way can you prove your loyalty to me? What else but destruction of a planet would show me the depth of your love?"

A smile curled the young man's lips. "Of course, master," he acquiesced. "I can never repay your goodness to me."

"Swear you will obey me," Malevolence ordered. "Swear to me by your blood that you will destroy Wynaeria."

The young man lifted his eyes, a devilish look on his face. "More," he breathed. "I vow to you that I will destroy Wynaeria. Take my blood, my life, and my breath if I fail you."

"Seal the promise."

Lifting one hand, the young man transformed it into a scythe. He pressed the tip into the palm of his other hand until it drew blood, a pitch-black liquid. He dropped the scythe and raised his bleeding palm to Malevolence.

The Burning Ember took the hand gently in both his own. He raised it to his nose, breathing in the scent. Dropping it once more, he grasped the wrist of the bleeding hand and smeared the blood over his forearm.

Leering, he answered, "I accept your vow."